MY NAME IS MAHATAA

By Jikun Kathy Sankey

For my parents who gave me life

Dedicated also to

my maternal grandmother, Mahataa

my spiritual teacher Zen Master Shodo Harada Roshi,
http:www.onedropzendo.org

my Tai Chi teacher, Master Kai Ying Tung of Los Angeles

my first Yoga teacher, the late Marie Chase

"...and to all beings, both known and unknown to us, may they be
freed from the path of delusion and suffering and equally attain the
way of awakening..."

Zen Buddhist Chant

The Sanskrit term *upaya* is defined as a means, a device or method to bring others to a spiritual end. These skillful devices are employed by teachers to assist beings in suffering. In some circumstances even trickery can be an upaya if they help someone to wake up. In other words, even if a technique or view is not ultimately true in the highest sense, it may still be employed by a teacher to bring a person to the path.

May this book serve as an upaya.

HISTORICAL INFORMATION

In 600 AD Chinese ambassadors were sent out beyond China's frontiers by the Emperor who, like so many of his predecessors, was eager to find the Secret of Immortality. Court magicians and Taoist priests assured the Emperor at Lo-yang that the secrets could be found. They spoke of an elusive Land of Happy Immortals in the distant Eastern Seas.

The first attempt to reach the Land of Happy Immortals, made in 607 AD by the Sui People, was unsuccessful, but in the next year, an expedition reached the islands in the Eastern Seas. These islands were not peopled by happy immortals as legend had promised. Nevertheless, the Chinese envoy commanding the expedition advised the primitive islanders to yield to Sui rule and to acknowledge the Chinese Emperor as their ruler. They refused, a battle ensued, and many captives, said to have numbered a thousand persons, were taken back to China.

The exact location of these islands has never been determined; the annals are vague, and for centuries the Chinese referred to all the islands lying between Japan proper and the Philippines as Liu Ch'iu. There is a strong presumption that the Sui expeditionary force had indeed reached the island of Okinawa.

OKINAWA: The History of an Island People
By George H. Kerr

*Great-Grandmother once said to me, "We women are very lucky.
We have the choice to give birth to children or to give birth to our True
Self right out the tops of our heads."*

CHAPTER 1
MY BIRTH

My name is Mahataa.

With a huge birth cry on the early morning of July 27, 1902 in the Year of the Water Tiger, I announced my arrival. I was born to Kana, who was the granddaughter of Hanaa, a diviner and seer.

They say my cry echoed beyond the borders of our rural village nestled in the northern peninsula of an island in the East China Sea. Great-Grandmother said my cry was so huge, in fact, that it could be heard for miles and miles.

"There was something mysterious about your birth cry," she once said to me. "It caused a handful of people who were karmically ripened to awaken."

Great-Grandmother was not talking about awaken in the ordinary sense. Certainly many villagers were rustled from their sleep when they heard the long drawn out reverberations of my cry. But what she meant was that the consciousness of a handful of people suddenly opened, and they were able to know things in ways they could not have known before.

A few kilometers from our village, a fisherman who had cast his net before daybreak gasped at the unearthly cry. He stooped frozen and suspended for a time as he clutched the rim of his small boat.

"The cry was so bone-chilling it caused my heart to pound right out of my chest!" relayed the fisherman out at sea on the day of my birth. He told the villagers later that he paused for a long while as he steadied himself against the swells of the ocean while hauling in his net. Although he did not know the origin of the cry, he experienced its result. His attention was sharply gathered and not one thought entered his mind.

At the moment of my birth, a lonely soothsayer in the North Mountains deep in meditation opened her eyes and smiled a knowing smile. She knew that her life would soon be complete. At the same time, in a small monastery near the craggy limestone cliffs of the South, a young boy in training stirred from dreams of events to come.

Fifteen years have passed since that extraordinary morning when I emerged in our blessed northern province to fulfill a task too great for one small person such as myself. We are in an era where the three poisons of greed, anger and delusion have fueled leaders of many nations. Because of their misguided ambitions for personal power and profit, they will bring calamity and misfortune to many peoples of the world.

The mission for which I have been sent will require arduous training and the gathering of kindred spirits, with heightened awareness and wisdom, to coalesce as *one mind* to turn the tides of destruction. I have met many guides along the way, all of whom had infused me with their wisdom. As I prepare for my voyage by sea from my northern village to the town of Shuri in the South I look to a new life with heartache and with hope.

A collage of memories pours over me as I sit back on my tiny putt-putt boat on my way south, of Mother and Father waving goodbye to me as they boarded their Chinese junk, of the time my best friend En and I moved seashells with our mind, of the old Monk who showed me how to sew, of all the experiences that brought so much to my path of light. But I must withdraw inward soon, dimming my light, knowing that I will need to suspend my knowledge for the time being.

As I recall details of my birth from the deepest places inside of me, I am transported to a time long ago. As I drift into sleep, I recede back into time, and it is the summer of 1902 again.

Mother is dawdling about in the small, stony courtyard in front of our home, adjusting her hips, sighing and whooshing. Her hair is swept up in a *kampu,* topknot, and loose strands moist with perspiration are stuck to her forehead and cheeks. Her cotton kimono barely covers her large, round belly even though the light summer robe had been altered to accommodate the growth spurt this last month. She clutches both sides of the robe as she walks slowly around the small courtyard. She would have cast off the garment entirely were it not for the mosquitoes.

Modesty is the last thing on a woman's mind at a time such as this when the one and only driving concern is to birth the baby she carries. Her child holds the blood of ancestors from China and Portugal and from her own island that was in itself a mixture of central Asian and Native North American influences.

The heat of the summer night is penetrating and Mother splashes water on her cheeks and arms from a small wooden bucket she brought outdoors as she slaps away at the insects.

There's no breeze and the thick summer night sounds with the monotonous chirp of crickets. The farm animals are asleep. Only a hen sitting patiently on her roost lets out an occasional cluck as if in sympathetic resonance. Like the mother hen who generates heat to birth her chick, the chick, too, in the interior of the shell, must peck confidently and perseveringly, doing its part.

My mother Kana has had a restless night and senses the birthing will come soon. She had left her bed to amble quietly about the courtyard so as not to wake my great-grandmother. Though it is several hours past midnight Great-Grandmother is not asleep at all. She had been listening and patiently waiting. She finally hoists herself up from the futon mattress and twists her long white hair up into a small knot on top of her head. Her hands grope for a *jifaa,* a thin wooden stick, to hold in place the kampu on her head.

Our house, constructed many generations ago from local wood, supports a heavy roof made of thick bundles of straw. The house still stands strong and sturdy even after countless rainy seasons of treacherous typhoons. This very night the sliding wood panel doors of our home are wide open. A tiny pine candle barely flickers indoors. Its flame, moved by the flutter of a moth's wings, causes the silhouette of the mosquito netting to stir against the wall of the front room.

The moist air is thick and still as Great-Grandmother yawns and makes her way outdoors. Her shadow looms indoors as Mother peers back at her, leaning her hands on the thick stone slab that serves as a gate jutting up at the entrance of the courtyard. She leans against the stone slab to ease the mounting pressure in her lower body.

I am in the womb's water world and I want to come through now! Mother helps me glide into position for birth as she continues to pace the grounds and I make ready for my descent.

Great-Grandmother greets her with a tired smile and encourages her, "So happy to see you walking about! Keep going! Keep going! It will help the birthing."

Mother nods. Her senses are heightened, and a faint scent of tobacco in the heavy night air makes her nauseous. As she re-enters the home she lurches toward one of the wood posts and stoops with her head bent forward pushing against the post to release pressure that continues to build in her lower body. Mother lets go of audible exhalations. She moans on the verge of crying and then sniffs up an inhalation and whooshes another out-breath. Great-Grandmother slides instinctually in back of Mother and presses points in her lower back to relieve the tension that has collected there.

"Ahhhhhh," murmurs Mother, grateful for Great-Grandmother's healing touch. It is still dark as Mother moves further inward toward the small room recessed from the entrance. This special room was built generations ago with its dedicated purpose as a birthing room. My brother was born there and so were many of our forebears. Clean and unadorned, its only permanent furnishing is an old cedar chest with a facade of small double doors that swing open. The hinges are rusty and the inset drawers squeak when pulled and fit awkwardly when replaced. The rectangular alcove faces north and remains cool and shaded. North is the direction associated with reproduction and the basis of life so it is appropriate that birthing should occur here.

Great-Grandmother lights another pine candle and places it on the cedar chest as Mother makes her way into the small room. Mother's queasiness dissipates as she draws in the clean air of the birthing room that is slightly cooler than the rest of the house. She eases herself down onto a thick mattress on the *tatami,* straw floor, and moans softly as she leans against large linen sacks of dried barley that support her upper body. Great-Grandmother kneels next to Mother and slides her hands under Mother's aching lower back, using Mother's body weight upon her strong fingers to apply pressure to points along the spine to ease the throbbing pain.

Mother's bedding is arranged so that she lies with her head to the east, a most favorable position because east is where the sun rises and gives life to all things. Great-Grandmother lovingly tends to her while Mother waits with quickening breath for the village *katii,* the midwife. The moment Mother let out her first groan, her mother, Machi, rushed by foot to beckon the local midwife who lives just at the outskirts of our village.

Grandmother Machi stumbles upon the little house of the midwife and carefully taps on the exterior wood panel door.

"Wake up! Wake up!" Grandmother Machi whispers loudly. The midwife stirs easily from sleep. Accustomed to the demands of her profession, she slips out from under the light cotton cover without waking her husband and ties her hair up in a bun. Her face is pale, unlike the other villagers whose skins are dark and wrinkled from years of farming or fishing under the sun's intense rays. Her work keeps her indoors and her smooth face shows no sun damage. Even at the age of sixty there isn't a trace of a wrinkle and the glossy pitch-blackness of her hair is a result of the bountiful seaweed in her diet.

The midwife has encountered difficult births in her long years of practice but because of her skill, there have been only a handful with tragic outcomes. She is revered for her long experience but is most known for her keen intuition and uncanny ability to speak to the unborn. She delivered many babies in our village and, in fact, welcomed Mother's firstborn, my brother Jiraa, ten years prior.

The midwife splashes water on her face from a small basin in a tiny washroom and glides to the entrance where Grandmother Machi waits. She grabs a small cloth satchel with five items necessary for birthing and slips on her straw sandals. She also grabs a small square of personal effects which includes pieces of clothing neatly folded, a couple of toiletries, a small comb and towel in case she might be required to stay awhile in the home that calls for her services. She is punctilious about having these items ready and parked in the same place by the entrance in the event she must dart from the house at some strange hour as is the case this very night.

Grandmother Machi insists on carrying the satchel and precedes the midwife as they make their way to our house. They must rely on the stars to guide them on this night of the dark new moon, and there's a shared sense between the two women of the auspiciousness of the time. They know that from this darkest place, the light of the new moon will emerge to signify a new beginning.

"I had a strong intuition last night that my grandchild would arrive today," says Grandmother Machi to the midwife as they make their way. "I was awake all night long. I even gave in to the urge to smoke a bit of tobacco in the ceremonial pipe," she chuckles.

It is just before dawn as the two women slip out of their straw sandals and rush into our home when they hear coming from the back room Mother's groaning and Great-Grandmother's coaching. There's some laughter, too, between the moaning and coaching and the atmosphere is not tense.

The midwife is led quickly to the birthing room where she gives humble greetings and bows to Mother and Great-Grandmother as Grandmother Machi rushes to light another candle. The midwife kneels on the floor and opens her satchel bringing out its contents and laying them carefully on a clean cloth. There are scissors for cutting the umbilical cord, thread made of the inner skin of bittersweet for tying off the umbilical cord at the navel, sagebrush cotton and the inner skin of the wild hydrangea for use in place of soap and to accelerate difficult labor. She also brings out a powerful herbal medicine to help build blood in case Mother experiences excessive blood loss.

The early morning air is humid and warm and Mother's entire body is now soaked in perspiration.

"I poured some boiling water into the washbowl and it should be sufficiently cool now," says Great-Grandmother who had placed the water bowl next to Mother along with a neat stack of dry, clean washcloths for the midwife's use.

The midwife bows slightly in a gesture of 'thank you' and kneels on Mother's left side. She manually examines the abdomen as Mother lets out gasps and groans. Determining that this is not a breach birth, the midwife lifts her face to the heavens and sings a song of protection calling the help of the birth deities. Her voice reaches very high notes and for a moment the insect world is hushed and the air carries only the midwife's crooning.

Lightly placing her left hand on Mother's huge belly the midwife speaks to me, yet unborn, "You have received a name already, little one! Your father Machuu will be home soon to be the first to call you by name."

The midwife's face is lit by a ray of light from early dawn. She closes her eyes and whispers, "You are protected and safe as you make your journey from the water world."

Mother is cradled in the hands of loving spirits as her face glows despite the labor pains. She is brave and feels no anxiety. Under the command of the powerful midwife, Mother is afforded quick moments of rest now and then, allowing for the necessary respite before the big push. She appreciates the highly unusual and sublime nature of this birthing so different from that of her firstborn.

Every detail of the birthing is etched in Great-Grandmother's mind as she witnesses my birth. She will tell this birth tale soon to our villagers. In her mind's eye she sees herself as village bard ascending to the high seat where she will recount step by step the birthing of her great-grandchild.

The midwife positions herself on the floor by the mother's feet. She places her left toe on the area just above the mother's tailbone to support her. When the infant's head shows, the midwife moves her toe to the tip of the tailbone to push it upward and gently places her forefingers around the scalp without touching the sacred aperture at the top of the baby's head. She gently introduces her hands slightly into the passage.

When the baby's cheeks show, the midwife places her forefingers on each side of the baby's chin and slides her hands slightly forward. That action causes the baby to tuck in her chin and makes the movement easier. When the baby's head is almost out and the neck begins to show, the midwife feels the neck with the forefinger of the hand that will catch the baby.

The midwife's left foot and toes work together to support the sacrum, making it easier for the hips to open. She touches the baby's neck bone and lets her fingers glide forward to the base of the neck. As the chest is coming out, she feels the tiny bones of the upper spine and slides her fingers from the neck down toward the hips. Giving gentle stimulation to the little bones of the back helps to awaken the baby's nerves.

The midwife finally catches the little one onto her hand!

At daybreak on that humid summer morning, I slid into the loving hands of the midwife and began my life with a mighty exhalation. With the assistance of the Original Wise Ones I had chosen the family into which I incarnated. The

Original Wise Ones are, as their name might imply, the ones who came before humankind. They looked for the best possible combination of persons who could provide the loving care and special grooming I would need.

During my birthing, my brother Jiraa had been sleeping soundly in an adjacent room partitioned off by sliding wood panel doors. My birth cry made such an explosive sound that it caused him to bolt up from his futon mattress and snag himself in the mosquito netting as if he were a wild fish caught at sea! He had been savagely thrown out of his slumber. How could he ever forgive me? Poor, poor Jiraa.

After the delivery Grandmother Machi and Great-Grandmother took me to the washroom for bathing. Grandmother Machi was quite ordinary as was my mother, but Machi's mother, Great-Grandmother Hanaa, was the exceptional one. She was a diviner and seer and, more importantly, our village storyteller.

When they returned, Great-Grandmother beamed at Mother. "We all heard her cry," she said. "It was an enormous bellow that will echo for generations."

"Her birth cry was unlike any other. So fierce the ground shook with trepidation!" screeched Grandmother Machi with exuberance. They proudly teased and bantered about my birth cry.

Mother, momentarily lost in thought, searched Great-Grandmother's face for an explanation.

"She is born with great karma," whispered Great-Grandmother.

And so it was, I was born in our simple birthing room, a womb within the body of the house, protected from outside influences. I came as a High Born One and although one might assume that I came to teach my family, it was they who taught me.

CHAPTER 2
THE UNINVITED GUEST

We lived in the village of Gushiken in the northern peninsula of the largest island of an archipelago that stretches for 1200 kilometers from the southern tip of Japan to Formosa in the Pacific Ocean. The long string of hundreds of tiny coral islands, known at one time in history as the Liu Ch'iu Kingdom, is bordered by two great powers, China and Japan. China was our first mother but it was Japan who would come to own us. The Japanese named our island, Okinawa. The written character for Okinawa suggests narrow islands lying offshore. Some even say the character calls to mind the image of a rope in the open sea rising up to the sky.

Although we are known as Okinawa-jin (jin means people) we call ourselves *Uchinanchu,* our rendition of the name, Okinawan, in our native tongue. Prior to being named by the Japanese we referred to ourselves as Doo-choo, our pronunciation of Liu Ch'iu.

After the Satsuma Clan of Japan invaded our islands in 1609 we were forced to form a tributary relationship with Japan in addition to our ongoing relationship with China. Our islands were heavily taxed, and our people suffered tremendously.

"Our people pay too many taxes," my father Machuu would often complain. "We can barely make ends meet especially with the terrible typhoons." What he said was true but he was resigned to the fact that he was just as powerless to stop the taxes as the typhoons. Whenever Father spoke about the severe taxation and the devastating storms, the family knew what that meant. He would have to leave for China to seek work. And it was because of this that he was not present for my birth.

My mother Kana was an ordinary woman with no particular gifts. Ordinary, one could say, because she was not schooled or especially talented but she was a mother through and through, caring for her family and placing our welfare above everything else.

She never once exhibited vanity about her exotic beauty with clear, flawless skin and eyes that slightly turned up at the outer edges revealing hints of her one-quarter Chinese blood and wavy hair from her half-Portuguese mother.

Like all new mothers of the village, Mother was cared for by friends and neighbors so she could properly rest after childbirth. Women arrived with freshly prepared food and helped with household chores. They chattered happily in muffled voices as they moved quickly through the house. They brought *champuru,* a popular dish made from tofu and vegetables that typically included roasted carrots, wild greens and boiled spinach. Tumeric was sprinkled on the vegetables, a spice that kept everyone's liver strong and high functioning. Someone was sure to bring stir-fried bitter melon, a food excellent for heart function. Although there were a variety of foods, the portions were small in keeping with our motto *hara hachibu* that we fill the belly only eighty percent for good health so that we are never entirely full. It is important to remain a little bit hungry our people say. Just like we must always remain a little bit hungry for knowledge and wisdom.

As helpers scurried about, a strange, cloaked figure appeared in the tiny vestibule of our home. An old woman, unknown to the family, peered into the little entrance of the house. "Hello," called the visitor softly, "I am here to see the mother of the child."

"Bring her to me," Mother's voice echoed from her bed as if she had been waiting for this meeting. Great-Grandmother Hanaa, sensing the portent of this visit, quickly rose to greet the stranger and our startled neighbors began to gossip quietly amongst themselves.

"She must be a witch or a ghost," whispered one of our neighbors, judging the old woman by her countenance, her dress and by her movements. Her face was hidden by the shadow of a dark hood draped over her head. The look was unusual and she stood in stark contrast to the casual, open dress of our villagers. But the woman did not seem to hear the whispering around her or perhaps she just did not pay attention.

As Great-Grandmother approached, the old woman extended something to her. "I hope Kana can use these herbs when she prepares the paste for the protection ceremony." In beautifully folded rice paper she handed sweet smelling herbs and flowers that had been dried and ground. Recognizing the herbs were not locally grown, Great-Grandmother curiously tilted her head to take in the aromatic scent and was certain these rare herbs were from a temple in the southern seas. She accepted the gift for Mother and, with a bow, welcomed the stranger into our home.

The visitor was led into the birthing room where she spoke directly to Mother who had been resting in the cool shade of the recessed quarters. She quietly spoke words of congratulations and good wishes.

"I have brought special herbal powders for your child," she said, repeating once again the intention of her visit.

"It is so odd," whispered a neighbor in the front room, "that no one recognizes her. Could she be the famous one who lives in the North Mountains?" The guests bandied back and forth about whether the cloaked one was the powerful soothsayer who lived far north of our village.

Barely containing her excitement, a woman blurted, "Quite an auspicious sign that she should appear here."

"I heard her say," whispered another, "she's brought special herbs for the protection ceremony." More whispering ensued and an atmosphere of awe and respect enveloped our home.

For three hundred years the Japanese government had prohibited the practices of these extraordinary ones from whom villagers sought fortunetelling and advice. In an effort to eradicate these practitioners the Japanese government as recently as 1900 had offered a reward to anyone who reported the *yuta,* soothsayers, to authorities. This was why the famous soothsayer had relocated to an obscure place in the north where villagers could find her only through word of mouth.

These special ones are respected and protected and would never be reported despite the large reward. That was one thing you could say about us. We are a closely-knit people with strong bonds to one another and we trust our own traditions and practices. We rely on our soothsayers for their wise counsel. We are not Japanese. We are Uchinanchu.

Consulting soothsayers is commonplace, yet, the villagers regard them in awe and sometimes fear. Their fear springs mostly from not wanting to hear news that goes against their hopes.

"Why do you think the stranger has come? Couldn't be just to bring herbal powders. What do you think?" whispered a woman to the others.

"That child gave such a *big* birth cry," stated a young man who lived nearby. "Maybe there's some connection with the cry and the appearance of this strange woman."

"I overheard Great-Grandmother say that her great-grandchild is a High Born One," said a young woman. "That's all I know."

"Maybe she will announce it at her story-telling," another offered, "and then we'll get to find out once and for all about this strange woman."

In the midst of the buzzing of the gossipers, the stranger stealthily slipped away. No one saw her exit.

CHAPTER 3
FATHER'S RETURN

Mother and I remained secluded in our home for almost a month after I was born. By the time I came along, ten barren years had passed since the birth of Jiraa, my older brother. Mother thought perhaps those ten years were not really barren but were necessary to enrich the soil of the womb to bring forth, in the words of Great-Grandmother, "this great one."

Infants, having recently come from the world of water should adjust gradually to the sights and sounds of the dry world, our women felt. It was our custom, too, when girls were born that special prayers were given to *Hinukan,* the Goddess of Fire of the Hearth. The hearth was located in the kitchen so that *utoto,* prayers, were conducted there. We also had in the front room of our home a *buchidan,* a small altar area that housed a memorial plaque with inscriptions of our ancestors to whom we prayed after placing incense in a small bowl.

Mother continued to wait patiently for Father's return. He would have been home were it not for the heavy storm that passed through our islands before whirling over the Chinese port where he had been working these past months.

One day, after praying in front of our altar for Father's safe return, Mother turned abruptly at a familiar voice shouting a greeting in the vestibule. "I'm home! Hello! Hello!" It was Father. He had returned.

Mother cried upon seeing him so thin and dark. His clothes were more tattered than usual and she knew he must have been working so very hard. He had a beard, a mixture of grey and rust, and had slung cloth bags on both shoulders, weighing him down. "Here," he said, handing his bags to Grandmother Machi who had run in upon hearing his voice. "Now let me have a look," he said extending his hands towards me.

"She's so beautiful," he cried out as he took me into his arms and refused to let me go. Father was so happy to be home and relieved to hear that my birth had been uncomplicated.

"Our daughter has come with a huge task," Mother explained as Father held me. "The High Born Matriarch Sandaa visited me in a dream and told me that we must not be frightened of our child. The Great Sandaa said to me something mysterious. She said, "Your child is born here in the North where the people are closest to nature, where the sacred energies of the northern province have drawn high teachers who will bring her the knowledge she will need to fulfill her destiny."

My father nodded. "Yes, we are closer to nature. And as compared to many places I have visited, our northern province is special, indeed."

"What will you name her?" Grandmother Machi asked as she handled the small packages of herbal medicines and seeds for planting from Father's bags. Father insisted that he had selected just the right name for me and kept everyone in suspense. Great-Grandmother stood back certain the name would be a powerful one, a name that would vibrate close to her heart.

Father had brought home a small gift for me in addition to various goods to barter. It was a tiny windmill with brightly colored wings on a wooden stick that one could blow to make the windmill rotate. I couldn't take my eyes off of it.

"Where is Jiraa?" Father asked, seeing out of the corner of his eye that his son had been hiding behind the sliding door to the kitchen. "Come, Jiraa, I have a gift for you!" Father had brought back Jiraa's favorite sweets.

"You are such a lucky boy that your sister is a High Born One," Father said, trying to draw Jiraa out. But, no luck. Jiraa would not come out to greet Father and instead he frowned and walked away. Everyone had seen the shift in Jiraa since my birth. He was jealous of the attention given me and pouted whenever the family attended to me. But more than jealousy, he was frightened of me and ran away whenever anyone spoke of me.

My brother was indeed very uneasy, but he himself did not understand why. My birth cry had created such commotion and his fear of me only continued to mount.

It's true that my brother had been the king-jewel of the household for ten years with the matriarchs hovering over him. And then, abruptly, with my birth, their attention moved to me. Perhaps it was just this simple reason, the family thought. But he became so distraught that this kind of reasoning seemed superficial and inadequate. The family grew more and more concerned about him. Mother tried to embrace him, but Jiraa violently pulled away.

One day, Jiraa went missing and did not return from school. He was in the fourth grade and apparently did not show up for his classes. Neither did he sleep at home that night. It had been only two days since Father's return from China and Jiraa had left without telling anyone. He had never done anything like this before and it worried the entire family. They checked with neighbors and learned from one of his friends that he was probably staying in a cave in the mountain where the boys played. Sure enough, when Father, with one of Jiraa's friends as guide, went to look for him, there he was, crouched near the entrance of the cave, hungry and dejected.

Father was angry and scolded Jiraa for worrying everyone. "You will come home immediately!" said Father. Jiraa frowned and followed Father down the mountain. On the way back to the house Jiraa said, "The baby is bad."

To which Father, shocked and dismayed asked, "Why would you say such a thing? Where would you get an idea like that? She is just an innocent baby."

"But she's not innocent," retorted Jiraa. "I had a bad dream about her. And, besides, she screamed like a monster when she was born."

"I heard about her unusual birth cry. We all know about that. But that is no reason for you to dislike her so much. You must have other reasons."

"I don't know. She scares me," Jiraa said looking at his feet.

Detecting Jiraa's fragile emotional state, Father softened. "You can have these thoughts for now." He was not going to battle Jiraa on this point. "But do me a favor," he continued, "No more running away. I have an idea. Help me after school in the fields and let's see if your feelings change over time. Will you do that?"

"Sure," shrugged Jira. And that was the end of the conversation about Jiraa's bad feelings.

The following morning when Jiraa left for school, Father, who had gone earlier to the fields, returned to consult Great-Grandmother.

"What do you suppose is going on?" asked Father.

"I don't know for sure," said Great-Grandmother but I know that I will soon be guided to help Jiraa heal."

Grandmother Machi, overhearing the conversation piped in, "It is so very strange, isn't it? Why should the boy be so frightened of the baby?"

Great-Grandmother took a moment. "What I do know is it has to do with past life karma," Great-Grandmother said accurately. "I am unable to see exactly what it is, but perhaps they were enemies at one time, and now they have the opportunity to correct their mistakes."

There was truth to what Great-Grandmother said. Whenever I looked at Jiraa, my heart reached out to him for forgiveness. Through our incarnations we have all been sisters and brothers, mothers and fathers, paupers and princes, monks and thieves. We have run the gamut of roles.

As I grew older I would come to know my own incarnations and would be able to see in which life I made horrific errors and deviated from the spiritual path. Like many humans, I have had to learn the lessons of power. But I am here now, and I have chosen this time to meet my brother and fulfill a destiny that has been calling me throughout the ages.

CHAPTER 4
PROTECTION CEREMONY

"Should I fetch the priestess to give the baby blessings?" inquired Grandmother Machi. "No, I am performing the ceremony myself," replied Mother. Jiraa laughed from the side, "How can you? You're not a priestess!"

That was true. Priestesses were trained in these sorts of things and Mother was not. They used chants that were unique to each child and they selected appropriate songs and invented special utterances when inspired. Sometimes they used incense to chase away bad spirits that hovered around a child.

Mother sighed and tried her best to explain that, though she was not entirely sure how she would conduct the ceremony, she was confident that she would know what to do when the time came. She was sure that through some unknown process the instructions for the ritual would spring up spontaneously in her. And sure enough, in the days to follow, Mother instinctively gathered plants from the hill behind our house. Her hands, like magnets, were drawn to certain botanicals. She apparently did not set out in search of any particular plant. She just trusted her intuition.

After gathering the leaves and stems of wild plants, she rinsed and dried them with a cotton cloth. She pulled the mortar and pestle from the kitchen shelf and crushed the botanicals. Mother created a special paste and then added the unique combination of the fragrant herbal powders from the mysterious visitor.

When she was done, she called the family together for a simple post-birth ceremony to protect me from evil influences.

Grandmother Machi lit some incense as Jiraa dragged in and stood next to Father. Great-Grandmother then took me in her arms and, as soon as everyone was ready, Mother recited a prayer.

> May you fulfill your destiny, my child, and
> May our ancestors guard you against all evils.
> May they inspire you without end and
>   bring to you all you need to fulfill your karma.
> May each of us in your family rise up to our own highest potential
>   to support you to prepare you for your task.

With that, Mother brought her hands together in *gassho,* hands in prayer, as the rest of my family prayed with heads bent in humility and high hopes. She then covered her finger with the paste she had just made and dabbed it on the little triangular area between my eyebrows.

The ritual was designed for my protection and also set in motion the quickening of my spiritual advancement. We are all born with a spiritual seed in the belly but for most the seed does not sprout and remains dormant for a lifetime. In my case, the seed had begun its gestation at the moment of my birth. When Mother placed the herbal paste at the center point between my eyebrows, the ingredients of the paste began to call the energy in my belly to rise. And so began the development of my mind and spirit. From that very day of the ceremony, I absorbed all that I heard and my senses registered everything around me.

The sacred paste Mother applied hardened in a short time and, when dusted off, left an indigo stain on my forehead. "Oh dear," said Mother, unable to rub the color from my forehead. "It looks like a tattoo." Jira laughed but when Father looked his way, he became quiet and respectful.

"Not to worry," said Great-Grandmother. "That indigo stain on her forehead resembles exactly the dark blue mark on her tailbone. And that blue mark is a stamp that comes from the Wise Ones to spread its influence into the lower belly."

Mother nodded but really had no idea as to what Great-Grandmother referred. "It is true," Mother thought to herself, "that we are all born with the blue mark on our tailbone. But what has that to do with our bellies?"

Great-Grandmother, intuiting Mother's question, said, "Tell Jiraa to ring the village bell." Jiraa didn't want to but went to ring the bell anyway. The big bell stood in the middle of our village and was rung to call people to our home whenever Great-Grandmother wished to recount tales.

In ancient times the King of Korea had sent a great bronze bell as a gift to the city of Shuri in the South and a smaller version to our village in the North. Although small by comparison, our bell could be heard for such a wide radius that it became a marvelous tool to communicate warnings or to call neighboring villagers to gatherings.

It was mostly Great-Grandmother who used the bell to announce her storytelling. For more than seventy years she had served as village bard. She told tales that were handed down through the bards and plucked new tales from a hidden place inside her vast, rich psyche. She often received tales from high sources right on the spot. The villagers looked forward to being entertained by her. Bearing witness to the clan's history through oral tradition was a way for them to remain linked to the Original Wise Ones.

Like many gifted women, she was aware of the power of her voice but insisted that, in the end, hers would never equal the one I would come to possess. She was *my* great-grandmother, but everyone referred to her as such. In many ways she belonged to everyone. "Great-Grandmother, tell us another story," they often called out. And when the bell sounded, they would come running.

"My goodness," panted an old man who made his way from the center of the village, "it was so warm I had fallen asleep under the banana tree when Jiraa's bell woke me up! Goodness! Goodness!"

A young girl, waving a rumpled shirt and laughing, ran behind the old man. He apparently had spread the shirt on the ground creating a makeshift bed and had forgotten it under the tree.

"On my way," yelped a neighbor who was boiling soybeans to make tofu. "I guess my soybeans will have to wait!"

As people started settling in, the old man who had fallen asleep under the banana tree joked about how the bell was so loud its reverberations surely could be heard in the South. People laughed and nodded.

Great-Grandmother took her seat. She was inspired to speak of an ancient tale about the power of the tattoo. Tattoo had played a spiritual role in our culture as well as one of beauty. Most women in ancient times tattooed their hands and faces. Perhaps it was the lighting in our courtyard that day that lent shadows to accentuate those darkened areas on Great-Grandmother's cheeks giving her face an eerie authenticity to her tale, which she began by becoming Tattoo Woman.

I am the first Tattoo Woman of our people. The Original Wise Ones gave me the power to insert spiritual energy into the tailbone of every newborn of our clan. You must now understand why you are all born with the dark blue stain on your tailbones. The tailbone is the base of our energy-body. Remember, we are not just physical flesh.

I take the black ink from the octopus together with crushed herbs and spread it on the tailbone of every infant. With this special instrument, I tattoo a dark mark there.

Great-Grandmother pulled out an ancient relic from her sleeve and showed it to the assembled group. The tool, used for tattooing babies, was a thin, cylindrical piece of obsidian that came to a blunt end. Its handle was a beautiful wooden stick of intricately carved animal motifs.

Tap, Tap, Tap…I leave a blue stain. The area at the end of the spine will then absorb the special ink and stimulate the spiritual energy to rise. And I become witness to the awakening of the spiritual potential of every child.

We practiced this ritual for thousands of years of tattooing infants' tailbones until the day came when every child was born with the dark blue mark. It was no longer necessary to continue the tattoo ritual on infants.

Is there one among you who was not born with this dark blue mark on the tailbone? The mark on the tailbone remains for many months, sometimes a few years. Whenever a child is born into our clan, the stain is a reminder of our spiritual potential. When the child grows into adulthood, the blue spot fades. Just as the blue spot fades over time, so has its meaning. I am here now to remind each and every one of you the truth of its purpose.

Great-Grandmother sighed and was then released from her role as the Tattoo Woman. She continued to explain. "The profession of tattooing belonged always to women. Eventually the tattoo artists sharpened the instrument made of obsidian to a razor-sharp point and tattooed the hands and faces of young women because it was thought to be a sign of beauty."

Later that evening, Great-Grandmother spoke to Mother, "So you see, the stain in between her eyebrows mirrors the stain on her tailbone. And while both marks will eventually disappear, the power they hold will always be present." She went on to explain that the special spot between my eyebrows where the paste left an indigo stain was the Third Eye, a psychic eye that remained closed in most people. When proper events fell into place the spiritual energy in my lower belly would rise to my Third Eye to help open it. With one's Third Eye closed, one was limited in seeing and knowing. When the Third Eye opened, one could see beyond ordinary sight. One was able, in the words of Great-Grandmother, "to finally perceive the obvious."

But she issued a warning along with her explanations. "Potential for the greatest spiritual progress is highest among the stamped ones. However, the potential for spiritual growth, if not cultivated in one's self, lies dormant and is essentially wasted."

My family knew that my spiritual cultivation could be interrupted if the right teachings did not come my way. Great-Grandmother was prepared to teach me all that she knew, and I would be groomed in a number of ways that the Wise Ones would arrange.

That evening Great-Grandmother rocked me to sleep by the light of the flickering oil lamp. She witnessed the unusual glow of the stain on my tiny forehead. "I can see the energy pulsating on your little forehead, my sweet one. The magical ingredients of the blue paste will pull the spiritual energy upward from your lower belly, and you will develop much more quickly than the other children."

You can see it in her eyes!" Mother whispered proudly. "She will grow to be a special child, indeed."

CHAPTER 5
FATHER GIVES ME A NAME

Father returned early from the fields, carrying pieces of fine wood. Jiraa had been waiting patiently to learn the art of cabinet-making for some time, and Father planned to start their project the next day. He wanted to let his son know that although there were special considerations for his baby sister, Jiraa was just as important.

The night before, Father had asked Jiraa to come home directly after school with the promise of showing him the wood. He had also requested that Mother prepare a special meal of rice and millet with pumpkin soup.

"Something smells good," Father said as he entered the house. Closely following his entry was Jiraa who returned promptly from school as requested. He immediately saw the pieces of wood and ran to examine and admire each piece Father had selected.

"Let's get started now," exclaimed Jiraa, practically breathless. "Tomorrow!" father waved his hand. "We need a whole day for your lesson. Besides, it will be dark soon." Jiraa was beaming.

"Today," Father continued loudly, "I think we should perform the naming ceremony." He smiled at his announcement because he was sure it was a surprise to everyone.

"Oh, really? Today?" Mother responded as if taken aback although, of course, she had already guessed that's what Father was up to. Grandmother Machi who had been chopping vegetables in the kitchen and Great-Grandmother who was stirring the soup both chimed in, "Great! What a wonderful idea."

Father stood in one place tapping his toe. Jiraa who was still inspecting his wood nodded in agreement, happy to have not been forgotten. "In fact," Father said unable to contain his excitement, "let's do the naming now before the meal." Great-Grandmother stopped what she was doing and rushed to get rare incense from a sealed wooden box behind the memorial plaque of the altar. Mother put me on a tiny mattress that she placed in front of the altar and Jiraa laid hibiscus flowers and leaves to decorate the area around my head. My family gathered around me as Great-Grandmother lit the special incense in a clay bowl. Rare and most precious, aloes wood was used in religious ceremonies. Great-Grandmother, waiting for an appropriate time to burn it, had stored the small cone many years ago.

They knelt on their knees, in *seiza,* on the tatami floor flanking both sides of me. Father took the head position facing me in my makeshift bed in front of the altar. The ceremony started with an ancient call and response chant sung on special occasions by our clan. Great-Grandmother sang the first line, and the family responded with the verse. The scent of the incense was exquisite and the smoky trail curled and lingered around us as if to offer its subtle fragrance for as long as it could. As they finished the chant, Father placed his hand on my forehead and uttered my name for the first time, "Mahataa."

The others glanced at Father and then at each other. They had never heard such a name. Father stroked my face, "Since she comes to us with such high birth, I thought she should have a unique name. I will explain."

It was a simple but sweet ceremony, and Mother picked me up immediately afterward, softly repeating my name. Jiraa paused to wonder if they had done the same for him and since the family had never mentioned it, he decided that they had not accorded him the same attention. He felt dejected until his eyes caught the beautiful pieces of wood for his cabinet.

"*Maha* means great in Sanskrit," Father announced proudly and then launched into the story about the name he had chosen.

"The first Liu Ch'iuans who made their home at the port of Ch'uang-chou were early settlers taken from our islands as prisoners by Chinese expeditions that came here looking for the Elixir of Immortality. Those expeditions never found the Immortals nor the Elixir. Skirmishes ensued on the island and the Chinese mariners rounded up at least a thousand of our people and took them to China where our people founded the community at Ch'uang-chou."

Great-Grandmother fell into a momentary reverie and revealed the truth. "The Elixir is indeed here in our archipelago somewhere hidden and so are the Immortals. The Immortals materialize only when they need to establish rapport with inhabitants of our islands. Otherwise they reside in spheres not visible to humans."

She paused and continued, "The reason the expeditions were sent to our islands was because our islanders, far back in history, had the reputation of living a long life well into our 90's and 100's. We've always been known for having secrets of longevity which countries around us have coveted. Despite our hard life we are long-lived."

The family nodded and Father continued his story. "The port of Ch'uang-chou was practically home to my great-great-great-grandfather. Although he was born and raised here on our island, he spent quite a bit of time as a young man in the Okinawan settlement at Ch'uang-chou and eventually died there. He lived in the seventeenth century and was a strong, adventurous fellow with a great sense of humor.

"My great-great-great-grandfather treated everybody kindly for which he, in turn, was well loved. On his frequent visits he stayed with his brother's family to work alongside other families who made their home in the commercial seaport. Whenever my ancestor arrived at his brother's home in Ch'uang-chou, he was fed hot delicious meals. After sailing for over a week and living off of dried, salted fish and sweet potatoes that were beginning to turn, he enjoyed the hot home-cooked meals."

As I lay cooing and gurgling, the rest of my family was entertained by the story. Even though Mother had heard bits of it before, my father was in rare form. We were fortunate to learn about our family so far back in history and to be given an education about earlier times. According to Father's story, merchant seamen from all over the world came to trade at this port—Arabs, Indians, Malays and Siamese. Wafting from the open marketplace was a mixture of odors from sweet meats and curried tofu from Siam to roasted garlic and cabbage delicacies from Korea.

Father's great-great-great-grandfather developed a close friendship with an Indian man whose life he had saved. This Indian man had accidentally fallen from his boat one night a few miles out at sea, unnoticed by his comrades who, while singing and making music, were tossing liquor down their throats along with delicacies they had bought at the port. He lay drifting on a piece of wood for a couple of days when Father's ancestor fished the Indian up from the sea. The Indian man spoke the Chinese language of the area and knew a bit of the Liu Ch'iu dialect as he had spent quite a bit of time in the port bartering with merchants from our islands.

It turned out, the Indian had set sail from Goa on the western border of India four years prior and was a Hindu of the kshatriya caste whose family came originally from Punjab, an area in the north of India near the Kashmir border. What tales he had to tell of the warrior caste into which he had been born and how his family disowned him for taking to the high seas to romp around with those of the lower merchant class.

My father said that the Indian, when he was a little boy, dreamt of becoming a pirate and of navigating the oceans of the world but he took a radically different path when he met a holy man in his earlier life. He actually studied with the Guru, a spiritual master, for a number of years near his village in Punjab. The boy's adventurous spirit eventually got the better of him and at the age of sixteen he ran off to sea to pursue his first dream. He soon found that he needed to make a living along the way and he became a trader and adventurer in the Pacific Ocean, traveling throughout all of Asia.

By the time he met my ancestors, he was already in his early thirties and looked much older than his age because of his rough living on the seas. Whenever he came to the port he stopped off to visit the family and stayed as long as he could. Gradually they got to know each other quite well, sharing stories and learning about each other's cultures. The Indian taught my ancestors verses from religious texts of India and was regarded as a very spiritual man. He had learned to play from one of his fellow sailors, a *tambura,* a long-necked instrument tuned in fifths, and he plucked it to bring forth the most delightful sounds. He sang songs of his homeland enter-taining the family whenever he visited, and, he visited often. His trade ship came through the port of Ch'uang-chou several times a year. The entire family treated him as one of their own and made sure he stayed with them whenever his ship docked at the port.

"You should marry soon," the family teased as they shared a meal together. Because he had been out at sea so long, he hadn't had the time to settle down.

The Indian turned to Father's great-great-great-grandfather and answered, "I will return one day to your tiny island of the archi-pelago and find the woman of my dreams. Perhaps I will marry one of your family!" he joked. Everyone burst out in laughter. They wanted very much to claim him on the spot as one of the family.

But he had been only half joking. He was a man of his word. Whatever he said he was going to do, he did, never making empty promises. "My word is all I can give," he said to my ancestors.

It was this Indian warrior who came to the aid of the family when Father's great-great-great-grandfather fell ill during a malaria epidemic. Due to severe illness, Father's ancestor was unable to return home to our island and had to be cared for by his brother's family in China.

The Indian man offered solace to the family when Father's ancestor died. The Indian presided over the memorial service recit-ing touching poems from his native country and wept alongside the family.

The Indian man's name was Mahataa, which was not a typical name even in his country. It was a name given to him in India by the famous Guru under whom he had studied as a youth. When the Guru saw the potential in the boy, he handed him the cloth, which was a gesture to take him as a disciple, and then, with divine guidance, gave the boy his name. The boy studied with the Guru for many years but left because the training was so very severe. He had been an excellent student studying the Vedas and Upanishads which were sacred texts of India, however, he was restless. One day he simply decided to take to the vast ocean to become a pirate. The Guru thought that the boy was choosing to waste his life but, in an unexpected way, his student was able to spread his Guru's teachings far and wide by meeting people and passing along all the wisdom and knowledge he had acquired in his former ascetic life.

The story of Mahataa, the Indian trader, was passed down in our family because he made such an impression with his kindness, intelligence, wisdom and brilliance. Many maxims learned from Mahataa were repeated in our family over the generations and to keep credit where credit was due, those teachings were always attributed to this generous Indian trader.

Having heard all the family stories connected to this unusually gifted man, Father wanted to bless me with the name of the one who would be remembered in our family for generations to come. Father hoped the name would inspire me with the same high spirit of adventure, kindness and magnanimity that the Indian had possessed.

"I have often wondered if the Indian ever traveled to our islands to find the woman of his dreams," said Father at the conclusion of his story, his thoughts drifting to a faraway time.

Great-Grandmother, prompted by a stirring in her heart, said, "Yes, he did! But, in a *subsequent* life!" Everyone turned to look at Great-Grandmother whose face was flushed and whose eyes glowed with tenderness. There was a karmic connection between this Indian man and myself whose name became mine, but our connection would remain a secret in Great-Grandmother's heart.

CHAPTER 6
GREAT-GRANDMOTHER TELLS THE BIRTH TALE

Father cleaned our courtyard to prepare the grounds for Great-Grandmother's storytelling. Great-Grandmother felt that by repeating the story of my birth the villagers who heard it might be catapulted spiritually. The syllables of my newly given name, if voiced properly, carried special vibrations that could stir the spiritual seed in others. She had spoken of my birth to neighbors, but this was her first telling to a large audience. News had spread that a great soul had incarnated in our tiny village and a large gathering was anticipated.

Although I was just an infant when my ears received Great-Grandmother's telling of the tale, the images and words settled mysteriously in my being. The storytelling comes to me as if in a dream.

It is the end of a blisteringly hot, humid day and I am hovering above crowds of people who are making their way along narrow, dirt trails to a tiny thatched-roof house in our rural village. People of all ages are chatting nervously, buzzing with excitement, as they collect in our tiny courtyard. I float above the villagers, yet at the same time, I am cradled in Mother's arms close to her breast, just a month old. Sitting near the sliding wood panel doors of our home, she rocks me and sings softly to me.

Women arrive in patched house kimono, and men come in cotton trousers and western-style shirts that are rumpled and faded. They are soaked from the penetrating mugginess. Some try to cool their faces with fans made of straw and reeds but the air is so thick and hot that the effort it takes to wave the fans generates even more heat.

All eyes are on Great-Grandmother as she kneels in seiza on a special dais designed and constructed by my father and brought out only when Great-Grandmother tells stories. Fashioned out of a large tree trunk, the dais stands as one piece with no joints or dowels. On top of it is an inset tatami straw mat upon which Great-Grandmother sits.

Latecomers, some from remote areas of our island, continue to trickle in to hear the birth story. They squeeze themselves into the mass of people in front of our home. The smell of perspiration from travelers who walked great distances in the heat of the midsummer's day permeates the crowd. Mingled with sweat is the acrid scent of coiled incense to ward off mosquitoes. Still, people occasionally slap their exposed arms and faces. What overrides their annoyance with the pesky creatures is the anticipation of what they think Great-Grandmother is about to reveal. They had been gossiping back and forth about the rumors of my birth.

Great-Grandmother is in her middle nineties and her bright eyes, surrounded by fine lines on her forehead and cheeks, glisten and warmly radiate her wisdom. Her hair, once black as coal, is wound up in a snowy white knot on top of her head. She slowly sips tea from a ceramic bowl made from local red clay. The heat of the summer's day, still trapped in the earth, is strong and rises up from the scorched ground causing beads of sweat to appear on her brow and upper lip. She shakily reaches into the pocket-sleeve of her kimono and pats her face with a tiny handkerchief that she retrieves. The kimono is made from patches of tie-dyed cloth with sleeves sewn from remnant strips of silk fabric she had manufactured that billow even in the still air whenever she moves her arms. The kimono's pieces come together in muted blues and greys with splotches of white that spring out in typical tie-dye fashion.

While Great-Grandmother sits on the simple wood platform with the house to her back, Jiraa peeps out from a tiny room inside the house clutching a cricket cage he had constructed with reeds plucked by the stream where we wash our clothes and sometimes bathe during hot summers. Grasshoppers and crickets have delighted him since he was a toddler. Now he grasps the cage to his small chest practically crushing the innocent creatures. It is as if someone were going to snatch it from him. The funny, once-happy-go-lucky boy is nowhere to be seen, and he moves about unsteadily, worried and scared.

My brother trembles as he peeks between his fingers, trying unsuccessfully to cover his eyes. And when Great-Grandmother rises from her seat with her arms raising up to the sky as if some spirit has come to occupy her, Jiraa becomes most upset.

Great-Grandmother grows taller and taller and, although she is small and shrunken in stature, the audience imagines that she has grown to an immense size. It is as though they are under a spell. Great-Grandmother's eyes emit flashes of light, and the crowd, all too familiar with her powers, comes to attention.

"My name is Mahataa!" Great-Grandmother roars. Just then, I see and hear a loud gushing of water spewing out the top of her head like a geyser, and for that moment the waterworks are so spectacular, so grand that there's no space for even one thought. The water, rather than pelting the villagers, rains down softly on them like a ghostly waterfall.

"My name is Mahataa," she insists carefully this time. Great-Grandmother allows for some moments to pass and the villagers nod to one another because they know her style of storytelling. She *becomes* the character of her tales.

"I can see you raise your eyebrows when you hear my name. It's a foreign name that hangs on your tongue when you mouth it. The sound of it has begun for you a questioning.

"Listen carefully to my tale. You must listen with the whole body. Listen with the eyes, the ears, the nose, all of the senses. Listen through the pores. You must hear in this total way to begin the process of awakening."

She summons from them as delicately as she can, as one pulls silk from a cocoon, their reason for being alive, their purpose for incarnating.

"My name echoes for each of you who hears it a deep, deep yearning. Mahataa, Mahaataa, Mahaataa...."

Great-Grandmother's voice trails and quivers as she repeats my name. Then, deep silence. Not a single sound issues from the villagers except for the faint gurgling of one infant boy in the arms of a neighbor. That boy's name is Li En Gong and he is part of my destiny. Even then, as mere infants in our mothers' arms, a peculiar thread of energy connects the crown of his head to mine. I can feel it.

I sense a kind of steamy, misty blessing as Great-Grandmother speaks in tones so low I can barely make out what she is saying. There's a kind of whirring sound where Great-Grandmother transmits the entire story of my birth through the mist.

And then, the unpleasant smells are gone, the mosquitoes have disappeared, and the villagers are sparkling and cleansed. I am nestled in Mother's arms, and the cool beads of water caress and moisten my spirit. My heart is settled. Our people are united, finally, in our collective purpose.

Great-Grandmother truly believed to the depths of her soul that I was born to do great things. Trusting also that her telling of the story would inspire the villagers, she told the story again and again, standing up and raising her voice, then quieting down again speaking in a whisper. She was a stern teacher, frightening ghost, wise soothsayer and tender nursemaid, all woven together.

When she told the birth story, she sometimes spoke in first person, sometimes not. It depended on her inspiration.

She always drank a special tea before she began her storytelling and when she finished the tale, she would characteristically swirl the tea in its clay bowl with both hands and sip the remaining drops of the special blend she had prepared for herself. It included a medicinal leaf harvested from a tree in Southeast Asia that tapped her inner vision and ensured her alertness. The rare leaf most likely imported from Thailand or Malaysia had been thoroughly dried and kept in a jar. She first got the potent dried leaves from the black market in the South where she met Mateus, the Portuguese trader who traveled the Pacific waters and with whom she was once in love. A vendor in the South, whom she befriended, sent her tiny packages every so often of these exquisite tea leaves. She was grateful and used the special leaves frugally and only when she recounted the tales.

At the end of this most recent telling of the birth tale in our courtyard, Great-Grandmother's eyes sparkled like never before, and my brother looked even more anxious at hearing the story yet again.

CHAPTER 7
JIRAA'S HEALING

One morning Great-Grandmother walked to the center of the village with Jiraa and asked him to ring the big bell again. He looked hesitant, afraid perhaps that Great-Grandmother was going to repeat my birth story. "This is for you," she said, encouraging him. He took a breath and struck the old bronze bell. The overtones reverberated for quite some time, announcing that she would soon begin another storytelling. On this day Great-Grandmother had finally gotten the inspiration to help heal Jiraa.

The villagers streamed into our courtyard and whispered and gossiped as usual until Great-Grandmother took her high seat. Muffled sounds echoed through the crowd until complete silence fell upon the gathered.

Great-Grandmother announced that she would be telling a tale from ancient history that took place in China's royal court in early 608 AD. It was a story, she said, that would reveal many things. She gave a special nod to Jiraa as their eyes locked for a while and then she began the tale.

"What do you mean they didn't find it!" bellowed the Emperor of China at the top of his lungs. His dull fish eyes bulged under wrinkled brow. His voice boomed for one so frail and so very ill. He had just received news, very, very bad news from the Court Magician that the recent expedition to find the Elixir in the Eastern Seas had failed.

It had been a whole year since the last group of seafarers, dispatched from their eastern seaport, came back empty-handed and now this expedition had also failed on one sole mission: to find the Elixir of Immortality. The Court Magician came to the Emperor to relay the unfortunate news from the captain of the expedition.

Soaking in every word Jiraa sat wide-eyed directly in front of Great-Grandmother.

The Court Magician had prophesied that there existed just off their continent in the Pacific Ocean The Land of Immortals in the Eastern Seas. He was referring to the islands of our archipelago! The Emperor had trusted the abilities of the Magician but had seen only one failed expedition after another. Still he believed and waited, hoping his own weak body would not give out before obtaining the Elixir.

The Court Magician cowered now in the corner of the Emperor's quarters, trembling like an animal already in its death throes. He dared to bring such dreadful news again of another failed attempt and was sure to be beheaded. The Magician shook with fright.

The Emperor called his guards with mad clanging of his service bell and in rushed two armed soldiers with curved blades drawn, their faces flushed, ready for attack.

"Execute him!" the Emperor growled. The Court Magician had promised to find a potion so powerful that would render its drinker immortal. The old ruler's anger mounted for believing such a thing possible. "What foolishness," he muttered to himself. He had achieved imperial supremacy but it was incomplete without eternal life to enjoy it. He gritted his teeth and clutched his failing heart as he collapsed onto his kingly divan in utter defeat.

Great-Grandmother's face was twisted with anguish as she became the Emperor. Something about the tale kept Jiraa on edge. His very soul stirred to its deepest place, and a strange understanding crept sinuously into his bones. As if the tale were laced with some kind of medicine to heal him, Jiraa relaxed and something profound was revealed to him.

My infant ears, too, drew in the tale to the deepest recesses of my being. The tale would remain in my psyche until it surfaced when I was older. Something about the story vibrated close to my heart. I would remember the events of the Chinese court and the emperor and the magician, all of it. A boy, a very young boy witnessed those events in the ancient Chinese court. Great-Grandmother, recognizing the powerful remedy inside her tale, continued the story.

A little boy, the son of a servant-maid, had run into the Emperor's chambers to fetch his pet cricket when he happened upon the poor Court Magician's sentencing. The poor boy grasped his artfully crafted bamboo cage and scurried to one side of the room. The Emperor was so enraged, and the Magician completely paralyzed that they were both unaware of the boy's entry.

The Magician had been a friend and confidante of the boy for the entire ten years of the boy's life. The boy, seeing the Magician just moments before his execution, trembled with fright and his heart pounded in great consternation. He shrank behind a large jade statue of Kuan Yin, clutching it from behind and pleading with her to grant his friend the highest compassion.

Great-Grandmother cleared her voice and explained, "Kuan Yin is the Bodhisattva of Compassion and the Hearer of the Cries of the World. Sometimes the actions of powerful men cannot be intercepted. Their will is enforced despite all efforts to curtail their mighty blows."

But on that fateful day, the little boy lost his confidante just before the summer solstice. And from that day forward he prayed and prayed that he would see his magical friend once again in another life. He knew his prayers would be answered. He had great faith in the Lords of Karma to grant him his wish.

My brother heaved a sigh of relief as Great-Grandmother finished her tale. He did not know why, but he felt resolved. His fear of me subsided. It was a rebirth for him, and my family was thrilled and humbled to witness it. Great-Grandmother finished the tale with one last detail about an incident between the boy and the Magician where the Magician showed his highest sensitivity in teaching the boy.

When one of the boy's pet crickets died, he sadly told the Magician about it. The boy was surprised by the Magician's response.

"Well that's the most fantastic news I've heard today," said the Magician to the little boy. "Because of your deep caring for him, your cricket will be catapulted to a much higher existence. Because of your kindness the cricket will ascend from the lowly life of an insect. Just look at what a wonderful owner of the cricket you have been."

Great-Grandmother threw a quick glance at Jiraa and knew the emotional healing was complete. It was a healing that came not from an intellectual understanding but rather from a deep shift in the ocean of his psyche.

CHAPTER 8
GREAT-GRANDMOTHER: MY FIRST TEACHER

Since hearing the Emperor's story, Jiraa softened considerably, and we were all grateful for the profound shift in his attitude and behavior. He was his cheerful self again and left for school with the kind of excitement he used to have. The cabinet-building project with Father was spread out over several weeks, working only on their free days. Especially evident after Jiraa's healing was that his awareness was much more crisp and relaxed as Father taught him during the final stages of the building project. This involved loving attention to fine detail, such as smoothing the corners of the finished piece. The pressure of the rough tool applied on the cabinet's surface needed to be just the right amount and uniform. And Jiraa was able to complete this task with a calm and even mind.

After Jiraa's transformation, Great-Grandmother, confident that the entire family was ready to support my development, began to instruct me.

Every morning my parents and Grandmother Machi left to work in the fields while Jiraa went to school. It was during this time that Great-Grandmother would care for me and teach me what she knew.

She introduced many advanced ideas right away, unconcerned that I was just a toddler. Maybe she knew she had only a few years left, as she would die before I was seven. But she was also aware that, despite my age, anything said to me registered in my cells and would become available to me when I was older.

"Your birth cry was not from you," Great-Grandmother said to me one morning as I managed to stand up and waddle toward her. "It came from the other world, which is why it had so much power. Your small voice now no longer holds the power of the original cry. But you will develop yourself soon enough and your voice will become strong." She picked me up, put me on my futon bed and began to weave.

As a young girl, Great-Grandmother learned to weave on a giant loom. The fibers of a large plantain tree produced an extremely fine textile known as *basa,* suited to the hot humid climate. It was similar to Chinese gauze and was an important industry in many of our homes. Our Liu Ch'iuans introduced this special craft to Japan many centuries ago.

"Learn to encourage the energy in your belly to rise up and your voice will become strong," Great-Grandmother spoke as she wove. "Only when the energy rises to your head will your voice have the quality of your first cry. Then you will tell stories that are embedded with powerful catalysts to help others embark on their spiritual journeys."

From the beginning, I absorbed Great-Grandmother's teachings in a way that cannot be adequately explained. Words are powerful and contain meaning beyond themselves. The heart can pick up the meaning when words are spoken by one as passionate and formidable as Great-Grandmother.

Great-Grandmother did not only leave me with esoteric wisdom. She taught me practical lessons as well. She often dyed the threads that she selected and applied to the loom with painstaking care in order to bring out a desired design or pattern. She taught me about various plants and seeds that created dyes in deep indigo blue, red, yellow and gradations of brown. Some of the plants used for coloring and staining were also used as medicine.

Great-Grandmother pointed to a bunch of *ukon,* turmeric stems, that yielded a yellowish-brownish dye. "Not only is this a dye," she instructed. "It is a wonderful spice for cooking and is used also in India's Ayurvedic medicine to treat many ailments such as liver disorders. It is used too as an anti-bacterial agent and as an antiseptic for cuts, burns and bruises."

My mornings with Great-Grandmother were precious. I would always remember the way her old hands worked with the speed and energy of a young woman.

Whenever she was done with her weaving, she would hold it up with pride, "Just look at these beautiful pieces of material," she might say. Great-Grandmother loved every garment she made and believed that the inspiration she received as she worked mixed with parts of her to create the perfect cloth.

Or she would exclaim, "Look at this exquisite *basho-fu,*" as she held up a light cloth processed specifically for summer kimono. The light cloth was made out of special banana leaves from plantain trees growing in the dense vegetation. The leaves were large and resembled those of the fruit-bearing banana trees but were instead of a non-fruit producing species.

Great-Grandmother also knew the tie-dye methods and stencil dyeing that were introduced to our islands from Java and Sumatra. I was fortunate to witness her skills since most of the creativity in the arts and crafts took place near the bustling seaport of the South. Great-Grandmother was resourceful. She harvested silk-worms to cultivate a meager amount of silk for her own use. She learned the art from her own mother who learned it from her Chinese mother. Great-Grandmother's mother, whose name was Uto, was born in 1812 of half-Chinese ancestry. Uto then would be my great-great-grandmother. Uto's father was the ancestor related to the most recent High Born One, Kamadaa.

A few years before Uto was born, her father, as a young man, left the Liu Ch'iu islands on a two-year expedition. He returned five years later with a Chinese wife and their young daughter Uto. The couple had met in the marketplace of a port in South China.

Uto's mother came from a family of herbalists and had acquired knowledge of hundreds of herbs and medicinal preparations which she passed along to her daughter. Also, Uto received by way of her ancestor, the Great Kamadaa, the ancient tales that were handed down. Uto, in turn, passed all of her knowledge of the tales and chants to Hanaa, my great-grandmother. Although Uto was not able to breathe life into those songs that held secret catalysts, she nonetheless was able to recount the tales to the syllable.

One morning Great-Grandmother had a sudden urge to teach. "Please call our villagers for a storytelling," she said. We never knew from where her inspiration came, but we were always grateful when it visited her. Today she would speak to us about the history of our clan. She gathered in her mind the various stories handed down through the lineage of bards in the way she gathered threads at her loom and wove those details from intuition.

Our people are a mixture of races. We come from nomadic people of Central Asia who separated from the greater clan to make their way through Korea and down through Hokkaido, the northernmost island of Japan. Some migrated south from Central Asia to areas now known as Tibet. Others moved east down the Bering Strait to North America.

They were driven south by the cold and found themselves in our archipelago where they mixed with descendants of indigenous people who held in their being remnants from an ancient culture known as Lemuria or the Land of Mu.

"I've heard of the Land of Mu," whispered one of the villagers known to be an intuitive one. "It's true. The huge continent of Mu sank into the Pacific waters, and there are huge head statues built by the Lemurians that remain on one of the islands that managed to stay above water as proof of this ancient culture."

Hearing this, Great-Grandmother expounded,

Lemuria was a continent ruled by matriarchs that eventually sank into the sea. There are written records about the continent of Mu in certain monasteries in the high mountains of Central Asia. The Great Sandaa who rose to promi-nence soon after that time and led our people is thought to have come from the Lemurian race. She took a strong name for herself. In fact, the name Sandaa belonged to men and she adopted the name for herself knowing that a masculine name would enhance her physical powers.

No one knew for sure the origin of the Great Sandaa but legend says she was Lemurian and ruled our people with fairness and with the integrated power of both male and female. It was Sandaa who came to my granddaughter Kanaa in a dream to prophesy the coming of another High Born One in our time, my own great-granddaughter, Mahataa.

Little known is that migrants crossed the Strait in a reverse migration from North America down through Hokkaido to our islands. North America was settled by indigenous beings before the arrival of the Central Asians to their continent. We have traces in our blood of many peoples.

"No wonder I feel an explicably deep connection to the Tibetan and the Native American," said one of the villagers after the story.

"Me, too," confessed a young teen. "I have always been drawn to wear owl feathers in my hair," said the youth whose mother nodded and said, "My boy is so silly. He collects feathers, and since he was a child has glued the ends of the feathers together with sticky rice and worn them on his head." Everybody laughed and made their way out of the courtyard as the storytelling ended.

For several generations in our village of Gushiken, because of a certain family karma, it was only our family that produced bards. A storyteller was born almost every generation in our lineage. I would learn the stories, too, but for an entirely different purpose.

"The women of our ancient clan were great warriors," Great-Grandmother said to me. "Their fearlessness was expressed through how they faced life's trials and tribulations. Our women were powerful because they faced their own demons and were able to experience them in such a way that the demons naturally receded."

"Demons are ghosts," I babbled to which Great-Grandmother let out a hearty laugh.

"Yes, indeed!" She chuckled. She could almost not believe that those words rolled off my toddler's tongue.

"You are so right," she said. "But when I said demons, I was referring to the dark qualities that we have. Emotional qualities existing inside of ourselves like anger, jealousy and fear that arise naturally in all of us," she said, "and these emotions come and go every moment so they *are* ghosts in a way. They are not substantial."

"You will grow to be one of our women warriors. You will develop yourself as they did long ago. They developed their true power by *using* the energy of their emotions rather than being used by them. By working on themselves in this way, these women demonstrated their high development and led by example. We can allow our emotions to be just as they are, not grasping or rejecting them. That way they then tend to lose their power over us."

She said, "It's easy to be a big bully, but can we look inside our self to root out our own bully? By asking these kinds of questions, the women warriors worked diligently cleaning out places in their psyche that could hinder them." The potency of her words settled in a deep place within me.

"In the end we cannot truly help others without clearing our own selves of our mistaken ways," Great-Grandmother looked away and muttered under her breath as if she still had misguided places left inside her psyche. Occasionally when she taught me, she would lift her head and gaze off like that, as if frozen in time. Although her mind drifted to other worlds, I knew she was acutely aware and always listening to me with her heart.

CHAPTER 9
FATHER AND OUR PROPERTY

The women raised me, taught and disciplined me but it was my father who brought the spirit of adventure and curiosity to my young mind. He regretted having been away during my birth and wished he had heard the cry that everyone still talked about. "But the past is the past," he would say. "Can't get it back. What we can do though, is make up for lost time," and with that, he would take me away from whatever I was doing just to spend a little time together. He loved to tie me onto his back whenever he took his creaky bicycle on rides. In the same way the other villagers carried their children, he used a long wide piece of cloth that he wound around the both of us as I straddled his back. The cloth criss-crossed underneath his armpits and over the shoulders and wrapped around the top of his head. Father stopped the bicycle frequently to point out funny looking insects or unusual scenery.

"Let's go to our neighbor's farm. Their mare is giving birth to a colt," Father might have said excitedly. And off we would go, venturing to the outskirts of our village to witness such a birth.

My father was a jack-of-all-trades. As farmer and sometimes-carpenter, he produced adequate crops for our family and crafted practical furniture, like our personal cabinets or our dinner table. Because we sat around the table cross-legged or on our knees, he made sure to fashion short yet sturdy legs.

My father's major crop was the *tumai kuru,* the Okinawan sweet potato. He planted those in addition to barley, wheat, millet, soybeans, peas and taro. Those were grown on very small plots of land,

and even with such variety the quantity was rather meager. He had sesame seed plants on the edge of the farmland and grew cotton, sugar cane and tobacco, too. At one time we owned our own rice paddy, but we sold it to a nearby farm when we were quite desperate. After that he bartered for rice from nearby paddies.

"Let's put you on the horse again today," Father would often say as he smiled and placed me on the back of our mare that was harnessed to walk around and around a stone press to squeeze the juice from the cane that produced molasses. It was such fun and I happily rode as he walked alongside me. The blackest and most beneficial form of molasses is formed after boiling the sugar a third time. This was another food source that contributed to the longevity of our people.

Although my father was a farmer, skilled carpenter and seaman he was deep inside a dreamer who started a number of businesses that failed. He was a good man but had no business sense. He once built a bathhouse, digging a well just outside our property to access underground water to fill the tubs. Then he put Mother's brother, who lived in a nearby village, in charge of running the bathhouse business. My uncle was a bit of an eccentric and we rarely saw him except for when Father recruited him for the job of running the bathhouse. He was free spirited and mostly absent from our lives as he was off on his adventures. The tubs sat on wood stoves and my uncle would light and fan the fire managing the temperature of the water.

The bathhouse, built rather crudely, was still functional and should have succeeded as a viable business but there wasn't enough underground water from that well. There was also the problem of the villagers being too poor to afford it. Farmers generally bartered both produce and labor among themselves so their pockets were mostly empty.

My uncle became bored in a very short time and ran off to war one day almost immediately after the bathhouse was built, leaving no one to maintain it and shortly thereafter the bathhouse simply fell to ruin.

"He enlisted when he heard about the war that the Japanese were waging against the Russians," Mother cried, "and I pleaded with him not to go but he wouldn't listen and ran off to war." The story was that no one ever saw or heard from him again and after many prayers, the family gave up hope and eventually knew that he had died.

Grandmother Machi kept hidden the pain of losing her only son but my mother spoke openly and often affectionately about him. From time to time my mother's voice would break when she spoke of losing him in the Russo-Japanese War when I was just a toddler.

My uncle became a statistic. He was part of the ten percent of Okinawan soldiers in the Japanese army who lost their lives in the war of 1904. His bones were lost on foreign soil and could not be properly recovered and cleansed to be housed in our family tomb. The village *kaminchu*, priestess, and Great-Grandmother, who was a diviner in her own right, performed a ritual for the safe passage of his spirit to the land of the gods.

Our property included a small hill at the edge of Gushiken. Seven stone steps led up to our house, which was nestled against the hill. Our house was unlike the others in our village as it was built with a small vestibule area. The other houses did not have this feature and had instead an *engawa*, a long plank that lined the front of the home so that after removing one's sandals one would step up onto the plank to enter the home. The houses stood slightly above ground on a number of short stilts that protected the homes against floods during typhoon season, typically late summer and early autumn.

Our house was constructed on high ground so that rain would run off to the fields below. Next to our house was a smaller structure built on high stilts with a ladder attached. It served as a storage area for grains and other staples. The exterior of our house had well built wood panel doors, strong enough to withstand storms and the interior was divided by less sturdy, removable, sliding wood panel doors. My father had built extra shutters for the exterior that were stacked in back of the house and could be brought out for additional protection during storms.

One feature our house did share with the others was that our house had a name. The house that we lived in was known as Teira-ya (ya means home), after the presiding matriarch seven generations before.

"Do you know why our houses have women's names?" Father asked me as he moved to a section of the courtyard to plant some shrubs. "My guess is that because a house is a structure that protects us and keeps us warm, perhaps our ancestors saw the house as naturally female. And why wouldn't we then give it a woman's name?"

According to the custom in earlier history, as soon as a house was constructed it was named after the woman head-of-household. Consequently, houses had names rather than numbered addresses, and villages were small enough so that people could easily find their way with major landmarks and house-names.

Our house had a thick thatched roof that could withstand heavy rain and wind and was replaced every thirty years or so. A stone fence covered with dark moss and lichen surrounded the house. The fence was made of medium-sized stones stacked and fitted to perfection. A freestanding rectangular slab recessed a bit from the ten-foot wide gap at the entrance of the fence hid the house from view. Between the stone slab and the house was a small courtyard and Father had planted a plum tree in the middle of it.

"This stone slab protects our house from bad energy," Father explained to me as he continued planting around the courtyard. Although I was still little he instructed me as did the others in my family.

Father said he used *funshii,* our native, logical, natural science that uses principles of water, wind, sunshine and direction while working in the garden. In planting trees and building structures, Father also incorporated similar laws of the more elaborate Chinese *feng shui* to ensure the free flow of Yin and Yang energies around our home. Most special was the birthing room where we were born. The houses of old had this feature as if the ancient builders with knowledge of funshii and feng shui were also attuned to creating each living space with unique purpose.

"By positioning buildings in a certain way, we can avert negative energies," Father taught. "The fence's wide gap is directly opposite our house and would have created a forceful energy flow into our home if we hadn't built the stone slab that hides the house from view and averts the harsh energy."

"These shrubs," he said pointing all around him, "redirect good energy and slow it down to allow it to flow throughout our property. Good funshii and feng shui in our courtyard bring good energy into our home. It's that simple. A beautiful garden delights our senses and refreshes our energy and provides protection too."

"If we attain a high level of sight," offered Father, "we will know intuitively how to arrange things. We can rely on our inner sense to place things appropriately for the cultivation of the highest harmony in our environment which in turn creates order in our personal lives."

"Hopefully the heavy rains won't rip out these plants," sighed Father as he worked. "We cannot survive another storm like the last one."

My mother overhearing him speak with such concern commented from the house. "There's nothing we can do about that, Machuu. Let's pray to our ancestors to protect us."

My parents were not wealthy landowners although they owned more land than most. They had to be resourceful to make up for economic setbacks brought on by fickle storms. An added fact was that the island was barely arable with soil too poor to grow abundant vegetables. Father experimented quite a bit and produced a wide array of produce than most surrounding farmers.

We never had a plentiful supply of food but we had enough to eat most of the time. Our typhoons were ferocious and unpredictable and could obliterate our crops in an instant. That sometimes left our bellies wanting.

In the kitchen I watched the women prepare the purple potato. They boiled, steamed, fried or sometimes mashed it. This purple potato became extremely popular because of its delicious flavor but, more practically, because it was typhoon-resistant and became the mainstay that rescued many people from famine when natural disasters struck. Its leafy tops were also cooked and eaten as a nutritious green vegetable, and its vines yielded lovely flowers that resembled morning glories.

"We have to wash them first," said Grandmother Machi as she took me outside to the well and settled on her haunches, hunched over a metal bowl filled with well water where she dipped a bristle brush to scrub the potatoes. I watched her wash the leafy tops of the potatoes and a small bitter melon too that would be stir fried with some fish shavings. Our evening meal would be simple and sparse.

I was especially happy when Mother mashed the purple potato. Whenever we had mashed potatoes there always seemed to be a bit left over. My friends and I, as small children, carefully crafted round lanterns from stolen bits of mashed potato and placed fireflies in them. We giggled at dusk and relished watching the potato lanterns glow as the light of day slowly receded.

For daily meals it was tradition in our family for the men to be served first in a separate area while we women ate in the kitchen, but during festivities we all ate together. Mother always gave our men the best food first, and we were content to have what remained. I don't think Father gave much thought to this as it was simply the way things were done. The men were accorded special honors but we women were the true leaders of our culture. Perhaps that is exactly the mark of true leaders. We serve and remain invisible.

CHAPTER 10
GREAT-GRANDMOTHER: OUR VILLAGE BARD

A time long ago, between the Fifteenth and Sixteenth Centuries, our Liu Ch'iu Kingdom emerged as the main trading intermediary in East Asia. There were items that you cannot imagine. There were minted coins and foam-green, glazed ceramics. There were brocades of the finest quality and other textiles that were traded by China and Japan for Southeast Asian sappan wood. It is from the sappan wood that we derive many, many things such as red paints and inks and medicines.

"Ohhhhhhh!" sighed our villagers as Great-Grandmother described precisely with brilliant detail the images of luxurious wares that were bartered among the various Pacific countries during a time before she was born. For centuries, the Far East was traveled by seafarers of many nations including Europeans, southeastern traders such as Indonesians and Malaysians and adventurers from India. All of these cultures influenced our islands of the Liu Ch'iu Kingdom, not just in customs, food, and dress, but also in the blood that coursed through our veins.

Traders sailed from port to port throughout all of Asia buying and selling goods the likes of which were unseen by the villagers in our northern Motobu Peninsula. Trading took place mostly in the South and only on rare occasions did a cargo ship make a stop at one of our two tiny northern ports. Great-Grandmother was delighted to oblige as historian and painted breathtaking images that captured the imagination in the minds of the villagers.

Practical items, too, were traded, such as tin, sugar and iron. But more interesting were ambergris from huge whales that swam the icy, northern sea and Indian ivory carved into jewelry. There were religious statues and Arabian frankincense, folding screens with bronze hinges fit for royalty. There were brilliant swords, Japanese silver, fans and shiny black lacquer-ware with beautifully painted designs of flowers. There were Chinese medicinal herbs of the exotic variety to make men virile and strong and women fertile.

"You know what medicines we've been taking all these years," laughed a fellow sitting with his nine children who were instantly embarrassed by their father's remark. His wife lightheartedly slapped his arm as her friends elbowed each other, and bursts of laugher from the women overrode the bantering of the men. The older men joked noisily about the rare rhinoceros horn that was prized as an aphrodisiac as if they were still enjoying its potency.

Our tiny islands of the Liu Ch'iu Kingdom served as a go-between for the bigger nations surrounding our archipelago, and its ports witnessed the barter of these magnificent wares.

The richness and variety of these wonderful material things that Great-Grandmother described stood in sharp contrast to the simple functionality of our native Okinawan goods.

But the wise bard brought her audience back to the essence of what was most important. "Material riches are nothing compared to the true wealth that comes from High Born leaders among us. They guide and inspire us to meet our highest expression." She always cleverly tied my birth to whatever story she told. It was her way of encouraging the villagers to rise to their potential.

Holding Great-Grandmother's deep teachings close to their heart and inspired to breathe humility into their art, local craftsmen brought their skills to excellence and produced fine wares. A sensitive and astute eye could appreciate the grace and beauty of the unpretentious earthenware and textiles produced by some of our island's potters and weavers who rose to prominence, gaining fame quickly throughout Asia.

"How is Mahataa coming along?" a local potter asked at the end of Great-Grandmother's tale. With the grace that comes from great wisdom, she explained to the villagers straightaway that they were not to interfere with my development. That is how the Original Wise Ones wanted it. I needed to grow up without hindrances that would slow my progress. If people around me focused on my uniqueness, they might interfere by overprotecting me. Overprotection is never a good thing. It makes us weak.

I wasn't as impressed as the other villagers were by all that Great-Grandmother had described. I found the funny bugs in our courtyard to be far more interesting. I wandered off to look at them. A large spider had woven a huge web and was perched in the middle of it. A green praying mantis was busy chewing on a blade of grass.

CHAPTER 11
SHIRASHI: NOTIFICATION TO SERVE

"You'll be given the responsibility to draw water when you are a little bigger," Great-Grandmother said as she threw the wooden bucket into our well. I watched exactly how it was done. There was a metal pulley suspended at the top of a wooden crossbar that helped to draw up the bucket tied to a thick rope made of hemp. "But for now, your only chore is to keep memorizing the stories I tell you."

"Great-Grandmother," I whined, "why do I have to learn these stories? And, why do I have to be special?" It was a day when I just did not want to memorize another tale.

Great-Grandmother stopped what she was doing and explained, "You have to learn these stories not because you will become the village bard. You must learn them for an entirely different purpose. The special sounds inside the stories will be imprinted in you so that you will be able to use the power of the sound to guide others. That is what I know about your calling. But what your true purpose is, you will come to find out later. Every gifted woman, whether she becomes a priestess, healer or diviner first receives *shirashi,* notification. A woman does not decide for herself to become a high servant of the people. She must be informed."

Detecting I was not satisfied with her answer, she sighed and admitted, "I too, in my early years rebelled about learning these stories and taking my position of village bard," said Great-Grandmother.

"The way we bards were selected was simple. The storyteller of the village would see potential in one of the children and begin to tutor her. A child who was most curious about the stories and who showed highest aptitude by repeating stories from an early age was selected. The child naturally fell into the training and was taught meticulously so that the tales were passed down syllable for syllable. When I was a child, the established storyteller in our village was my mother Uto and it was obvious to her that I should be selected.

"In the beginning I was fascinated by the tales, but as I grew older, I became distracted by worldly things. From time to time there was a merchant from the South who came up to sell interesting items and I wanted to know more about these fascinating objects such as lacquered trays and shiny mirrors inlaid in fine wood.

"I was attractive in my younger day and could have married sooner but here I was at the age of 26, practically a spinster, because I had stubbornly decided to wait for a man who could buy me beautiful kimono and novelties owned only by the privileged, someone who could afford me a life beyond this meager existence in our village. Eventually I decided to find my way down south to browse the black market and witness the trading of the most stunning arts and crafts that came through the port. Because of my beauty I was able to bribe the boatman to take me in his small boat that resembled the canoes used in the Dragon Boat races in the South. I say *resembled* because he had painted the boat with images and colors of those racing boats, but, unlike the authentic Dragon Boats, his canoe had a small sail.

"The South was an exciting place with the liveliest festivals. The Dragon Boat racing we call *haryu-sen* was borrowed from South China by our ancient Liu Ch'iu people. Also borrowed from the Chinese was a popular tug-of-war where people gather on either side of a huge, thick rope woven of strong hemp, the diameter of which is almost one meter. Villagers would have contests, and as you would imagine," said Great-Grandmother, "when one side won, the villagers immediately launched another contest and people ran to the losing side to lend a hand so that they would have a chance to win too." She looked off and smiled as if watching one of those contests.

I tugged at her sleeve and Great-Grandmother snapped out of her delicious musing to continue to explain her calling as storyteller. "I learned all the tales from my mother Uto but refused to take her place as village bard," continued Great-Grandmother. The idea of repeating the stories over and over again, I found tedious to say the least."

She spoke to me as if I were her confidante. "Oh, I was quite selfish in my early years. The idea that I would have to sit for long hours in front of crowds of people and tell stories again and again did not appeal to me. For goodness sakes, I thought to myself then, why can't someone else carry the burden of village bard? So, you see, my child, many of us question our calling. And unfortunately, because of my hesitation, there were many lost years where our villagers could have learned so much about our clan and about many, many important things. It was during the time that my mother Uto was too tired to continue the storytelling. I just found excuses to not replace her as village bard and selfishly kept high knowledge from our people. But, alas, the deep feeling of wanting to serve others cannot be hurried and comes in its own time."

She tugged at the rope to pull up the water bucket. "No one knows when shirashi, the notification to serve, will occur. It is rare for a very young girl to receive notification because maturity and life experience are needed to assume the responsibilities of the role. It is a mysterious thing. No one knows at all how it comes about. Shirashi comes usually as a strange illness or bizarre occurrence. My notification was no different," revealed Great-Grandmother.

"When I was twenty-seven years old, I woke up one day unable to get out of my futon bed." She carefully balanced the bucket on her head and I followed her into the house.

"I had just given birth to Machi. I named her after her father, Mateus, a Portuguese trader I met in the South. Mateus was your Great-Grandfather. The name Mateus means gift of the Lord and I wanted to name my child after him because I truly felt she had been sent to me as a divine gift. I wanted to give little Machi a name that resembled her father's. Besides, she had his eyes that turned down a

bit at the outer corners giving her a look of regret. Thank goodness
she did not inherit his nose that had a distinct bump where the nose
left the brow!" Great-grandmother let out a hearty laugh and then
almost immediately became serious again.

"When Mateus and I parted I did not know that I was with
child. We were both deliriously happy, knowing that we would be
together within the year. I looked forward to seeing him again and
when I discovered I was carrying his child I hoped to surprise him
with our sweet baby." Great-Grandmother's voice, all of a sudden
sad and wistful, trailed off.

"We had such a short time together," said Great-Grandmother,
"and when I returned home to the North, I was elated, my soul was
complete. I waited for many months but I never saw him again. My
poor Machi, born with a sadness for which I am responsible, was a
quiet child, never asking for anything."

"Our wretchedness can soften us and ripen our hearts," she
sighed. Although Great-Grandmother's pain would never leave her,
she managed to transform her attitude so that she was able to shine
brightly with tremendous love for all beings. She was wise, my great-
grandmother. She let her heart break and discovered her kinship
with all beings who know this place of pain. She spoke to me as a
contemporary. She spoke as if she were speaking to a close friend.
She knew that I was not capable of grasping what she was saying
at the moment, but that when I was older I would be able to pluck
from my memory this very day and everything she revealed. And
she was right. When I think of that particular morning that I spent
with Great-Grandmother I can conjure up all that she recounted. I
see the story of Hanaa and Mateus as a kind of romantic play.

The two lovers in the black market alley in the South. Great-
Grandmother Hanaa, as a young woman, dressed in her best kimono,
which by standards of the South was simple, leisurely browsing the
open marketplace lined with vendors. Her eye instantly catching
beautifully woven fabrics of *bingata*, a traditional cloth produced
by local craftsmen. Displayed on the vendor's cart are handcrafted

obi belts exquisitely painted with bright red and yellow flowers with vibrant green leaves.

As she bends to examine the beautifully crafted belts, loose strands of hair fall out of her topknot that she hadn't secured properly with the wooden jifaa that angles through the knot of hair. There is something delicate and alluring about the nape of her neck as she picks up some obi belts to admire when a deep European voice startles her.

"I think you would look best in the one with red flowers," the tall handsome man says, grinning broadly with gorgeous white teeth surrounded by a stubbly beard that has missed several days of shaving. He isn't as hairy as most of the Europeans she has heard about.

"They are like monkeys covered with hair," a friend in the North told her about the European traders who frequented our ports of the South. In fact, his brawny upper chest doesn't appear to have any hair sprouting from his collar and his arms are muscular and almost hairless. His skin is bronze from too much sun and he looks like a god with his brilliant sea blue eyes and thick black lashes. He points to one of three obi belts she holds in her hand. He speaks well enough in her native tongue despite the fact that it is probably his second or third language.

"What is your name?" the young man asks and Hanaa replies shyly. She speaks the dialect of the northern province and had difficulty understanding the southern dialect but manages to comprehend.

Even though the island is small, only 112 km long and 11km wide at its narrowest place, there are numerous dialects, and sometimes people from one province have tremendous difficulty communicating with someone from another.

Hanaa thanks him for his help in selecting the red obi, makes her purchase and moves quickly away as she is embarrassed by her sudden attraction to him. She has come to visit the South for a couple of days to browse the marketplace and purchase only a few items that she can barely afford.

The following day, in another section of town, near Naha port, she sees him again. He is lifting heavy cartons of cargo into a huge net that are to be lifted onto a large trade ship. When he looks up, he sees her in the distance, where she waves and shouts a greeting. He lays down the cartons and runs to her.

"Hello, Hanaa!" he smiles. They spend the afternoon together and make plans to meet again. He is a Portuguese trader who courts her and persuades her to prolong her stay so that they can have more time together.

"My name is Mateus and I am an islander like you," he says to her, his bushy eyebrows arching with enthusiasm under a thick head of curly dark hair. "I was born in the Azores, an archipelago off the coast of Portugual in the Atlantic." He says his father is a trader like himself and taught him everything he knows. He is unlike anyone she has encountered and Hanaa is swept off her feet.

Together, they browse the marketplace and when they come upon the obi vendor, Mateus grabs two other beautiful obi belts, both fit for high-end kimono and purchases them on the spot for her. Although the young Hanaa doesn't have enough time to get to know him, it is love at first sight and she trusts this is the man for her. Not only is he well to do and handsome too, he is kind and generous. Could there possibly be a man in the whole world who could surpass him? No, she knows without a doubt.

Soon, they make plans to marry within the year. He promises that he will travel to the northern port of Toguchi to come for her.

"My house is called Teira-ya in our village of Gushiken," she tells him to which he promises to jot down the address in his journal. Before they say their goodbyes, he pulls a small pouch from his vest inside which was a piece that has served as a good luck charm.

"I want you to keep this family heirloom as my promise that I will return to you. It has been held close to my heart since I left my country years ago. It is most precious to me, a necklace that belonged to my mother who gave it to me before my travels to protect me on the high seas."

Hanaa accepts the gift and leaves for Gushiken the following day. In the month that follows, she is thrilled to learn that she is going to have his child. She tells her mother she will introduce her soon to the wonderful man who will return to be her husband. Her mother Uto is very unhappy and can not hide her disappointment at the news but holds her tongue because she has accepted that her brilliant daughter is *different*. Hanaa has always been an unusual child. She rebelled about practically every convention there was since she was a young girl and has done everything her own way. Uto is resigned to accepting her gifted daughter as she is. Hanaa knows that her mother, no matter how angry or disappointed she is, will eventually come around.

One day, Hanaa receives word once from a Portuguese trade ship that stops at the northern port carrying a short letter from Mateus explaining that he has some problems with his family and would return as soon as he could. Uto knows that her daughter will never see him again but keeps those heartbreaking thoughts to herself. They will never know the real reason for his inability to return. One could conjure up many stories, but he was an honorable man. That, Hanaa knows for certain.

When the baby comes, Uto is so overjoyed that she forgets her disappointment and anger and welcomes the beautiful baby girl. As custom would have it, they kneel in prayer to the Goddess of Fire of the Hearth giving thanks for a healthy baby girl.

"Shortly after Machi was born," explained Great-Grandmother about her notification, "when I had barely begun to nurse her, I suddenly developed the most painful joints.

"I was bed-ridden for weeks and, thankfully, my mother Uto helped me through the difficulty. In the middle of the tortuous ordeal, delirium set in. I began to have visions and my intuition sharpened. It was then that I realized my calling, my shirashi. I became a diviner and could see and know things.

"I knew in my heart that Mateus would never return, and my heart ached from the unbearable loss. I resolved, however, in a moment of clarity that I would allow my broken heart to experience the depths of suffering. I had a sense that he had wanted very much to return but his family had pre-arranged a marriage for him. I would allow my feelings to be just as they were and to not push them aside. We bury our true feelings sometimes and that does little good. Instead, we must openly accept whatever our feelings are."

The birth of her daughter, the painful illness, the realization that she would never see Mateus again and receiving her calling to become a diviner marked a death and rebirth for Great-Grandmother. So much happened all at once that it was too much for her nervous system. She had to compartmentalize in some way and part of her went a little bit mad. Then one day her mind cleared and she stood up and began to share the stories she had learned and even some that she just knew. Her madness continued to visit her only occasionally but for the most part she was available as teacher and mentor to everyone.

In moments when she was not her stable self, she would speak out loud to herself. Sometimes it happened when she was within earshot of others. She would mumble or laugh to herself as if she were being told a funny tale.

"There she goes again," The villagers giggled and whispered but they were never mean, never rude. Why would they be? They loved her storytelling and just accepted that she was two people occupying one body. Her odd quality was more endearing than anything. The rumor was that when Great-Grandmother came into her full powers of divining, she was split in two. What used to be her ordinary self shrank and shrank until it reduced itself to less than half of her person so that most of her energy could be used for divining, which brought greater depth to her storytelling. That is what they believed. They didn't know the whole story.

Great-Grandmother was a highly developed soul and was awake in many ways. The path to full awakening, however, is an arduous journey that requires a singular undivided attention to which she could not apply herself due to life's circumstances. Had she not had the karma with a certain Portuguese trader, she might have become the one to unify our people. She might have been chosen by the Originals. Beneath that even voice and radiant face, this lofty storyteller hid a deep sadness that could never be extricated. It was a pain that she would live with her whole life.

"From the moment of my awakening," Great-Grandmother said, "I knew my calling and shouted, 'Yes, I accept the responsibility to see all things as they are. I will serve my people to the best of my ability and become the village bard as I was chosen to be.' As soon as I uttered those words, the pains vanished, and the full powers of divining were bestowed upon me."

Great-Grandmother carefully set down the water bucket, "I could now see beyond the stories I had memorized, and my storytelling was catapulted to new heights with my new powers of divination. The tales handed down from the clan vibrated with a huge aliveness that was not there before."

What Great-Grandmother described about her sudden illness was the typical way in which notification came. My case was different. I would experience no such notification, no physical symptoms whatsoever, and would be led, instead, into my full powers in a sequence of events from my birth. In the case of a High Born One, told the bards, shirashi came to one of the relatives, usually the mother. The High Born One's status was determined before birth. This was not necessarily so for the gifted women. No one knew exactly how the gifted ones were selected but one thing was for sure, notification came late in life.

From an early age I wrestled with the idea about being a High Born One and whether I had a karmic obligation to fulfill. I asked myself from time to time if this was really what I wanted to do and wondered if I had a choice in the matter. All the while, Great-Grandmother fantasized that one day I would prove to be as powerful as the Great Sandaa, the first High Born Matriarch. After all, it was Sandaa's spirit who had visited Mother in a dream foretelling my birth. The ghost of Sandaa had come to give her instruction.

"She had a deep, resonant voice that could have been male or female," recounted Mother. "She was covered in the fur of wild animals with a snake skeleton draped around her neck and she held a stick made of tree bark. Her hair was long and silver with a crown of feathers."

Sandaa was the first known High Born Matriarch who led the people in ancient history. The High Born One was said to be extremely powerful and gifted such that she embodied the wisdom and knowledge of prayer, divining and healing.

By way of mind-to-mind transmission Sandaa communicated to my mother. "You will soon give birth to a High Born One. It is time for such a one to incarnate to lead the people. The child will come into the world a ripe vessel to receive high knowledge. She must, however, grow up as other ordinary children without interference so that her powers can develop easily and naturally."

Upon waking from her dream, Mother pondered, "How can this be done? How can my little one receive high knowledge and at the same time grow up like other children? And from where will those teachings come?"

Sandaa answered her query the following night. "The High Born One should be schooled alongside the others but since she will have high aptitude for spiritual matters she will require special grooming. She will need the combined attributes of the three gifted women of our culture, the *noro*, high priestess, the *yuta*, soothsayer and the *yabuu*, medicine woman."

CHAPTER 12
THE THREE WISE WOMEN

One morning Great-Grandmother showed me how to pray, *utoto*, to the Hearth Goddess by placing a pinch of sea salt in a tiny dish alongside a tiny bowl of water, and then placing these two items on a small ledge above the hearth in the kitchen.

It is our tradition for the eldest matriarch of the home to lead prayers to Hinukan, the Goddess of the Fire of the Hearth. Great-Grandmother and I prayed together and then she plopped me onto the kitchen floor and began mixing some ingredients.

She said longingly, "A dear Portuguese friend of mine taught me how to make a delicious dish we call *po-po* and I am going to make it for you right now." It was interesting that she chose not to mention his name even though I had just learned the whole story.

Great-Grandmother grabbed a skillet and said, "Today I will teach you about three wise women from our islands. You will learn from each of these women one day. Know that the power of each woman is unique and must merge with you to complete you as a High Born One. Each gifted woman holds a piece of the energetic puzzle that you will need to receive. When you finish your training with the gifted women, each of your senses will have developed from its mundane use to a transcendental one."

"I'm ready," I said excitedly. "Will you teach me now?"

"After our meal," promised Great-Grandmother. She whipped up flour with a bit of black sugar and water, adding an herbal powder used for baking. "Just a tiny dash of salt brings out the sweet," she said, adding a pinch of sea salt to the ingredients. She placed a greased pan over a small fire and while it heated, she stirred a bit more water to smooth the mixture. Then she poured just enough batter into the hot pan and immediately rotated the pan until the thin batter covered the bottom.

"Hurry and tell me about the wise women," I prodded her. Great-Grandmother answering my impatience said, "The noro are our high priestesses, the yuta are our soothsayers and the yabuu are our healers."

She lightly browned both sides of the po-po, and began to teach, "In ages past, our ancestors used flint and iron to light fires. Every village had a noro high priestess who kept the fire going and ensured that it never went out. The noro was given the huge responsibility of being Keeper of the Fire of the Hearth and fanning the fire for the entire village."

"When we talk about *fanning the fire* it also has spiritual meaning. You will learn the deeper meaning of fanning the fire when you study with one of your teachers sometime in the future."

Great-Grandmother and I sat at our low table and enjoyed the warm, delicious treat. As we ate, Great-Grandmother explained that historically the first noro to arrive in our islands came from Kudaka Island just off our southern coast to work closely with the King of Shuri Castle in the South. She advised him on many important matters. There was an invisible thread of energy from the crown of the noro's head to the heavens so that when she would have a vision or receive a warning from the Original Wise Ones through her psychic hearing, she immediately advised the King. In this way she acted as liaison.

With the noro indirectly leading society as the mouthpiece of the Originals, the people enjoyed sustained peace in the Liu Ch'iu Kingdom until political freedom was lost partly to foreign rule and partly to lack of understanding on the part of the islands' rulers. When the noro's position was diminished and the connection cut between the King and the Wise Ones, there was an unraveling of the good work established until then.

Great-Grandmother asked, "How can a people disconnected from the Wise Ones know how to properly proceed?" Even though she wasn't looking to me for the answer, I shrugged, I didn't know.

"When people lose divine connection, they become blind," she warned.

Great-Grandmother led me outdoors to the well to rinse our bowls and chopsticks. "The next gifted woman is the yuta, a sooth-sayer, somewhat like me," Great-Grandmother taught. "I do not practice as yuta because my work as storyteller consumes so much of my time and now I have you to teach. I am able to use my divin-ing skills in another way. Rather than giving counsel to others I can dig deeper into the tales with my sight to bring out hidden meaning that I was unable to access until I received my calling."

"There are different levels of yuta," Great-Grandmother con-tinued. There are yuta who can see and simply describe what they see but are unable to *interpret* what they see. The most advanced yuta are seers who guide seekers by emphasizing the positive attri-butes of their situation. We seers have a responsibility to emphasize the positive aspects of a person's situation and not dwell on the negative. We must always choose to bring light to all matters no matter how dark the situation."

After she had washed the dishes, I followed her back into the house and sat transfixed on the kitchen floor. "The most famous Yuta lives deep in the mountains," Great-Grandmother said as she dried the utensils and put them away.

"Seekers go to yuta for advice but this famous Yuta paid you a visit right after you were born. People go to them about love, fortune, marriage, illness and death, and yet, this famous Yuta, on the occasion of your birth, traveled the long distance to visit you."

"Tomorrow I will take you to visit the third type of wise woman, the Yabuu, our healer, since I have to pick up something from her. You'll get a chance to see her clinic and learn a little about what she does. Besides, you'll be studying with her when you're older so an introduction to her now will be good.

The following day, just as Great-Grandmother promised, I accompanied her to meet our local Yabuu. Great-Grandmother carried me on her back as we set out. I was capable of walking but I loved riding on Great-Grandmother's back. Because I was a bit spindly, I couldn't have weighed much.

We were on our way to a neighboring village to purchase a rare mushroom from the Yabuu because Great-Grandmother was going to prepare a medicinal soup for a sick neighbor. On the way, Great-Grandmother said, "The Yabuu can see on the level of the physical and emotional body. She cannot tell your future but she can lead you to your highest health."

As soon as we arrived at the Yabuu's house, which served as a small clinic, Great-Grandmother put me down. "Hello!" she called. "This visit is long overdue. I am so sorry for not coming to meet you sooner."

The Yabuu dressed in loose-fitting cotton trousers that were soiled with dirt and grass stains from her garden came out to greet us. Her long hair looked like a combination of crushed black and white sesame seeds and was tied in a ponytail that fell below her waist. She was considered eccentric for not donning the typical top-knot and sometimes when she wandered in the mountains searching for wild herbs she wore her hair tousled and free so that from a distance the villagers thought she was a witch.

"Please come in," she said as she lifted off her patchwork apron made of crude linen. The apron had even more stains than her trousers and underneath it was a kimono top that had been cropped at the hips and tied at the waist with a braided cord. The sleeves of the tattered kimono were shortened considerably but altered to retain a bit of the pocket-sleeve design so that she could use the sleeves to store small items for her work, sometimes a tiny pair of scissors to clip herbs in her garden or a stick for stirring herbal decoctions at her wood-burning stove.

There were strange and exotic smells that permeated her clinic and a young assistant who looked no more than twelve was there as apprentice. She came to help clean the hut and observe in the late afternoons and wouldn't begin hands-on work for another two years. She was dressed like the Yabuu in old trousers and a stained kimono with the corners of both sleeves attached to strings that were tied at the back of the neck so that the long sleeves were out of her way as she worked. She had an impish grin and probably caused a lot of mischief when the Yabuu looked away. Her hair was wound up in the customary topknot and she was busy sweeping the entrance when we arrived. At the Yabuu's bidding she rushed to bring us some tea as the Yabuu disappeared to the back to fetch the mushrooms. When the Yabuu returned, Great-Grandmother apologized again for not coming to visit sooner.

"I knew your aunt who ran this clinic and it's been a while since I've been out this way," said Great-Grandmother. "Because I learned quite a bit from her, I have managed to treat my own family with simple medicines and techniques. I am forever grateful for all that she shared."

Great-Grandmother then asked the Yabuu to speak about herself and her work perhaps so that I might learn.

"I am from the South," the Yabuu said, "and I came here on a teaching rotation but ended up staying. My aunt and I used to live in the South where she raised me. She moved here to the North leaving me to study with a famous herbal teacher for several years. A couple of years ago my aunt asked me to come and help organize her clinic and teach some yabuu here in our Northern Province. Unfortunately during the early part of my visit my aunt passed away and so I ended up taking over her practice.

"Most yabuu learn solely through apprenticeship using only indigenous methods. I was lucky to be schooled in various healing arts not only through apprenticeship, but also through academic instruction from the master in the South. The master was affiliated with a hidden school that housed imported books from China and India. He had diverse knowledge of healing methods from around the world and I was fortunate to study with him.

"My aunt arranged for me to apprentice with the master in the South because her knowledge of healing was limited. I studied with him for five years and learned more than all the yabuu on our island." She bobbed her head and looked my way, "Do you know what this is?" she asked as she picked up a soft cottony substance and addressed me, "It is an herb, used to burn on people's bodies to heal them."

I already knew that yabuu heal through the practice of *yaachu,* a name in the old tongue for moxa-cautery where dried, pulverized mugwort is burned on specific points of the body. The burning method stimulates the organs and systems of the body. It feels like a quick touch from a burning incense stick to the skin.

With a glint in her eye and a slight smirk, the Yabuu extended the herb and looked for my reaction. She knew that some mothers threatened to burn their children with yaachu if they were naughty.

The young assistant who was cleaning a shelf behind the Yabuu turned around and, looking at me, made funny faces as if she were in pain from a burn. Great-Grandmother and the Yabuu had started talking so they both missed it completely. But I found it so funny that I burst out laughing. Of course, that was not the reaction anyone expected. Great-Grandmother turned to me with question and the Yabuu looked somewhat indignant. From that point, the Yabuu seemed to grow cold toward me, acting unimpressed by whatever I said. Realizing my laughter was not appreciated, I stopped and immediately focused on the furry substance of mugwort the Yabuu still held. It was different from the powdery substance that Great-Grandmother sprinkled into tiny mounds on my father's back.

"We use a powder," I informed the Yabuu and Great-Grandmother patted my head and nodded at the authority and assurance in my voice.

"Fine," the Yabuu said, not looking directly at me. "There is another herb with similar properties and is ground into a powder, but the more potent one is this fluffy gold-colored herb that feels like a ball of cotton."

"We must keep our body strong and healthy through appropriate treatments. From a strong physical foundation you can build a healthy emotional life. And from there you can pursue a spiritual path," the Yabuu rose, ushering Great-Grandmother and me out.

Before we left, she added, "To only focus on the spiritual and neglect the body is foolish. At the same time, to only maintain an excellent physical body with no attention to emotional and spiritual pursuits is a life wasted." And with that, she bowed and we said our goodbyes.

On my way home, I thought about the meeting with the Yabuu. She was informative but cool. She wasn't friendly but gave us any information we sought. Apparently she was a brilliant healer and so the villagers put up with her quirkiness.

Despite her peculiar traits, the Yabuu proved to us that she actually embraced spiritual principles. That came as a surprise to me. It didn't add up. I had ideas about healers and assumed that her personality ought to be a certain way. I would have to open my mind to accept her just as she was.

As soon as we got home, Great-Grandmother prepared the mushroom soup combined with ginger root and garlic, and brought her herbal decoction to our neighbor. The sick woman's family was grateful and gave us, in payment, some of the bitter melons they grew. Although Great-Grandmother refused payment, they insisted and had five pieces of bitter melon already wrapped to give us.

The next day, Great-Grandmother dressed me to gather some bamboo shoots for our evening meal. She fetched a small trowel that was rusty but still functioned well. Its edges were chipped from years of use, and the old wood handle was fastened by frayed, thick hemp. She plopped it into a small tattered bamboo basket and took my hand.

Off we went to the edge of a bamboo forest near our home. My steps were tiny, and I took two steps to her one, but Great-Grandmother was patient and walked very slowly, not letting go of my hand. We soon found a patch of shoots and as she bent down to dig them out she began her lesson. As usual, she spoke to me as if I were a full-grown person. Passers-by assumed she was talking to herself. They couldn't fathom that she would be speaking to me, a toddler, in grown-up language.

"Did you know that it was the Great Kamadaa who lived ten generations ago in our family line who put our gifted women into the three groups you just learned? She was considered a great organizer. Before Kamadaa's era our gifted women were scattered about and many never came to develop their full potential because of lack of organization," Great-Grandmother said.

"Do all the wise women get sick when they receive shirashi the way you did?" I asked Great-Grandmother. She laughed and said, "It's different for everyone but one thing is for sure. Each woman who is notified knows when she receives shirashi. There have been instances when a woman believes she is being called to be a priestess when in fact, she is being called to be, perhaps, a diviner. This is very rare but does happen.

"When we are fulfilling our destiny, there is a clear knowing through and through. We don't feel uncertain about it."

"Once the noro or yuta or yabuu receives her calling, she is guided step by step by an invisible force that she instinctually trusts. From the point of shirashi, notification, a truly gifted woman never questions opportunities that arise to help her along. From the day she is summoned, the world begins to bring her the things she needs to complete her tasks. Everything, all events, lead her to her goal. She is supported to develop herself in all ways necessary to fulfill her karma. No matter how great the challenges she cannot be deterred, and progression along the path quickens. She is propelled by an inner knowing, like an animal following a scent that cannot be thrown off the path."

"Look!" exclaimed Great-Grandmother, "See what I dug up."

She held it so I could see the root that looked like a white carrot with lots of tendrils and hairs growing from it. "A ginseng root! "I'll dry it when we get home."

She was delighted by the rare find. Ordinarily, ginseng did not grow in these parts and Great-Grandmother paused at the extraordinary discovery. Suddenly, we were overshadowed by an indescribably peaceful presence. It was that kind of feeling one has upon entering an ancient temple or a sacred field.

Great-Grandmother and I sat enveloped for a time in communion with spirit. Perhaps by speaking earlier about the Great Kamadaa we unwittingly summoned her.

"Kamadaa created a dome of protection over our people of the archipelago and during her reign our islands became more cohesive. Through her strength and influence our people enjoyed peace. The islanders trusted her and knew she had their best interests in mind. Then something interesting happened. The Great Kamadaa became invisible during her reign. She was there and not there at the same time," explained Great-Grandmother.

The spirit of Kamadaa stayed with us for a while as Great-Grandmother searched for herbs and shoots. We knew when Kamadaa took her leave, but the atmosphere remained charged until we left the sacred meadow.

"A true leader is one who makes the people feel as though they are completely in charge of their own lives. The people make excellent decisions and claim them as their own. A true leader works in this way, and her satisfaction can be likened to a mother whose skillfulness is visible through her children."

"The most interesting thing about the Great Kamadaa," said Great-Grandmother, "is that she ruled as a young woman, and before old age visited her, she came upon the Elixir of Immortality here on our island. She opted to join the Immortals and left as a young girl. To this day, when she appears, she comes as a child of twelve. When she came upon the teachings of immortality, she was able to reverse her aging. She appears in visions as a child but with the wisdom of an accomplished crone. Through the teachings of immortality, one can choose to grow young to any age one desires."

I wondered at the time if I could develop a friendship with Kamadaa. The fact that she was a little girl made me wish for her companionship. Maybe she could teach me how to make interesting toys. Grandmother Machi had sewn me a stuffed doll of dried barley seeds with beans for eyes and various fabrics for ears, nose and mouth. But eventually I came to understand that although Kamadaa appeared as a child, her interest did not lie in childish things. Instead she was concerned with the overall wellbeing of all people. She managed to rule our islands in peace and one day, I would have the hope she could share with me how to bring peace and happiness to our islands especially with our uncertain future.

On our walk home Great-Grandmother repeated her assurance that the gifted are not left entirely on their own. "Once the noro or yuta or yabuu receives her calling, she is guided step by step by an invisible force that she instinctually trusts."

My life would progress as was decreed, in a straight karmic line with all the assistance I would need. This being so, great faith lived with me but so did great doubt.

CHAPTER 13
THE ORIGINAL WISE ONES

Great-Grandmother knew I ingested every word she uttered. She taught with a bright energy that exuded from her core. She commanded a huge field around her. It was the most elegant means of communication. Those who entered her field were shifted in mysterious ways. Her ability to do this was granted to her by the Original Wise Ones. Persons who were developed to a high degree were encouraged to teach in this way, their bodies becoming instruments to spread light. I believed for this reason that Great-Grandmother had reached her spiritual peak but she insisted otherwise.

We had many outings together and I learned many facts about our clan while acquiring skills for daily living such as gathering edible wild plants and being cautioned about poisonous ones. Children are fascinated by all that their senses take in and I was no exception. Seeing a common bug for the first time can be an extraordinary experience. And Great-Grandmother always seemed to know exactly what these insects and plants were.

"Were you always so smart?" I asked. "You know everything— all the stories you tell, you know all about plants and bugs. You know everything."

Great-Grandmother smiled, "There are many things that I learned from my ancestors but the most important gifts were given to me by the Original Wises Ones."

I had heard Great-Grandmother talk about the Original Wise Ones before but a lot of my information came from overhearing the villagers talk about them. "Are they really as tall as the biggest trees?" I asked. "And, do they breathe fire from their mouths when they are angry?"

With a soft chuckle, Great-Grandmother replied, "I don't know if that's what they looked like at one time but I'll tell you what. When the time is right I will teach you and the villagers all I know about them."

"What about now," I said thinking of a way to convince her to tell the story that day. "What if you forget about them and we'll never learn about them?"

"I won't," she assured me.

Great-Grandmother waited for the right time to tell her tale. Following the cycles of moon and seasons she chose a suitable setting to create the right backdrop for her evening storytelling. She selected the perfect dark night to gather the villagers to speak to them about the Originals.

The Original Wise Ones who settled our Great Mother Earth came from a twinkling star in the northern sky. The Originals were a council of twelve who arrived when various species of humans who had come from other stars had populated parts of our planet. The Originals came eons ago to direct and guide the humans to establish high cultures. Those cultures disappeared and some say they left in large groups back to the stars. Although they disappeared completely, they left energetic imprints in the rocks and mountains and trees. When we sit on these rocks among the trees we are inspired by truths they left behind.

Among the assembled was an older village kaminchu, priestess, who sat deep in thought. She remembered years ago when the band of kaminchu to which she belonged was led by the village noro, high priestess, to a new meeting place.

They had brought with them special white robes they wore during ceremonies. The noro had asked each priestess to look for flat rocks to create seats around an altar. She held her hand over each stone to determine whether or not the stone should be selected. After setting in place the stone seats imbued with high resonance, they put on their white robes for the opening ceremony to bless the grounds.

"I understand now why the noro had been so fastidious about what stones could be used and what could not," the old village kaminchu whispered to another kaminchu friend who was seated next to her. An especially gifted noro could sense which natural objects held the highest teachings.

"Yes, the stones are living things and subtly call us," the friend replied. "And I do feel much clearer and more inspired when I pray in our sacred grove in the mountains."

The Originals had human features and appeared like radiant blueprints of us. They eventually lost what little physical form they had and became mere voices. They are not our creators, but they are highly developed beings who desire to help the inhabitants of our planet.

The Originals searched areas of every continent to locate zones most conducive to house high teachers. These zones were portals where the Originals could send spiritual beings to assist the people.

The twelve voices, referred to still as the Original Wise Ones, continue to influence and guide us. They live in the psyche of those who can receive them and house them.

A sudden chill ran up and down my spine. It was the first time I became aware of how my body served as an instrument to signal me when a truth was being spoken. Our origin was from the stars. I knew this without a doubt.

The villagers disbanded and Great-Grandmother took me for a walk. "I know you have discovered something very important," she said to me. "Our body is a fine instrument if we know how to use it. It is an accurate instrument and never lies."

Because of my fortunate birth, I would receive instruction from certain teachers under whom I would apprentice. The Wise Ones arranged for these special teachers to avail themselves to me. Every one of our people of the archipelago was greatly influenced by the Originals. Teachings from them came in many forms, often through dreams. We are all taught the way to longevity and a handful were shown the way to immortality.

This explained why some villagers never seemed to age. They remained very active until they were over a hundred years old, and yet, were unable to give precise instructions on how they did it. They naturally gravitated to healthful habits that prolonged life. They were influenced by the Wise Ones who lived in their psyche although the connection was not a conscious one.

Great-Grandmother let me know that it is only when we cut ourselves off from these ancient instructions by following our *thinking* mind rather than our inner *knowing* that we lose our way. She said the quest for immortality that lies deep in our marrow is fueled by our inner knowing of its possibility. Fear and disbelief about immortality are emotions that serve as protective measures. Immortality is a sacred path that should not be traveled by persons who are not ready.

What struck me most was the knowledge that the voices of the Wise Ones stream through us to guide and teach. I had decided to always be open to that inner voice in me that is directly linked to the Original Wise Ones. I had decided to let go of a layer of ego that told me I had to control my hearing. And although I didn't know exactly what that meant at the time, I sensed that my body did and that I would be guided to find out.

CHAPTER 14
TEA, PLUMS AND THE SEED IN THE BELLY

"You have a funny light coming from your head!" laughed one of my friends.

"Ha ha!" scoffed the others, and I looked at the ground, embarrassed that they could see.

"Stop making up such stories about Mahataa," reprimanded a farmer who happened to overhear the teasing. I knew then that the older people could not see.

"Do all people lose their sight when they grow up?" I later asked Great-Grandmother.

"No, not everyone, but most do," she sighed.

She explained to Mother, "My teachings are absorbed into Mahataa's very being. As the inner light of the child grows, other children around her glow brighter too. Her mere presence influences them and she shares rich truths as they play."

The teachings I received from Great-Grandmother continued to emanate from me, and my playmates were influenced by her wisdom through this mysterious process. But I still got into as much mischief as anyone.

I was free to climb trees and run about with the young boys of our village. When I fell and scraped a knee, I ran home to Great-Grandmother who always had a remedy. She poured a salt solution that contained an herbal decoction over the cut to clean it of debris and gently applied the gooey liquid of the aloe leaf for healing.

Her mother had taught her about simple folk remedies and also about various herbal teas, which is why Great-Grandmother experimented greatly in inventing all kinds of teas. Some ended up being quite medicinal with a flavor too strong to enjoy. Some of the tea recipes were handed down from healers through the generations within our matriarchal line.

When the women of our village came together in our home to learn how to heal with teas, Great-Grandmother served interesting combinations of dried herbs and skins of fruits. For example, she brewed skins of dried tangerine mixed with hibiscus flowers or dried wild flowers with ginger and a hint of molasses. She also stored in her cabinet a popular tea called *sanpinja,* made from jasmine flowers. She bought this from a merchant that occasioned the North once every few months. The jasmine flower has a most exquisite fragrance.

Her teas were subtly aromatic and tasty but at the same time used medicinally. When possible, she served tea piping hot with a tiny piece of black sugar as a sweet to be taken before enjoying the potent blend. She might say to her guests, "Here, have some tea to strengthen your heart and stomach." Not only beverages but food, too, was appreciated as medicine. 'Whatever we ingest serves to support the body or weaken it," she used to say.

When I had no appetite during illness, I was allowed to fast. Great-Grandmother encouraged our family to recover naturally, prescribing simple medicinal teas until our appetite returned. After an illness, she made plain rice gruel with sour plum. The mushy, sour plum was produced when Great-Grandmother marinated the plums in sun-dried sea salt that was full of minerals and then added *perilla* leaves to bring out the reddish-purple color. The perilla leaf has medicinal properties in the ability to remove poisons from the body.

Great-Grandmother learned this pickling process from a farmer in a neighboring village who obtained the perilla plant from the South and began to harvest it himself. The perilla leaves were known as *shiso* by the Japanese. The enzymes created by the pickling process of combining salt and shiso acting on the plum created a medicinal condiment that helped to cleanse the body and remove disease-producing factors.

These plums were not the sweet, juicy variety of purple plums. They were a different species and grew in the middle of our tiny courtyard in front of our home on a particular tree that in winter produced white blossoms. The soft white petals, when shaken off the branches from a cold winter's breeze, looked very much like soft falling snow although it never snowed on the island.

There was a subtle fragrance in the air when these petals first came, falling gently, creating a delicate scenery. One winter, when I was still a toddler, my family sat bundled together watching in silence. It was a silence that was full of joy and gratitude.

The white petals created a carpet of snow and I was aware of how the collective mind of our family was as clear as a mirror reflecting the billowy scenery. No thoughts. So exquisite!

It was as if in unison our singular wish to allow the moment of beauty to suspend itself was granted. Our united invocation carried us for a long while and it wasn't until our stomachs began to grumble that we slipped out of our lovely absorption. We slowly disbanded, and the adults worked together silently in food preparation, each person savoring the quality of that rich, prolonged moment.

At the end of each day our entire family, which included four generations, gathered round several lighted pine candles at sunset to continue minor unfinished chores of the day. Great-Grandmother re-stitched torn clothing while repeating old tales.

One evening she told us about the Great Warrior Sandaa who appeared just at the time our remote ancestors in Central Asia became despondent after unimaginable hardships. Jiraa ran to call some of the neighbors and dashed to ring the big bell. People rushed into our home, some sitting in the narrow vestibule as she spoke.

At one time eons ago, the weather all over the great earth became terrible. The skies were darkened for what seemed an eternity. The only light that could be seen in the heavens was our sun, which was covered over with so much black dust that it could barely be seen. It was just a small, hazy glow in the sky and the people shivered with cold. They knew how to make fire, but to keep the fire going was not such an easy thing. It was at that time that the clan decided to appoint one person to be the fire keeper.

They selected the wisest of them, an elderly crone. She was old but resilient and respected by everyone. Her name was Sandaa. She was kinder than any person of the clan but she could also destroy anyone with a glance. She was selected as the fire keeper but rose immediately as the clan's leader. Holding the most prestigious and most coveted position as fire-keeper and head of the clan, she maintained her post without opposition. She was known for her great love and compassion and fairness in meting out punishment consonant with crimes.

The people knew not where she derived her power. She had tremendous physical strength and wielded the heaviest tools. But it was with true inner strength that she weathered all calamities, all misfortune, with an even-minded clarity that only a true leader could provide. She led by example and taught others to be clear and strong.

During a certain period of her last years she spoke to them about a great waterfall that could be found deep in the canyons. She said if one were fortunate enough to discover it, one would be instantly catapulted to a place of profound wisdom. The one who discovered the sacred waterfall would have a mission that the Original Wise Ones had yet to disclose.

The Great Sandaa left the members of the clan with a deep desire to know about the mission. She placed a deep yearning and inquisitiveness in their hearts. The one hint she gave was that the one who discovered the sacred waterfall would hold a state of mind as clear and powerful as water."

I was mesmerized by the tale and repeated it word for word after Great-Grandmother told it. Many catalysts were embedded in the story and I experienced even at such a young age the shifting of my own perception.

"Listen with all your senses, with your whole body and mind," Great-Grandmother would admonish when she saw that I was distracted. There were parts of certain tales where I needed to sing the words, emphasizing certain syllables and keeping true to a unique cadence, and so Great-Grandmother demonstrated these for me until I could recite them with accuracy.

Although I complained in the beginning, I grew to love these stories that were told in my mother tongue, the language closest to my heart. The catalysts had remained intact in the sounds since the very, very beginning when the Originals birthed this method of assisting humans.

"Bits of information, carefully sifted, are hidden in the sounds that have been passed on as a code that cannot be broken," Great-Grandmother assured me while cutting a branch of pine to extract the tree oil into a small metal container where a braid of cotton thread would be placed in the middle to be lit for burning.

"Also," she added, "Each of us has a seed inside our belly, and when the right sound touches the seed, it will sprout and take life. But, to bring the seed to full maturity in order to birth the True Self requires meticulous cultivation that few people are actually able to accomplish." Great-Grandmother was introducing to me the practice of birthing the True Self out of the top of the head.

She explained that she was not advanced enough in the spiritual arts to give me instruction for the birthing of the True Self. In fact, it was a mystery to her and she did not know anyone who could guide us.

By the time Great-Grandmother left this world I had memorized all of the tales in her repertoire. Too young to replace her as village bard, I would not assume that role. She was the last of our lineage to hold that prestigious title. It was necessary however for me to absorb the magic of the catalysts so that I could, in turn, transfer the sacred sounds to those who could receive them.

CHAPTER 15
NEW YEAR'S CELEBRATION

Despite the fact that misfortune and calamity visited our people through taxation and typhoons, we never lost our ability to lift our spirits and have fun.

The Lunar New Year fell on February 13, 1907. Since the previous year's storms had not taken our crops, my parents invited friends and neighbors to our humble home for a small celebration. In preparation Grandmother Machi and Great-Grandmother scurried about excitedly cooking and cleaning for two days. Mother hummed her favorite tunes and brought out our best kimono from the attic to air them out. Hers was a rich deep indigo with a silky sheen. Ours were the typical cotton fabrics of blue and white, but they would be adorned by special obi belts that Great-Grandmother had acquired during her sojourn in Shuri long ago.

"Look at these beautiful bright colors of the bingata cloth," Great-Grandmother said to me as she laid out the colorful obi belts of exquisite flower designs for us to see.

"Can I wear one too?" I exclaimed.

"Why, of course," smiled Great-Grandmother. She paused momentarily to clutch the red obi to her heart and said, "This red one is much too bright for me to wear at my age. It will look wonderful on you!" Of course, an old woman would never don such bright colored clothing. When a woman became of childbearing age, she wore only drab greys and deep blues.

Great-Grandmother wrapped the obi around and around my waist. I had a simple child's kimono that would have been dull and drab but the bright bingata obi dressed up the plain kimono such that I could have paraded in the South with confidence.

"We might let you wear this obi to school when you start classes next spring," laughed Mother. Our school year began during the first week of April and ended the following year in March. It was not likely that I would be wearing such a bright, luxurious item to school but Mother was gay and spewing outlandish ideas. She was exuberant and letting go of the frustration from the last two years devoid of festivities. Here was a chance to celebrate.

Mother practiced some of her dance steps and looked forward to entertaining the guests with a popular court dance she learned as a young woman. And Father brought out his *sanshin,* a guitar-like instrument evolved from the Chinese sanxian. The sanshin has a thin fret-less neck with three strings made of silk and a drum-like body covered with tautly stretched *habu* (snake) skin.

Father encouraged Jiraa to pluck along on his own sanshin although my brother was not as experienced as the other players who would soon be arriving. Neighbors and friends streamed into our courtyard and entered our home with offerings of food and drink.

The mood was light and joyful. Laughter and joke-telling filled the room. The women drank barley tea and the men drank *sake,* a rice wine, and everyone shared the variety of food laid out on two small tables. There were dishes made with bits of pork and chicken and rice-balls with condiments. Grandmother Machi had also made a soup with chunks of taro that she harvested in a pond nearby.

My favorite was the *undagii* which are deliciously sweet, deep-fried doughnuts shaped into small round balls, crispy on the outside. Great-Grandmother whispered to me, "I have saved a couple of the undagii in the kitchen just for you."

As guests gathered food in their bowls, the musicians tuned their instruments. Two female musicians had brought their *koto,* a long rectangular instrument. They knelt on the floor and plucked thirteen long silk strings to compliment the sanshin. With thirteen strings they were able to pluck deep feeling from every person who attended the party. Stringed instruments, both sanshin and koto, resonated with the mystical workings of the heart.

One guest had brought his sanshin and another a small *taiko* drum. They joined Father and Jiraa in the corner of the large room. As the four men began a lively song, everyone joined in for the *kachashi,* a joyful dance. The guests jumped up to the strumming, drumming and whistling as they rotated their wrists in short choppy movements while waving their hands over their heads in keeping with the upbeat sounds. We had not heard so much laughter in years, and the merry-making was infectious. A few hours flew by so quickly.

Friends were animated, talking about recent events and sharing in discussions about their hopes and dreams. The musicians tuned their instruments again, and emerging from the raucous laughter and merry-making was the slow, deliberate, melancholy plucking of the sanshin.

Hearing the opening of her song, Mother excused herself from her friends and positioned herself for the slow court dance. People, tired from dancing, plopped down to the tatami floor and were grateful for a bit of respite. The bittersweet song was about loss and disappointment, and the group watched with silent admiration as Mother glided agilely with Tai Chi-like movements. The musicians sang with deep, penetrating sadness. The classical dance was very slow, and the movements, graceful and subtle. Mother was amazingly controlled in her movements.

This popular song and dance called Hanafu is a story of love lost. The island women were often left by men visiting from other lands. The men sailed off never to return leaving behind mixed-race children and ethnic influences from other countries.

As Mother danced with delicate gestures Great-Grandmother reflected on her karmic relationship with the Portuguese man she would always love.

CHAPTER 16
LAST MONTHS WITH GREAT-GRANDMOTHER

The last few months before Great-Grandmother passed away were filled with joy. She played hide-and-seek with me between my lessons and we laughed endlessly but despite our light-hearted play, now and again, uneasiness welled up in me. I sensed some challenges ahead but did not see the dark clouds that loomed in the future because my powers of divining were not yet developed.

The challenges that faced our people would be greater than anyone could possibly know or imagine. Our people had suffered so much through history—the invasion of the Satsuma Clan of Japan in the early seventeenth century, the heavy taxation that weighed down our people and the unpredictable typhoons that swept away our hard work in the fields. We were dominated by big countries and treated poorly. It is a wonder we were able to remain cheerful and hopeful. Our loving nature enabled us to withstand these harsh conditions.

The spiritual messengers who visited me in dreams did not reveal specifics of the future so as not to distract me from the very important work that lay before me. But I began to sense calamity ahead and felt the urgency for my development. Somber moments visited me now and again but I was still a child.

My playmates were oblivious. I played all summer with the boys, running barefoot most of the time. Our feet were tough and calloused. The islanders could not fathom the idea that people in other parts of the world lived a life in shoes. We found it strange, indeed. How could a human live his entire life with feet that never knew the earth directly?

Great-Grandmother said, "My goodness! It would be impossible to be a living conduit between heaven and earth if our bare feet never touched the ground."

She was referring to the ancient understanding that the human is suspended between heaven and earth and draws energy through the top of the head and bottoms of the feet. From special points on the head and the feet our body pulls celestial and terrestrial energies into itself. The point at the top of the head is known as Celestial Fullness where we receive energy from heaven. We draw earth energy from the points known as Bubbling Spring at the bottoms of the feet. We wore straw sandals only in cold weather or whenever we ventured into rough terrain, otherwise, we knew Mother Earth directly.

I learned all these things from Great-Grandmother who always spoke to me in the old tongue although she knew the Japanese language. Highly unusual and unlike her contemporaries, she was fluent in the Japanese language. Using the old tongue she imprinted in my mind pertinent information about the mysterious catalysts that were embedded in certain sounds.

"When you sing the stories that I have taught you, the catalysts hidden in certain sounds will be carried in your voice to ignite the dormant seed in the belly of the hearer," she whispered, reinforcing the lesson she had previously given me.

"The catalyst will be disseminated through your voicing. As you mature your voice quality will develop to its fullest potential," Great-Grandmother assured me.

"There are two sides to the voice. We use our outer voice in ordinary conversation," she said loudly. "The inner voice," she softened her tone, *"speaks to us* if we can listen for it. You must attune yourself to the inner voice."

"You must be quiet long enough to begin to hear the inner voice and when you have developed that ability, you will be able to help others through the use of your outer voice. The inner voice is the most highly developed aspect of ourselves and will inspire and guide us. As you have learned, the Original Wise Ones communicate to us through that inner voice.

"The Wise Ones whisper so softly," Great-Grandmother brought her finger to her lips and continued, "that unless our mind is very, very quiet we will not be able to hear the messages that stream through us, moment by moment."

Great-Grandmother explained just how an answer to a problem suddenly pops into our heads out of nowhere. These were messages from the Wise Ones as their communication flowed through the psychic center in the throat, the Fifth Chakra, which is an important station for sending and receiving information.

"When we are closed off to the communication from the Wise Ones," she cautioned, "we might, sooner or later, develop physical symptoms in the throat. Unusual and persistent coughing with no known basis might be an example of this."

"The magical catalyst embedded in certain sounds can help a common human develop into a high human," repeated Great-Grandmother. "Sounds that carry the catalyst are numerous and varied because not everyone is influenced in the same way by the same note or tone."

"You ought to know," she continued, "that every culture develops its own unique way of helping the spiritual growth of its people. We do it through sound but others have developed methods using other senses such as sight, smell, taste or touch. For example, some of our ancient kin journeyed from Central Asia to southern regions of the continent where the people developed artwork that could powerfully shift those who meditated on them." Great-Grandmother was describing a process where monks used pulverized sand dyed with bright colors to create sacred designs. Those patterns mysteriously transformed its viewers.

"Sometimes one can even have deep experiences by chewing roots of certain plants," she added.

I was not quite six when Great-Grandmother, at the age of 101, prepared for her departure from this world. A week before her *mahasamadhi,* the great passing, she led me by the hand to the back of the house and explained as we strolled together that she would be leaving us in seven days.

Since I was born, my family spoke often about death being one of the most natural things in life. We were all prepared to a large degree that we must pass on from this physical world. Even with this understanding, I was sad at the thought of losing Great-Grandmother.

"Why must you leave us now?" I asked with tears welling.

"I will never actually leave. I will always be close by," she reassured me. "We have borrowed this body for a time and we must eventually return it," she explained. "Don't ever confuse your *self* with this physical vehicle that carries you around. There's nothing to fret, my dear. My only concern is that I have not been able to complete my task of grooming you."

Great-Grandmother's time was limited, and she would not be able to complete what she had set out to do. Her main concern in her last few years was to prepare me for my destiny. That was her karma. She heaved a sigh and with downcast eyes apologized for not being able to explain in full, secrets she had been holding. She showed me a strange box stored in back of the house. The box was inlaid in the horizontal wood beam on the lower border of the house. She scratched away at the edges and removed it from its resting place.

"No one knows about this tiny treasure box," she sighed wistfully. "It was handed down to me by my mother Uto who in turn received it from her mother and so on from our ancestors. It was opened once by the Great Kamadaa ten generations ago but since then has remained closed."

Removing dirt particles that were clinging to the tiny box, she ran a soft cloth over it and whispered, "It contains some kind of message that will lead its reader to the mystical waterfall, which exists…but does not exist. The one who finds the falls will be catapulted to magnificent heights of knowledge and power."

She paused and looked directly into my eyes with jet-black seriousness. "But the box must not be prematurely opened or something terrible will happen." There was such a frightening look on Great-Grandmother's face that I gasped with my little hand over my mouth to suppress a yelp.

Great-Grandmother secured the tiny treasure box shoving it back into its snug place in the wood beam. I was so terrified that the incident was completely obliterated from my mind.

Since Great-Grandmother Hanaa, like many developed souls, knew in advance when it was time for her to depart this world, she made preparations by fasting for three days. Knowing the importance to cleanse the body before the soul takes its exit, she drank only water, and no more food passed her lips. It was early spring when she called our family together to announce that she would be leaving soon.

A particular species of cicada found only in the South began to sing its unfamiliar song here in the northern peninsula. We noted its mysterious cry on the special occasion of Great-Grandmother's departure. The cicada spends most of its existence underground, insulated from the world, finally emerging from its long hibernation to give its otherworldly cry.

The simultaneous cries of a thousand cicadas produced an atmosphere of timelessness in our village. Here was nature's reminder that we leave the body but live on in another way. In our part of the world the cicada carries philosophical connotations of re-birth. Since the cicada emerges from the ground to sing every summer, it is a symbol of reincarnation.

Great-Grandmother smiled as she acknowledged nature's way of calling her. She turned to each of us and thanked us for bringing her so much happiness. We spoke what was in our hearts and she informed us that she had only a little while longer.

"You've been the wisest and kindest mother, ever," whispered Machi whose voice cracked with deep gratitude.

"And you've been my hero since I was a child," cried Mother who always deferred to her out of tremendous respect.

Father touched Great-Grandmother's wrinkled hand and said, "Thank you so much for your great care of our daughter and son.

They are unique and special and regarded highly by our villagers because of your influence on them."

She nodded gently to all of us and then asked Mother to bring out a few simple items to her bedside. Great-Grandmother had carefully stored these mementos in our attic, and now she wanted to bequeath these precious gifts.

To Machi, her daughter, she left a tiny necklace that was given to her by Machi's father. It was a simple but elegant piece of leather on which were strung some beads with a focal piece shaped as a cross, carved from stone.

"Your father gave this to me as a promise that he would return, and now I give it to you. As I hand this to you, know that your father *has* returned. His good wishes are carried in this piece, and now you can hold him next to your heart." Great-Grandmother had kept it well hidden and now it rested in her daughter's hands.

To her granddaughter Kana, my dear mother, she gave a delightful patchwork quilt made of scraps from exotic places and shiny squares of silk she had harvested and processed.

"You know very well that many of these squares are remnants from kimono you made from bolts of cloth you brought back from China. After you put the worn out kimono to be used as rags, I managed to salvage some good pieces and worked on the quilt secretly whenever you were away. Look at this little square from your very first kimono that you sewed! Great-Grandmother was teaching until her last breath. Here was the idea that we recover and re-use, not letting anything go to waste, giving new life continually.

Jiraa received a handy hammer that Great-Grandmother had found many summers ago in the southern port where she had gone to witness the trading of fine wares. The object with its beautifully carved handle was both utilitarian as well as an interesting piece of art. Great-Grandmother catered to my brother's love of carpentry and his refined appreciation for well-crafted objects.

To my father, she bequeathed a rare book on the study of our ancestors. She had traded this for several from her collection. "I have never seen anything so exquisite," he sighed. "I will make the time to appreciate the knowledge collected in this fine book." Although Father rarely had time to read or study, Great-Grandmother was encouraging him to do so.

I was the last recipient. I craned my neck to look for a fifth gift in the empty space where the other four gifts had been. But there was nothing there.

Great-Grandmother turned to me and lovingly held my little hands for a long, long while. At first I began to feel a lightness of being. The entire room grew sunnier, and I felt as though layers of my skin were lifting off. I was suddenly weightless. For a moment Great-Grandmother and I were two beings of light. The room glowed with our presence as everything and everyone else faded away.

Great-Grandmother looked different. Her whole being glistened with youth, and the sparkles that filled her eyes zoomed into mine. In that moment I understood. She transmitted her wisdom that could not be given in words.

The entire family witnessed the shimmering event as they stood outside the luminescence. Gasping and gripping each other's arms, each of them experienced the scene in a unique way. Curiously, not one member of my family ever spoke about the event because soon after the transference was complete, the Originals erased the incident from their memory. My family went on as if nothing out of the ordinary had happened. Mother had a faint recollection that I had squealed with delight as if I were being tickled when Great-Grandmother gifted me. Beyond that she remembered nothing.

What was transmitted to me would remain private. Speaking of it to family members would dilute the magic of the transference and decrease the power I received. If the family simply forgot about it, the concentrated energy would remain sealed. And so it was.

I recall vividly the moment of her transition when Great-Grandmother with a trace of a smile nodded to me and rolled her eyes back into a deep mahasamadhi, the soul's conscious exit from the physical body. It was time, and it happened just so. It is simple and elegant how great souls depart. From exhalation to exhalation we enter the world and exit. The leaves of the trees began to rustle, and there stirred a huge wind as if announcing a storm. The winds whipped up for a while and then quieted to a kind of stillness where each of us could hear the sound of the sea in our inner ear.

Great-Grandmother had turned 101 just a couple of months before her departure, and the villagers gathered now to celebrate her illustrious life. Her daughter Machi and granddaughter Kana bathed her body and dressed her for the villagers to come and pay their respects. Her face maintained a luster as villagers bowed deeply and streamed through our house all day long. Close friends offered cooked vegetables to our family. Each person spent a bit of time by Great-Grandmother's motionless corpse, lovingly stroking her arms and hands. They spoke out loud to her and gave thanks to her long service as village bard.

The day after the visitation, my mother and grandmother readied the body for burial. They carried the body, dressed in a clean kimono, in a wooden coffin to a remote area near the sea to a special tomb where her body would be left for three years. At the end of that time our family would remove the bones, wash them, and carefully put them into a huge urn to be placed next to urns of our ancestors in the large family tomb. The design of our family tomb shaped like the back of a turtle came from China. It was quite large, almost a miniature house. The older tombs were large like ours and resembled wombs. We come from the womb and return to it.

One of our family designated to clean the bones, would first pick out the small bone from the throat thought to be in the shape of the Buddha seated in meditation. It is said that the more the Buddha-bone resembles the Great Buddha, the more elevated the spiritual development of the person.

I knew my connection with Great-Grandmother was forever and, for a time, I spoke out loud to her every day.

Great-Grandmother continues as my spirit guide, and she has never left my side. She hovers nearby and is right here to help me whenever I call out to her.

CHAPTER 17
MOTHER AND FATHER BOARD
THE CHINESE JUNK

Great-Grandmother's mahasamadhi remains a strong memory for me, perhaps the most powerful in comparison to many events in my early years. There is also a particular night at the end of summer 1908 when I was just six years old that is equally memorable. That night revisits me from time to time and remains my last recollection of our family nestled together in silent connection.

We had suffered severe typhoons in late summer that practically destroyed all our crops and my parents needed to sail to China. I was too young to understand the devastating impact of the storms, causing ruinous conditions on the island. Our family was left with only a few small pottery bins of stored grains and some farm animals, including a few chickens that yielded some eggs.

My parents, like other villagers, had prepared for bad times by stocking rice and millet in our storage hut and protecting the farm animals in sturdy pens but we did not have enough rations to last through the winter. They had worked so hard on our farmland but due to poor soil and fickle storms the yield was sparse. They decided to sail to Ch'uang-chou port where my father's distant relatives were settled. My parents would help till the land, plant vegetables on the Chinese farm or sell goods in the market place and then would return home in two months with various items to sell and trade in our northern port.

So, in October of the very same year that Great-Grandmother had passed on, my parents prepared for their excursion to China. If conditions were favorable, their journey might take only a week. They packed fried sweet potato, rice balls, dried fruit, dried fish and canteens of water to last two weeks. They also took some fresh tangerines, persimmons and bananas.

I will never forget the night before their departure when Mother leisurely combed her long hair with a lovely strip of black lacquered wood upon which were ornate, delicate paintings of Chinese court ladies and a row of very narrow teeth that untangled her soft tresses. She had acquired this treasure on one of her ventures to China and carefully kept it in a beautiful, perfectly fitted silk pouch. She stored it with other valuables in a special case that she allowed no one else to touch. Mother told me that it would someday belong to me.

As she combed her long wavy hair, Mother gazed off into the twinkly night sky, and the fireflies competed for her attention. I saw Mother's beautiful profile by the light of the pine candle. She was born in Nakijin, a small village on our Motobu Peninsula. Her blood was a mixture of races. Our islands had seen the comings and goings of so many traders from other lands that it seemed as though we were a part of all people and all people were a part of us.

My father dreamily watched her, and my brother intently shaved the edges of a wood cabinet he was fixing. Because of economic difficulties, Jiraa had put off advanced schooling for another two years. He wanted to help my father in the fields.

I thought if Great-Grandmother were here, she would be re-stitching some piece of clothing. Just as the thought crossed my mind I felt a soft wind caress my cheek and I recollected a strange incident when I was a toddler. Great-Grandmother had taken me by the hand on a warm, quiet afternoon to go herb gathering in the hills near our house. Suddenly out of nowhere strange gusts of wind whipped up around us. She immediately stood straight up and placed her hands in gassho, hands in prayer. She muttered something and bowed deeply.

"When a great soul passes, there are high winds," she had explained. Sudden winds that announce such a passing come in the midst of ordinary calm and disappear just as quickly as they arise, and we are left with absolute stillness.

This vision of Great-Grandmother consoled me and soothed my mounting uneasiness about my parents' departure.

My parents assured us that they would return in two months with food, exotic plants and various wares to sell and barter to return economic stability to our family. The poorer villagers could not afford the items that my parents would bring, but merchants who sailed through our northern ports from time to time might purchase such wares.

"We'll bring fine paper and ink with writing brushes," Mother said excitedly, "and colorful bolts of cloth and small glazed ceramics." Grandmother Machi reminded Mother not to forget the medicinal herbs that were becoming scarce in our tiny medicine cabinet.

My parents appointed Jiraa to be man of the house and he volunteered to toil in the fields alongside the other workers. Grandmother Machi would care for us children, keep the home in order and manage our few months of rations during their absence.

My mother turned to me. She was no fool and reiterated that she did not want me to get into any mischief. She was well aware of my thirst for adventure. I loved climbing tall trees and swimming in our ocean and taking hikes into our mountains. Mother was concerned that in their absence I might feel freer to explore.

"I'll be careful," I said. "And, I promise to ask Jiraa's permission."

In case Jiraa would not permit me, a brilliant thought crossed my mind. I'll just bribe him. I would promise him my share of sweets that our parents would bring back and for that, he would keep quiet. I was wrong about this. Jiraa was a responsible boy and would never accept a bribe. But, it was a fun thought to entertain.

So, in October 1908 my parents, Kana and Machuu, set sail for Ch'uang-chou. Busy with the inventory of food she would have to dry and store, Grandmother Machi excused herself from seeing them off, but even she, stubborn as she was, gave in to my cries of protest and walked the entire distance to wave goodbye to her only daughter and son-in-law.

Grandmother Machi, Jiraa and I accompanied them on the long walk to Toguchi Port. Our mare pulled a small cart of boxes of food, water and some medicines. Despite the strange disquiet deep in my soul and a tight knot in my stomach, I was brave and held back tears.

They boarded a small Chinese junk with a tall sail. The boat was large enough for eight passengers with two men alternating at the sails, and everyone was expected to bring their own rations of food and drink. Jiraa helped Father hoist the boxes onto the vessel. It looked like a tiny houseboat with a small covered area for sleeping. The seas might be a little rough and surely cold at night. But my parents had brought along a heavy futon to keep them warm. My father was a great navigator and could lend his help to the captain of the vessel.

After loading everything, the boat slowly drifted off picking up a little speed as the captain worked the sail. Our parents yelled their goodbyes and hollered that they would be returning very soon.

As is the custom, everyone waved until the tiny trade boat could no longer be seen on the horizon. As Grandmother Machi, Jiraa and I turned homeward, I silently cried and gave a prayer of protection.

CHAPTER 18
THE ORACLE

Our parents did not return at the end of two months like they had promised. Jiraa sent a letter to our relatives in Ch'uang-chou inquiring as to whether our parents had decided to prolong their stay. We somberly moved through the winter with one piece of communication from relatives indicating that our parents had happily loaded their trade boat with plenty of goods and left the port of Ch'uang-chou in high spirits. That was all we knew. There was a time our local fishermen sailed out in every direction but returned exhausted and dejected from empty searches. The sea authorities were notified too, but still no word. It was a complete mystery.

In March 1909 our parents were still missing. It was five months since they had set sail into the East China Sea after the islands of our archipelago came to the end of a disastrous typhoon season. Jiraa and I often wondered if we could have dissuaded them from going to China.

"The typhoon season is over," Mother had exclaimed confidently, "and we'll be back soon with lots of interesting goods to sell." Those were Mother's last words as she waved goodbye.

They should have returned by the end of November or, at the latest, early December. Grandmother Machi, Jiraa and I sat together at our evening meals anxious and depressed. We suffered many sleepless nights. The gloom was building day by day and we cried together with worry. The three of us had no appetite and we had to struggle to get our meals down. We invented stories of why they must be alive and then we fell into complete despair crying ourselves to sleep.

With our parents' failure to return, Grandmother Machi's health deteriorated. She forced herself to care for us by trying to complete her daily chores but her emotional exhaustion caused her to curl up and sleep during the day to escape her pain. We feared losing her soon.

After a time we accepted that our parents would probably not return. We had so little food but we eked by. We stretched our grains in watery soups, and Jiraa and I went frequently to the ocean in search of seaweed and clams. Our neighbors stopped by from time to time to bring small amounts of food although they, too, were barely surviving. They tried to ease our grief with kind words. The months went by and we managed somehow to get through the dreary winter until spring was upon us.

I was entering the first grade in early April. During the two-week school break from mid-March to early April, the older students graduated and other children were shouting and running happily about but Jiraa brooded. He felt it was surely bad karma to lose our parents at such young ages. He was seventeen and I was almost seven. He could not comprehend why such a thing should happen to us.

He challenged me, "You are a High Born One. Why would the Originals abandon you now?"

"They have not abandoned me, Jiraa," I said to him. "The Wise Ones work in mysterious ways, and we cannot blame them when things do not go according to our plan. Although they influence us subtly, we still have free choice. Who knows what choices Mother and Father made while sailing the vast ocean?"

Jiraa nodded but I could tell he was barely listening. He went on to broach the subject that had been on his mind for several months since the anticipated date of our parents' return came and went.

"We should visit the Yuta," he said quietly. He was referring to the soothsayer secluded in the mountains north of us. "Some say she is over 100 years old and may have already passed on. Hopefully she is still alive and giving counsel."

I agreed. We could have consulted another yuta closer by, but this one in the north was known for her extraordinary power and exactness with which she understood the past, predicted the future and brought profound understanding to the present. She had sight and was able to interpret what she saw in the most sublime way.

We made Grandmother Machi as comfortable as possible and asked a neighbor to check on her. Jiraa prepared two simple meals and asked that the neighbor feed her during our absence of a few hours. I left small bowls of water and tea by her futon bed. She was listless.

Jiraa and I set out in the cool morning with only a small snack and one canteen of water. Our trusty mare would carry us along a treacherous trek into the mountains to the Yuta's cottage.

"We can return by afternoon if we hurry," said Jiraa even though we were not entirely sure of where we were going. We had only vague directions from the neighbors but we were determined to find her. At the end of the dirt road that led east out of the village, we headed north on a windy trail infrequently traveled. Keeping the East China Sea within sight we slowly climbed upward. Our mare stepped sure-footed along a narrow path through tall grass and thick brush. The morning chill quickly burned off and we rode under clear and sunny skies.

At one point, I complained of thirst and hunger and Jiraa slipped off to help me down. He said he was not the least bit hungry or thirsty and handed me both water and snack, which I gobbled quickly. At the height of the afternoon heat we came to a small stream where he refilled his canteen and quenched his thirst. I saw then that he must have been very, very thirsty. I began to observe Jiraa and his sacrificial ways. This characteristic of prioritizing another's welfare over one's own is typical of our island people. Kindness is inculcated in the culture to such an extreme that foreign visitors criticized our island men as being effeminate.

"According to a famous Chinese scholar who visited our islands, our men of the Liu Ch'iu resemble the highly developed sages of the Golden Age in their attitude and conduct," Great-Grandmother had shared on numerous occasions. "The ancient sages, such as Lao Tse and Confucius were brilliant men of high caliber, who knew the way of gentleness and had great concern for all beings."

My brother was most definitely exemplary of such kindness. We rode deeper into the mountain until Jiraa pointed to smoke coming from a tiny hut.

We had finally found the Yuta's cottage and made our way through the thicket that surrounded her thatched dwelling. A bubbling brook gurgled nearby, just outside the south gate, an auspicious layout of the land.

As we approached, we called out a greeting, "Hello! Hello!"

In a scratchy tone, she answered back. "Come through the south side of the house." Jiraa peered at me suspiciously and whispered, "She sounds like an old witch!"

Great-Grandmother once told us, "Yuta are feared by some who think they practice sorcery. They have the power to reduce someone's bad karma, but even the worst karma cannot be taken away completely. We must face situations resulting from seeds sown in the past. One thing is certain, the yuta will never bring harm to anyone."

Bowing and greeting we entered the hut. There was a familiar scent filling the entrance. The interior was dimly lit just as I imagined it would be. The old soothsayer welcomed us again in her deep rough voice. She was kneeling just to the side of the stone hearth on a worn tatami mat with dried straw stalks sticking up in scattered places. Grey, loose strands of unkempt hair fell from her topknot through which ran a thin craggy twig. She was shrunken and wizened with beady eyes that reflected the light of the fire flickering in the hearth. There were several small black iron pots near the hearth, some probably for preparing food and others for exotic herbal decoctions.

The Yuta drank various herbal potions to sharpen her sight before giving counsel. Great-Grandmother had also used similar herbs before storytelling. The unique scent I detected as we approached the entrance was the very same herb used by both crones.

The Yuta knew in advance when clients were coming to visit because of her sight. She knew specifically who the visitors were because a phoenix would appear to communicate to her about them. At least, that was the rumor.

The phoenix in our part of the world was a mythical Chinese bird known to have unique physical characteristics. It had a bird's beak, a swallow's jaw and a snake's neck. The front of the body of the phoenix resembled a giraffe, its back, a tortoise and its tail, a fish.

I looked around, hoping to catch a glimpse of the strange creature. But no luck. Instead, what I found was a small square space housing all her needs. It appeared that she ate, slept and cooked in this very space she received clients. There was a tiny altar of incense and small prayer books.

Jiraa asked her, "May we offer incense to your ancestors?" The Yuta nodded and Jiraa signaled me as we both stood and took three incense sticks and lit them, carefully placing them in the incense bowl. We put our hands in gassho and prayed.

The pungent smell of her medicinal herbs mingled with the scent of exotic incense acquired from foreign traders who came for her divining and wise counsel. There was also the distinctive scent of a special resin she had burned during a brief ritual prior to our arrival. The aroma of the special resin was delicate, yet, seemed to grow more and more intense, overriding the smells of the strong herbal decoction and various sticks of incense.

The resin's smoky trail wove its way around us with an intelligence of a slithering snake as Jiraa and I took our places in front of the Yuta, kneeling in seiza and bowing reverently, bringing our foreheads to the floor. The scent of the resin grew ever stronger and, at once, our senses were sharpened, wherein our vision was enhanced and our hearing was extended beyond its usual limits.

The Yuta informed us that prior to our arrival she had faced the rising sun to perform her prostrations. She had murmured an invocation to her special guardians and ancestors and now faced south to receive us as she set two steaming bowls of an herbal brew before us.

The Yuta was known for occasionally pulling out an ancient book called the *I Ching* and on this day she had a tattered copy on a small table next to her. I couldn't take my eyes off the book. There was something mysterious and compelling about it.

I confessed, "That book is mesmerizing. It's so beautiful." Although the book was old and tattered it had a regal presence. "It is a book of oracles containing 64 hexagrams," said the Yuta.

"Who wrote it?" I wondered out loud.

"The origin of this mysterious book from ancient China has been debated over the centuries," she answered. "One story of its origin is that the mythical King Fu Hsi, the famous Taoist Hermit Sage, viewed the back of a turtle shell and immediately saw the configuration of the hexagrams and learned divination. I keep the *I Ching* next to me whenever I give my counsel. The wisdom of the book pervades my mind and heightens my awareness."

Jiraa had prepared his questions long before our quest began. Yet finding himself in front of the Yuta, he could not speak. Overwhelmed by the power that surrounded him, he was unable to utter a word. After a time of silence the Yuta, intuiting the reason for our visit, spoke in a whisper and carefully revealed what we already knew in our hearts.

"Your parents are gone."

Although I imagined that our parents had perished in a storm on the high seas, the Yuta explained otherwise. My ability to see was not yet sufficiently developed.

"They were attacked by pirates who stole their boat with all their goods. I am sorry to say......that all passengers... were thrown...

overboard." The Yuta gently enunciated to soften the blow, but each word cut deeply and painfully into our already suffering hearts.

"Not everything that happens to us is a result of something we initiated in the past," the Yuta said, addressing a shallow understanding that we held about karma. "There is such a thing as generating *new* karma. These pirates have generated evil and will have to pay the price. All deeds must answer to karmic law."

Jiraa worriedly asked, "Are their spirits wandering about lost and distressed? I've been told, should we die an unnatural death or should we become lost at sea unable to have a proper burial, there will be problems for our descendants for many generations."

The Yuta replied, "I will perform a special ceremony to release their spirits and all will be well. When you return home you must sprinkle salt water in all corners of the house and outside the borders of the house as well. You must then light three sticks of incense and pray to your ancestors at your altar. By the time you return home I will have removed any evil surrounding you."

In a few years, through various events, I would come to heightened powers of divination. For now, I could only gasp and lament, unable to see the whole picture. The thought of Mother and Father helplessly drowning was more than we could bear and we wanted revenge. The Yuta read our thoughts.

"It is not a simple thing to rid ourselves of strong, hard feelings such as anger and vengeance. We cannot push away these emotions but we can learn to soften by holding compassion for others who are in similar situations. All wicked acts are engendered by the three poisons of greed, anger and delusion, and by working to rid ourselves of these three poisons we will contribute to reducing in others the wish to commit crime. To change the world, we start with ourselves.

"We begin to rid ourselves of these poisons by softening the areas where we hold bad feelings. These bad feelings will be transformed into light and we will be able to assist in reversing the negativity of the world."

The Yuta stopped abruptly. Her eyes misted over as her mind's eye hurled forward to a future time. She looked past us to a vision that left her helpless in the face of inevitable karmic tides.

"In your own lifetime," the Yuta announced, "you will witness catastrophe and destruction. You will experience great pain and loss but your harmonious and loving way will never die."

The old soothsayer continued in this vein with extreme sadness, "In the future when our people become divided by war and colonization, there will be fragmentation even among our gifted women, some of whom will lose touch with their extraordinary powers. With his constricted and unenlightened ideas our male colonizer will create fear among our people and rally us to create arms and ready us for war."

I could not comprehend the prediction. I was young and had only vague notions of what she described. I would someday witness the inhumanity the Yuta referenced. We were a peacekeeping people and though our men were influenced by our colonizers to take up arms and develop militaristic views, it was impossible to completely root out our deepest love for all beings. Many of our clan fought bravely in wars in distant lands but let it be known that we are intrinsically peacekeepers.

To conquer our own demons was the greatest battle and that required true discipline. Real power had less to do with subjugating others than challenging our own selves to do what was right and follow through with what was necessary to maintain the highest integrity in all situations. The true warrior is one who knows this, and time and time again this way of thinking was inculcated in the hearts and minds of our clan. It would be no different for the Native American and Tibetan brethren, save those who lost this truth by giving in to the ways of the small human.

The famous Yuta ended the oracle saying to me, "I was guided to your home soon after your birth to bring to your mother special herbs for your protection ceremony. You have latent powers of sight and healing.

"A number of teachers will appear to you in your early life to assist you along the way. Many secrets will be revealed to you as you develop yourself and you will bring hope to our people.

"And you, Jiraa, must continue to protect your little sister. The one who protects is just as necessary and vital as the one who carries and disseminates the teachings." Jiraa nodded. He already knew this and was not the least bit puzzled.

The Yuta faced me again, "You will continue to learn through your dreams. You experience nightly visitations by teachers from the spirit world. In two years your next teacher will come to you in the flesh to provide lessons in clearing the mind and strengthening the body. You will also meet an advanced priestess who will teach you the powers of manifestation. Then, in your twelfth year, the year of the Wood Tiger, you will begin to learn the art of healing." The Yuta bowed her head. The divination was complete.

After the oracle the Yuta sang a song of protection for Jiraa and me. Her voice quivered with the lilting accent of the old tongue. We thanked her and bowed deeply saying our farewells with tear-soaked faces and heavy hearts. The Yuta gave us dreadful news, yet at the same time she gave us hope.

I felt the presence of my parents during the oracle, and though I missed them terribly I knew they watched over us. Despite the horrifying news I sensed a welling of responsibility and wonder about my future.

Jiraa and I returned home carrying a deep sadness we could not hide from our frail grandmother. We needed to let Grandmother Machi know what we had learned from the Yuta.

"We are so sorry to bring home bad news," Jiraa said. While he saved her from details about the pirates attacking our parents, he did let her know they had died at sea.

Grandmother Machi had weakened to such a state that there was hardly any emotion on her face. She had known deep inside that her daughter and son-in-law were dead. And because of this, she had become numb. She had lost her appetite and was wasting away.

"I want to wither away in darkness," she whispered. She did not want to see the light of day and requested that we keep the panel doors closed.

Jiraa agreed to close the doors and then went quickly to bring two small bowls of salt water which we both sprinkled in and outside the house as the Yuta had instructed. It would take some time for the dark energy of the house to dissipate but Grandmother Machi's heaviness could not be lifted.

The despair was so heavy and thick that even the bright sun could only send its rays through tiny cracks in the wood panel doors leaving the interior of our living space with a cold blackness. Grandmother Machi ate like a little bird and although we did our best to comfort her, she could not be consoled. We cared for her through the beginning of summer and, during my summer break, she died in her sleep of a broken heart.

Our neighbors came to help us with the burial. A local kaminchu priestess came to assist although generally it was the family members themselves who took care of various details such as food offerings and prayers at the altar. The kaminchu kindly recited a long prayer to our ancestors and said she would return in 49 days to conduct another short ceremony. The spirit is said to move through after-death stages and at the end of 49 days the spirit has finished movement through the shadowy world.

Jiraa and I were now utterly alone. "We will find our way, little sister," he said. And, we opened the panel doors and brought in the sun. We prayed to Hinukan and dissolved salt in a bowl of water and sprinkled the salt water throughout the house as we had done when we returned from the Yuta.

The salt water cleansed and purified our surroundings. We burned incense at our altar and prayed. The dark energy in our home began to lift and I couldn't help but contrast this passing with the high passing of Great-Grandmother. We meet our death in different ways and from that our future karma is determined.

Jiraa and I decided that we would make a new life for ourselves and I grew closer to him. I wanted to help him in the fields but he said, "You are destined to receive higher education just as Mother and Father desired for you so you must devote yourself to your studies."

He felt with our parents gone, he would forego his plans for schooling altogether and take care of our land. We learned that loss could build us in ways other life events could not. It taught us to accept the ephemeral nature of things. We learned that by remaining pliant and receptive and clear we could weather calamity and misfortune and not be defeated. We both had times when we were sad but we helped each other through those times. Sometimes I cooked and cleaned so Jiraa could rest. We knew each other's moods and found ways to help each other adapt to our situation.

Our neighbors dropped by often so we still had the sense of belonging to a larger community. One of the strengths of our people is the closeness we cultivate with each other. We are friends for life.

CHAPTER 19
BLOOD BROTHERS

"Hey!" a voice called after me. I turned to face a skinny boy whom I had seen in school but never met. We were on a day off from school and here we were crossing paths. The boy was with three friends, all dressed alike, in shorts and rumpled, faded cotton shirts that were missing a couple of buttons and hung on them as if they were hand-me-downs.

"We're going to hike along the stream if you want to come," he invited as his three friends ran ahead. I had always imagined this boy to be quiet and shy and yet, today, he seemed bold and full of energy.

"Sure," I accepted. Girls were not much fun and I relished the chance to hang out with the boys. As we walked alongside each other, he kept giving me funny side-glances. Finally I turned to face him and, after an awkward pause, we both broke out into uncontrollable laughter. There is something strangely familiar about him, I thought to myself. Perhaps familiar was not the exact word. But I knew him. I wondered if he felt the same. We followed the other boys in comfortable silence along the stream until the calm flow turned to noisy rapids. It was there that his three friends decided to turn back, but something compelled me to forge ahead with my new friend. The hike was exhilarating although in a short time the sides of the stream became impassable. We swung from branches and hopped huge, smooth stones to get to its source. At the end of the hike was a tiny pool and small waterfall. We were breathless.

"How do you like it?" he shouted. The fall was gushing and noisy. I yelled back that I couldn't be happier, laughing loudly. The pool was icy and we stuck our feet in it and lay on the smooth surfaces of the huge stones. The sun was directly overhead and the cool from the spray of the falls saved us from too much heat.

As we lay on the rocks I realized I did not know his name but somehow it seemed unimportant. I was sure I already knew him. We meet people sometimes and we are linked to them with no explanation.

On our way home he told me his story. He was born a fourth generation Chinese. "My great-grandparents lost everything when their tiny boat was shipwrecked on these shores," he said.

"They had no intention whatsoever of landing here. They had plans to travel to islands in the north where they expected to find a better life. My great-grandparents had been scraping by in a very poor village in southwest China."

People had died of famine and disease there, he said. After they made their way from southwest China to the Pacific via an oxen-pulled caravan, they managed to acquire with their meager savings a small boat upon which they entrusted their entire fate.

Braving a violent storm, they barely landed on our shores in their dilapidated vessel. Our island villagers collected them from the wreckage and gave them immediate assistance. It has been the custom throughout history for our islanders to offer food and lodging to those who were shipwrecked. The villagers did it happily without hesitation and not just from a moral obligation. No matter how difficult the economic situation, the kind-hearted people of our islands never accepted payment in return. Recipients who were thoughtful would automatically return assistance to others who were less fortunate so that the cycle of giving and loving kindness was perpetuated.

His family settled in our northern village of Gushiken and learned the local dialect as well as Japanese. Although the boy's family had plans to leave once they were better off, they grew to love their neighbors and learned the customs of the island, and soon, talk of leaving the island was heard no more.

"My parents named me after my great-grandfather, Li En Gong, which means kindness and reverence," he said.

His family called him Gong, but I decided after mulling it over and repeating his name in my head, to call him En, because in the Japanese language En means one's karma or one's destiny.

From that day forward I developed a close friendship with him. He was a gutsy boy whom I found fascinating because he was so much like me. He shared my high sense of adventure, and together we planned many excursions that summer.

We were inseparable buddies for almost an entire year until my spiritual teachers came. Even then, we were able to see each other on occasion. His parents didn't like us playing risky games swinging upside down on branches like a couple of monkeys but we did it anyway. It is truly a wonder how we survived our childhood with all our exploits.

In addition to being a good playmate, En was a kind and thoughtful companion. En was a friend with whom I shared secrets and on whom I relied to carry me through some difficult times when I slumped into a dark place.

One afternoon the darkness of my parents' loss overcame me and I did not go out to play as we had planned. I yanked out my futon mattress and curled up in the birthing room. Suddenly, I heard En's voice, "Mahataa! Where are you?" He sneaked to the back of the house and tapped on the birthing room door.

"You must come out," he called. I was so sad that I did not reply. "Come on, I want to show you a funny bug I found near the stream! He has a million legs and speaks four languages and asked me to come and get you." He sounded so excited that it made me want to laugh. I muffled my giggling but of course he heard.

"I'm waiting," he sang. "I know you're in there and I'm not going anywhere until you come out." I stayed in bed for another few minutes but En waited patiently just like he said he would.

Finally I got out of bed and En greeted me with a huge smile. My mood lifted and I felt such gratitude for our friendship.

At the end of summer of 1909, En and I became blood brothers through a secret ceremony. We were both seven and took vows of loyalty to each other. Great-Grandmother had taught me a ritual that was passed on by way of our ancestors. It was a ritual that would bind En and me to each other as well as to our village.

One evening, I led En blindfolded to a clearing near our house, a small area that was once the foundation for the small public bath that my father had built. There were weeds now growing all around and the stony structure was in ruin. I had my friend kneel while I recited in the old tongue a song that would bind us in secret. He repeated a promissory line as I untied his blindfold, after which we each pricked our little fingers and held the digits together high in the air. En made a face and shrieked with pain even though it didn't hurt. We both giggled and our laughter traveled the faint breeze to all the corners of our island. He and I were now bonded for life. I would be obligated to give my life to save his and vice versa.

The mingling of blood occurred serendipitously under the full moon of August 1909.

"Chinese legends say that the August moon is at its brightest and roundest on this day," En taught me. "Under this bright autumn moon, friendships are made and renewed. Poets wrote about the August moon because long lost lovers found their way to each other on this night."

I think En was simply repeating something he had heard and knew nothing of these sorts of things. After all, we were much too young to be chatting about such adult matters.

We took our vows to protect and serve the village and to be forever bonded as brothers of this noble cause. The next day we carved the date of this most auspicious occasion with a sharp sliver of bamboo on a gnarled tree that grew between his house and mine so that posterity would be reminded of this important event.

No sooner had we carved the date on the tree, a poisonous snake slithered toward me from behind and En, without thinking, grabbed a stick nearby and rushed the snake, beating the grass to scare it away. It happened so quickly that I didn't even know that I was in danger. He had saved my life right then and there.

"We are truly brothers for life," I said, my heart still racing.

En laughed when I referred to myself as his brother once again. He grew serious when I explained that each person contains both male and female energies and that the male side of me was joined to his male aspect. He crinkled his forehead in question, but accepted the explanation just the same.

But he would come to understand this, along with many other esoteric teachings. In the course of a few years En's awareness was heightened beyond the ordinary, and I surmised that there must have been a catalyst hidden in one of the incantations during the bonding ritual I recited that ignited his spiritual seed.

From the time En and I were toddlers, the elders warned about the dangers of lethal snakes, habu, that inhabited the mountains. We children were also cautioned about the poisonous jellyfish that bobbed invisibly off the coral reef, not to mention the occasional sharks that visited the warm Pacific waters. The adults forbade us to play in the mountains and the sea because of these very real dangers.

Naturally these warnings just made the two of us more curious than ever. I felt deep in my heart that my friend was always braver than I, but I never once showed any apprehension. It was important to me that he view me as his equal.

It was En's unbridled curiosity about the world around him that drew me to him. His fearlessness was contagious and I took on the desire to explore the hills and mountains and the vast stretches of ocean lapping up on top of coral reefs. Those reefs extended out from shore for a few meters in parts. The waters surrounding the island were various shades of blue and green and in some places so crystal clear that the sandy floor could be seen from the shoreline.

Our coastline had irregular inlets where an imperceptible lapping of gentle waves refilled saltwater pools separated by craggy rocky surfaces. During low tide, En and I would go clam digging or sometimes break open fresh sea urchin to eat the roe right on the spot. Sea urchins are spiny creatures so we had to be extra careful when we handled them. Another find was a kind of green moss called *ahsa,* which grew in the holes of jagged rocks and was quite delicious in miso soup. The ahsa grew underwater in high tide and we scraped them out during low tide. In fact, whenever we hiked to the sea, we searched for ahsa to bring home.

"Let's head for the ocean," said En on a hot day in early September. And we trekked three kilometers or so from the village for a swim. He had in his possession rubber goggles that enabled us to enjoy the incredible underwater world. He only had one pair that had belonged to a cousin who had come from South China. She had used En's home as a kind of base to pursue her dream of becoming a deep-sea pearl diver.

She would dive the oceans in neighboring islands for pearls from which she was paid handsomely. Sadly, she lost her life when a shark attacked her on one of her outings. "She was barely twenty-four with lungs that could hold her underwater for hours," said En. That was a colossal exaggeration but I got the point.

The cousin was a free-diver and like all free-divers she was forced to descend to depths of over thirty meters on a single breath. Pearl divers manually gathered the oysters and opened them at random on the ocean floor. Often many pearls could be found on shoals at a depth of two meters from the surface. Divers went down twelve meters and sometimes even forty.

"She greased her body when the weather was cooler," En informed, "to conserve body heat and put greased cotton in her ears."

"When she dove down she wore a nose clip made out of tortoise shell and carried a large basket to hold the oysters," he described.

A fellow diver found her goggles floating on the surface after the vicious attack and brought them home to En's family as the only remaining vestige of a young life robbed of a promising future. En's parents packed the goggles away with her few belongings and came to forget about them. It had now been a few years since her death, and En recovered the goggles for his own use. His parents never dreamt that their son would be so daring as to venture the waters that so savagely took their niece's life.

So here we were with only one pair of goggles that were a little large for us. His cousin had had a large face, but the goggles could be adjusted enough for us to view the magical world off the shores of the island.

On one of our expeditions to the ocean we came across an abandoned circular tube by the side of the road. We were never sure what the tube had been used for, perhaps a bicycle tire, but it proved handy. Filled with air, it could be used as a flotation device. We welcomed it as sheer luck. Although En and I were superb swimmers, we occasionally needed a bit of respite when we swam far away from shore. We used the tube to rest momentarily as we handed the goggles back and forth, each marveling at the fascinating sea creatures below us.

We had found a stretch of pure white sand and transparent waters which became our own tiny paradise. There were many summer days when we swam out during low tide enjoying the sandy colored floor of the reef beneath us that seemed to stretch out for hundreds of meters. We saw starfish and sea urchins and small fish below.

We swam farther out following the brightest colored fish that wiggled their way directing our eyes to a number of indescribably peculiar sea creatures. As we swam out with our eyes on the sandy colored reef beneath us we were suddenly projected over a bottomless black ocean which gave us the sensation of falling off the face of the earth. It was thrilling and terrifying all at once.

We made our way often to the beach by following a long dirt path from the village. Well traveled by fishermen, a crude and narrow roadway emerged over time. En and I traveled the narrow dirt path up to a certain point and deviated left, away from the small ports. As we turned from the dirt path, we trampled through the high grasses and brush to carve our own way with the sound of cicadas buzzing in our ears. The buzzing was so loud that we could not think and because we were unable to think any thoughts what-soever we were transported in a kind of meditative state. By the time we arrived on the pristine shoreline we were so intensely pres-ent that we found ourselves in an altered state of consciousness.

We did not know then why it was so, but we were especially alert and could hear and see in ways that were not just magnified. Every-thing seemed to oscillate and beat with the breath of life. We dis-covered that we had special powers and could make things happen.

"Did you see that?" En asked. He was talking about a pink shell on the sandy beach that had seemed to magically move from one place to another. "I did that," he said proudly.

"Not possible," I said turning away. "No really," he grabbed me, "watch." And the pink shell actually moved from one spot to another.

"Oh my goodness," I whispered in disbelief. "How did you do that?"

"Can you still hear the faint buzzing of the cicada in your ears?" he asked softly. "I think it's giving us some kind of power. Go ahead, you try."

So, I did. I couldn't explain how or what I thought or even if I thought. But I moved the pink shell back to where it had been previously.

We spent time moving other things on the beach: shells, peb-bles, even creatures. There was a tiny crab with claws that emerged from one of the cone-shaped shells and we managed to move it closer to the water. In so doing, the crab slipped back inside of its shell and emerged again to walk away sideways.

We giggled as we watched the vegetation breathe, and came to appreciate how everything in nature was alive and could speak to us. The clouds in the sky were bestowing blessings and the lazy lapping of the tide was welcoming us. Insects spoke relaying tales other human ears would never hear.

We could not hang on to these powers and lost them as soon as we left the ocean. By leaving the sea we lost our special state of mind.

CHAPTER 20
I MEET THE OLD MONK

The island was a mystical place with so much to discover between mountain and sea. We children were exempt from the worries of the adult world and were free to experience the island's magic.

"I'm off!" I shouted to Jiraa as I slipped into my straw sandals. Filled with a sense of high adventure, I set out on a long hike. En and I were nine this year in the middle of our summer vacation that included the whole month of July. He was off with his friends so I headed for the mountain to explore alone. The day was sunny with wisps of stunning white clouds drifting across the light blue sky.

I found my way near the top where a beautiful monarch caught my eye. It was nature pointing the way, and following the butterfly, I stepped into a small clearing surrounded by tall overgrown grasses. This place evidently had been used for some special purpose. Three rows of stone seats formed a semi-circle and faced what might have been an altar. The area held a holy vibration. I curled up on one of the stone seats and wondered why it had been abandoned. I lingered for a while before making my way back down and decided to keep this discovery to myself.

Weeks passed and the image of the strange setting on the mountain would not leave my mind. I relished the idea of visiting it again, so here I was on another exploratory mission. As I made my way through the brush and tall grass, I suddenly heard in the offing the crunching of branches underfoot. Each step echoed down the steep slope toward me and seemed to be coming from my secret place.

"Who has discovered my special spot?" I wondered, annoyed at the idea. My hidden place had been well camouflaged by over-grown weeds with no worn path to guide others to it. "Impossible," I muttered to myself. I had been mindful on each excursion not to disturb a single branch or blade of grass. I had learned to move effortlessly, weightlessly, practically floating through the air. The Great Kamadaa taught me this secret way of travel in a dream. The formula for traveling in this way involved two important things. She taught me a visualization to place air pads under my feet and secondly, most importantly, I must hold a deep desire not to injure life, not even the tiniest creatures such as ants and crickets.

Suddenly I saw the silhouette of a tall man in a dark robe. The sun was at such an angle that the brilliant rays bounced off the ancient man's countenance. As I got closer I could see that it was not entirely the sun's reflection, but a curious radiation from his whole body, particularly from his face and head. A strange glow around his hairless head looked like a mixture of steam and scintillating light.

"Konnichiwa," the ancient one called out from a distance, his friendly greeting sending powerful waves my way and compelling me to go toward him. He spoke in the Japanese language which was unusual for a man his age. The older generation would have greeted in our native tongue, *"Hai Sai"* or *"Cha Gan Ju."*

"Good," he shouted. "You are the student I have been waiting for. I have been up this way a number of times to look for you. What good fortune that I have finally found you." His strong voice reverberated on the mountain. "Much work ahead of us and we must hurry. We have no time to waste because I am getting on in years."

"No time to waste," he exclaimed again and again.

This is one of the teachers the Yuta spoke of in the oracle, I thought to myself. This is an important karmic meeting.

When I walked up, the ancient one introduced himself as a simple monk and said, "I knew without a doubt that I would soon find the student to whom I would teach the mystical arts."

I knew a little about Taoist monks who had secret practices for longevity and immortality and Buddhist monks who brought teachings of how to clear the mind. It seemed that the old Monk was not simple as he claimed and that he was holding powerful knowledge and wisdom.

"I saw the perplexed look on your face," he grinned, "when you realized that I had found your secret place."

I nodded.

"Your hidden place was once a very special meeting area for the kaminchu. Those priestesses gathered together in this sacred grove to pray and perform rituals, but abandoned the grove several years ago when one of them was struck by lightning during a ceremony. They were nearly frightened to death."

"This place has a special aura and, whoever is drawn here..." his voice trailed off to a whisper. Though I strained my ear I could not make out what he said. Something about the answer to a prayer, but I was not sure and he would not repeat it.

"Most do not survive being struck by lightening," he continued, "so there is meaning when someone survives after being struck."

"The kaminchu who was struck went through a difficult recovery," he explained, "but soon afterward she realized why this had happened to her. She was being shaken by the great powers to know her true calling. She quickly left the kaminchu, the common priestesses, and became instead a yuta, a diviner and seer.

"The magical strike of the lightening transformed her instantly," the Monk's voice quivered, "and demonstrated the mystical workings of the universe."

"She confessed that as a priestess she often had an uncomfortable feeling of things not being quite right. Her true calling came with a jolt from the heavens that might have left anyone else dead. Perhaps you have heard of her, the most powerful soothsayer who lives deep in the northern mountains and gives wise counsel to all who visit," he queried with a glimmer in his eye.

"Yes," I exclaimed and recounted the details of Jiraa's and my meeting with the Yuta. Although I suspected that the Monk had knowledge of that meeting, he did not let on.

"The Yuta lives as a hermit and I came to know her when she summoned me," the old Monk said. "I gave her special energetic exercises to relieve the aches and pains she had suffered from the lightning incident."

"You summoned me too," he winked. I wrinkled my brow. What an odd thing to say. I never did any such thing.

"We do not necessarily consciously call persons and events to us. It happens that our soul decides what we need," the old Monk taught, "and then we draw to ourselves what our soul asks for."

"Often, major events that present themselves to us are orchestrated by unseen forces." He did not elaborate any further and waved his hand gesturing for me to let go of my inquiry.

I thought of the sudden urge I felt to visit the mountain before I discovered the sacred grove and the desire today to revisit it. The mere suggestion and the nuance of the moment led me to the next step on my path. I shared with the old Monk that only a whisper of a thought had inspired me to come to the mountain.

"Yes," he said, "if you do not pay strict attention, you will miss the call." Suddenly, his face shifted and his eyes cut right through me. "Far more critical than to miss the call is to hear the call and hesitate to act," he said sternly. I recoiled, not yet familiar with the deep compassion with which the old Monk taught. When he instructed, his carefree, playful glance could instantly change to a piercing look that lasted only a few seconds, just enough to get the point across, before resuming its normal softness.

We tend to shy away from teachers who bring us face to face with our fears and places of discomfort. If we are fortunate to come across such a teacher we can, with his help, root out those places of insecurity and fear.

"Face your fears," he taught, "then you will see they are all illusion."

"You must rely on your own knowing to determine the truth in situations," he continued. "True self-confidence does not arise from a bloated sense of self but rather from a quiet, humble place where all is well no matter what the circumstances, whether we are up or down, whether we are winning or losing. With self-confidence we can go along with whatever is, no matter what we face. We can assess a situation and decide instantly whether we are going to take action or let things lie."

"Study with me and I will train you to develop yourself," the old Monk offered. "Learn to hear your own voice that is guided by the wisest of the wise and follow your own heart that is nurtured by the deepest wisdom. We receive divine suggestions but choices we make are ultimately our own. You must not look to others to make decisions for you. That is not the right way." I took in what he said and knew that I needed to learn what I could from him. In my mind, I agreed to be his student, but before I could say anything, the Monk replied as if privy to my thought.

"Good then. I would like to meet your brother and ask his permission to teach you," he requested. I immediately invited him to the house, and we made our way down the mountain.

"You have a noiseless way of travel," he commented on our descent. I blushed and told him that I learned many things in dreams.

I waved to the workers in the fields as we passed and as we approached the seven stone steps leading up to our courtyard, I noticed a tiny soot-faced boy sitting outside our fence crying uncontrollably. I rushed to pick him up and he sobbed saying that his brother had stolen the bamboo stick he was playing with. He could not be consoled. I rushed to our attic, dragging the small ladder from the side of the house, and scrambled to find the small windmill toy that my father had given me. It was Father's first gift to me and I had kept it carefully wrapped next to the precious items that my mother left me.

As I held the windmill next to my heart, I knew that Father would have wanted me to give it to the little boy. I brought it down to the toddler and blew on the bright colored wings to make it whirl. He immediately stopped crying and his eyes filled with great joy. The boy had never seen anything so beautiful. It was like a gift from the gods.

"I'm so sorry to have kept you waiting," I said to the Monk.

"With that step you have just entered the path," said the Monk.

I wondered about his comment as I invited him into our home.

"You demonstrated the first of *the Six Paramitas,*" the Monk said, once again responding to my thought. "I will explain to you soon enough."

I rushed to light a fire and put on the kettle to brew some pomegranate-loquat tea. Great-Grandmother had created this particular combination as a healing tea. "Loquat leaves are excellent for lung function," she had once instructed.

A morning chore assigned to me years ago by Great-Grandmother was to pull water from the well to keep the kitchen kettle filled and it remained to this day a daily ritual. Our old well, circular in shape, sat in back of the house and was made of large stones much like the ones that made up the fence surrounding our property. I had seen other wells that were rectangular in shape but this had in common an infinite depth.

I glanced at the kettle that was beginning to steam, and my thoughts drifted to the fun I had the other day with my best friend. "Let's yell into the well," shouted En. We took turns yelling and screeching with laughter over the echoes of our voices that reverberated with endless overtones.

I smiled inwardly at the thought of the yelling-into-the-well game as I brewed a cup of tea for my guest. The vibration of my voice was in this very cup of tea. I was sure the old Monk would never need the vibratory assistance of my voice, but I found the idea to be delightfully funny.

I looked around for some sweets while the tea brewed and found a small tangerine, thank goodness, which I peeled and placed on a small dish. Mother sometimes brought out a small cube of black sugar or tiny sweet for guests if we had such luxurious items.

I poured the old Monk his tea in a special porcelain tea bowl, a prized possession that Mother had stored away long ago. It had been one of her guarded treasures which she kept wrapped in silk and stored in the crude chest where she kept her comb and a few relics from China. Those items now belonged to me. I was careful to take good care of them, and this was the first occasion to bring out the delicate bowl. It gave me great pride to serve tea to my teacher in such a treasure. I felt Mother's steady hand over mine as I placed the steaming bowl in front of my guest. He smiled and thanked me as he enjoyed the delicious and most unusual decoction and then said to me unexpectedly, "Your mother sends greetings."

I was not stunned. I felt her presence too.

As we waited for my brother, the old Monk sat quite still, cross-legged, spine straight as a rod. I again witnessed the energy emanating from his entire body, particularly around his head. In the subdued lighting, as the sun traveled across the sky, I saw a pale gold glow around his body, and around his head was a faint lavender. His kind and clear eyes brightened his soft face.

We sat together in silence for what seemed an eternity, and the usual lively sounds around the home quieted. His calm voice entered the quiet stillness in the most comforting way just as light seeps into the morning.

"It was the custom of the ancients to sit in silence for at least an hour when they met a stranger," he said, "so as not to rush things."

"We learn so much about each other in silence, in fact, so much more about the core of a person than when we speak. It is when we immediately speak to someone, that we are distracted from the true person," he taught.

Just then his eyes sparkled and he looked strangely familiar. Where had I known him before? I searched my mind for the answer but the odd feeling of familiarity vanished just as I heard my brother enter the vestibule of our home.

Jiraa, in his dusty, worn work clothes, removed his field shoes and called out, "Hello! I'm home!" He was nineteen and his skin was tanned from being in the fields every day. He was tall and thin in comparison to the other workers, who were all very short and stocky. Mother always said it was the European blood in him that gave him his stature. With a sweat soaked towel around his head, he entered the house and stopped abruptly as he beheld the vision of the Monk in meditation. Jiraa could not see the rays of light that streamed from the Monk's head and face, but he most definitely experienced the profound energy of our home.

Jiraa quickly removed the wet towel from his head and bowed reverently placing his hands together in gassho. When he looked up at our guest, I could see from the expression on his face that he, too, detected something familiar about this man. But Jiraa was not one to try to figure out the connection and was able to let the impression go as soon as it arose.

The old Monk in polite response to my brother put his hands in gassho as well. The ancient one smiled and quickly sized up my brother. Seeing that Jiraa was kind and generous, a trustworthy young man, dedicated to the wellbeing of his little sister, the Monk wasted no time in asking for permission to teach me.

Remembering the oracle, Jiraa beamed with joy and agreed, "Yes, yes. When will you begin?" The old Monk responded, "It would be best if I spend an hour or so of instruction at the house every day in the late afternoon. When school begins again I can visit at the same hour when she returns from school. We will have to create a special place in this house where Mahataa can begin to build her own power. It should be a place infrequently traveled by others, a quiet place where she can uninterruptedly develop her spiritual energy."

"Well, I think the best place," contemplated Jiraa, "might be the room where many of our family were born. The simple room looks out onto the side of the hill in back of the house. A few things are stored there but all of that can be moved out quickly and Mahataa can clean the room. It is where we were born..." Jiraa shared nostalgically.

"How appropriate," laughed the Monk.

"Ho, ho, ho! Yes! Yes! A birthing room is perfect! There will be another birthing of a different kind," he exclaimed, winking with an enigmatic twinkle in his eye.

CHAPTER 21
MEDITATION INSTRUCTION BEGINS

The next day I began my lessons with the Monk. I had a week left before I started school so I completed my chores in the morning, cleared the birthing room and still had time to run about with my friends before I met the Monk at home.

"Konnichiwa!" he greeted as he stepped into the vestibule holding a large cloth bag filled with various materials. I ran to greet him and invited him into the birthing room, where I served a small clay cup of *genmai-cha*, brown rice tea, on a wooden tray. He thanked me and took time to sip his tea.

I looked forward to this first meeting and could hardly wait for the Monk to teach me how to meditate, especially after experiencing the sight of him as he sat so very still the day before while waiting for my brother. I sat in a cross-legged position anticipating instruction, and was startled when he said my first lesson would be learning to sew. "To sew?" I asked.

"Today we will sew small cushions to use for sitting." I looked at him with question. "Everyone must be self-reliant," he said, "taking care to the minutest detail all of one's needs, not leaving anything for anyone else to do."

He brought sewing needles, sturdy thread and a couple of broad square cloths already cut to the proper size. He even brought dried barley seeds to fill the cushions, but I remembered the cotton batting that Mother had stored away in our attic. I moved the small trap door of the ceiling out of the way and climbed up into the dark attic, where cobwebs surrounded the wood beams of the

A-frame structure. There was just enough light to see small wooden crates with treasured family mementos, too precious to part with. I quickly found the batting in a keepsake box that had belonged to Grandmother Machi. I also found an old pair of scissors, a small sewing kit and remnants of silk.

The Monk had brought enough cloth for two cushions but I asked, "May I please use a piece of cloth from a bolt of silk my mother brought back from China? I just love the shiny eggplant color."

He jovially approved, "Your mother's good energy is stored in that fabric. You will sit with her support, and that is a beautiful thing."

I squealed with delight and gratitude upon hearing his words. Grandmother and Mother provided all the supplies I needed.

The Monk and I spread our sewing materials on the tatami floor and I began my sewing lesson. I used the outline of his cloth samples to cut my fabric to the appropriate size. I plucked a needle and some thread from the sewing kit and watched the Monk very closely as he threaded his needle.

"When you're threading the needle you must narrow your vision and focus. You cannot look away," he said.

I kept poking the tiny hole at the top of the needle with the end of the thread and grew frustrated because the thread would not go through. I made several more futile attempts and blew out an angry "Huuuuu."

The Monk looked up and said, "What is it that you are lacking? Just do it."

I finally managed to thread it and learned to tie a small knot at the end of the thread as he had done. I watched closely as he sewed with relaxed focus. Even when a noisy rustling occurred just outside of the house which made me jump, the Monk went on sewing, undisturbed, completely absorbed with the task.

At one point he looked up and said, "It is important to make each stitch the same length and sew in a straight line." This required tremendous concentration and patience.

At first, it was difficult to sit still enough to make even stitches, but as I relaxed, the sewing became easier. Every stitch followed the previous one, born from a steady calm. At the end of the afternoon we had completed our cushion covers, leaving a small gap on the side to allow for the batting. We sewed the last stitch after stuffing the cushions and closed the gap. I was pleased with what I had made.

"Wonderful!" he said. "Tomorrow I will give you formal meditation instruction."

As promised, the following day my teacher began the first of many meditation lessons. The birthing room where we worked was lined with two-inch tatami matting, soft enough for us to sit for long hours. "You must learn how to cross the legs in Full Lotus, but first we will work with preliminary leg positions. We will use the cushions that we sewed yesterday so that we will be comfortable.

"These postures require a specific alignment of the body and are not to be confused with casual ways of sitting. Our island people customarily sit in a casual cross-legged posture, but here, we must keep our backbone straight and keep our attention on our breathing," said the Monk.

He demonstrated the final form of sitting so that I would be able to see where we were going to end up in these series of postures. Having studied extensively with yoga pundits in India, the ancient one was adept in all yoga postures even at his advanced age. I awkwardly tried to cross my legs as he demonstrated and I found it impossible to bring my legs into the advanced posture that he so easily assumed.

"How can I possibly twist my legs like that?" I yelped with pain.

My teacher smiled and handed me a small book containing pictures of the various sitting poses and instructions on how to execute them. I flipped open the first page to a diagram of the first sitting posture. The Monk demonstrated as I simultaneously read from the book.

FIRST POSITION

As one sits on the floor the legs come together as if one is going to cross them but does not. The heels are tucked in toward the pubic bone, one leg in front of the other, with the knees falling to the floor. The ankles are not stacked on top of each other.

Because both knees should drop to the floor, it is necessary to hoist oneself up by placing the small cushion underneath the sit-bones. "So that's why we sewed those small cushions," I said as I positioned myself as described.

The Monk asked me to keep undivided attention on my breath as it seeped in and out of the nostrils. July was turning into August and this particular afternoon was especially sweltering. I wanted to splash water on my face from the stream and could think only of that while I sat there. I forgot all about the task the Monk had given me about observing my breath and I found myself daydreaming of dashing to the cool stream in front of our home and jumping in. I was lost in thoughts, images and feelings and only when my legs began to grow numb did I return from my reverie to my cushion.

The insects crawling into the birthing room where we sat were another challenge. The room opened to the side of a small hill that teemed with wildlife: insects, birds, caterpillars and occasionally snakes.

The Monk seemed undisturbed that a spider would find its way onto his lap. But many thoughts rushed through my mind as I brushed away a gnat that had landed on my cheek.

At the close of each lesson the Monk simply stood up tucking his cushion under his arm and turned to leave. It was not necessary for him to speak. I knew I would see him the next day.

He arrived every afternoon and I made sure to have fresh tea prepared for him. "I appreciate the kind gesture of your preparing tea for me," he said one day, "but I want to release you from that chore. I would prefer that we get started as soon as I arrive each day. We have limited time together and it is important that you progress as quickly as possible."

I agreed and we began the day's lesson. The Monk was patient and repeated the simple breath instructions, always reminding me to let go of my thinking.

My body grew accustomed to the first sitting position as I trained for the rest of the summer but my mind entertained itself endlessly. Just before autumn I picked up the book of diagrams and instructions and proceeded to change my leg position to the second posture.

SECOND POSITION

For the second posture the legs are crossed with one foot resting on the calf of the other leg. The legs are alternated from one sit
period to the next to equally strengthen both legs and open the hips.

I experimented with the second posture alternating the legs,
while the old Monk sat peacefully. I noticed his eyes were slightly
open but he allowed me to keep mine closed. He was patient and
worked with me step by step. Although the Monk encouraged me
to sit without moving, he didn't enforce the rule or scold me when
I moved. Besides, when the Monk fell into his meditation there was
nothing that could disturb him.

I was soon able to sit motionless for long periods of time, but
my mind continued to skip from concerns of the future to concerns of the past. One day, after sitting for half an hour I grew quite
bored and was glad when the Monk broke the silence. "Keep your
attention in your nostrils as if your life depended on it." That bit
of strong instruction helped me ignore my thoughts, at least for a
bit. But after a while, I sank into boredom again and my thoughts
returned to torment me.

The Monk spoke again, "Keep an awareness of your belly as it expands and contracts with your respiration." Giving me something else to focus on, I felt hopeful that I might really make some headway. I did as he suggested and another half an hour slipped by, ending our session for the day.

Very soon after the Monk's arrival the next day, winds whipped up around us as if a storm were approaching but my teacher kept very still, even as Jiraa and the farm hands rushed back from the fields to put up typhoon shutters.

The following day, despite the ongoing typhoon, the Monk arrived, ready for my lesson. Jiraa was surprised to see him in our vestibule and offered him some hot tea. My teacher, of course, declined the offer as he wished to begin my lesson straight away. I was impressed my teacher would not let the storm interrupt our teaching schedule.

He taught without interruption as if the high winds were only a minor hindrance. The howling of the wind and thrashing of tree branches were no distraction and he began the lesson with a few instructional phrases.

"Keep attention on your breath," he said. And when he knew my mind was wandering, he prompted me to come back to the breath giving me helpful hints.

"Breathe down into the lower abdomen and use the abdomen like a pair of bellows. The belly and the low back expand out on the inhalation and squeeze during the exhalation."

The rains and strong winds eventually left our island and we were lucky that the storm swerved away from our archipelago. My brother lost some days of work but the damage in the fields was not as bad as it might have been.

I worked diligently and was encouraged by the Monk to continue no matter the distractions around me. Another month slipped by and I made progress in reducing the turbulence in my mind. I was applying all the discipline I could muster and one afternoon my teacher said, "You might try the Half Lotus posture."

HALF LOTUS

In the Half-Lotus posture the Monk showed me to tuck my heel into the highest point of the opposite thigh. I practiced with one leg up and then switched to the other leg.

We sat again in silence and, although my mind had not completely learned to settle, my body had grown used to sitting. Seeing that I was not consistent in mind-stillness, my teacher expanded the breathing instruction suggesting I count my exhalations, one through ten and return to one again. He said to make my exhalations long and extended. Busy with this task, I could harness my attention a bit more. But it was still boring and in a short time my determination turned to anger. This wasn't any fun at all.

"Let go of all concerns," the Monk said calmly, seeing my agitation. "We are not our emotions, we are not our thoughts. Those are phenomena that change continuously. So how could we be our emotions or our thoughts?"

That doesn't help, I thought. Not one bit. But I went back to counting my exhalations and found that my mind actually had small moments of clarity.

"What is most important is to persevere enthusiastically," the Monk said. "You must develop the enlightened quality of energy, vigor, vitality and enthusiasm when you practice sitting. We must never sit lackadaisically. We sit always with diligence and persistent joyful effort."

The Monk stood and left, leaving me to savor the meditative mind.

Moving through the preliminary cross-legged postures helped me stretch the hips before coming to Full Lotus, the final preferred position. Once I mastered Full Lotus, I would be able to sit for much longer durations. The Full Lotus, called *Padmasana* in Sanskrit, is the ultimate pose in yoga. All the various yoga postures lead to this final meditation posture.

I studied the book's diagram of the Full Lotus prior to the Monk's arrival the next day.

FULL LOTUS

Under my teacher's meticulous instruction I placed my right leg on top of the left thigh, tucked the right heel into the belly at the highest point of the hip crease. I ensured that the right leg was tucked in deeply. Then, I placed my left leg on top of the right, tucked that foot in as deeply as I could and dug the left heel into the highest point of the lower belly. The soles of both feet faced up.

Full Lotus felt tight at first and a bit uncomfortable, but I learned to surrender to the initial discomfort and my hips opened automatically. The knees eventually relaxed downward, and the posture became easier to execute.

In the beginning, I was able to stay in Full Lotus for only a few minutes. I could not imagine anyone sitting in this final pose for an entire sit period. I spent most of the winter months practicing mostly in Half Lotus and only occasionally in Full Lotus. The Monk and I sat many more afternoons together in silence. He knew that for me what remained was practice, practice and more practice. His presence was a source of encouragement but my legs were often numb and my back and hips hurt.

"It takes time for the hip joints to open and for the back to become strong. We have to work at it little by little," said the Monk. He then taught me various yoga postures to open the hips to facilitate sitting and to stretch the muscles and tendons of the legs before assuming the positions. I persistently worked to maintain a correct, erect spine so that I could sit for longer periods without moving.

As I began to find physical comfort, I noticed that I started getting sleepy. I confessed to the Monk one day. "For me to sit still with nothing to do is not my idea of fun and it's putting me to sleep."

"Ah! An important point you bring again," said the Monk. "You must be ever vigilant when sleepiness or boredom overtake you. Those are the times when we must exert even more attention to the task of keeping our mind clear. Do you know why you become restless or bored or sleepy when you learn to meditate? It is because, for the first time in your life, you are taking control over the small self when it wants to maintain its control over you."

"Don't fret," said the old Monk. "We all begin this way. The practice of meditation is difficult to learn but you will begin to gain more and more influence over your small self by training morning and night."

Days turned into weeks turned into months where the Monk arrived to sit with me. The training was continuous without respite and in time I saw how necessary it was to stick with the task of sitting on a regular basis. I trained with the Monk for a total of three years and because of his urging, forged a habit of meditating morning and night.

My meditation was up and down in the beginning; one day I felt as though I had finally arrived at a mind that was utterly clear only to find the very next day that the turbulence had returned. It was like that, month after month, until I began to notice the consistency of a more relaxed mind.

In early spring the following year the Monk said, "You are coming along nicely and are now ready to take your meditative state of mind into your life of activity." He then introduced me to the way in which meals were taken in monasteries. He brought some nested bowls, wooden chopsticks, a lunch box of rice balls, cooked vegetables and some pickled daikon radish. "When we prepare food," he explained, "we must hold a clear mind because the food we prepare is imbued with our state of mind. We have a responsibility to always offer our bright, clear mind." He set the items he brought down and asked me to make some tea. He laid out the food and bowls on a small square cloth as I ran to our kitchen to make a tiny pot of tea.

"Monks eat together as a group and the activity is itself a meditation. We eat in silence and we learn important things about ourselves and others." He had brought two sets of nested bowls for each of us and we put food in one bowl and the daikon radish in the other.

"People who take food first must think of others who will take from the serving dishes after them so that everyone can partake equally."

We ate the humble meal in silence and, when we were finished, he poured some tea into the larger of the two bowls, passing the teakettle to me to do the same. He demonstrated the cleaning process using hot tea and a tiny piece of radish held by a pair of chopsticks. The pickled radish was soft and pliant and therefore easy to manipulate. In this way, the Monk taught absolute responsibility we have for our own lives, not leaving things around for others to look after. We wash our own bowls, clean up after ourselves, never expecting anyone to tidy anything for us. I learned by observing my teacher. He taught by example, never through criticism.

I reflected back to the day I met the Monk. I asked him to explain his comment then about my having entered the path. "You told me on the day I met you that I had entered the path and that I had demonstrated the first paramita. Can you explain?"

"Ah, yes," said the Monk. "The *Six Paramitas* are virtues that we cultivate as a way of purification. We purify our karma by following these virtues to live an unobstructed life. When we are fully awake, these virtues naturally express themselves in our word and in our action. Meanwhile, we can strive to practice these virtues as a way of purifying ourselves.

"Paramita means to cross over to the other shore, in other words, to cross over the sea of suffering to the shore of happiness and awakening. Paramita can mean perfection or perfect realization.

"The first paramita is the perfection of generosity. The essence of this paramita is unconditional love, a boundless openness of heart and mind, a selfless generosity. You gave something most precious by giving the windmill away. You gave it without attachment, without another thought after you gave it away. That is the first paramita and with its manifestation, you entered the path. True action is without a trace."

"What are the others?" I inquired.

"You have unwittingly demonstrated several of them already and the rest you will realize in the course of your training. The second paramita is the perfection of self-discipline. Through your consistent daily training of sitting meditation and other practices, you are demonstrating this paramita.

"When you finally settled down in learning to sew, you manifested the third paramita known as the perfection of patience. But, the work of patience is ongoing and you must continue to apply the fourth paramita, which is the perfection of joyous effort. When anger or frustration arises, remember to apply this perfection.

"The fifth paramita is the enlightened quality of concentration, meditation and samadhi. The mind has a tendency to be very distracted and restless, always moving from one thought or feeling to another. This fifth paramita has to do with training the mind so that it does what we want it to.

"The sixth paramita is the highest understanding that living beings can attain. It is beyond words and completely free from the limitation of mere ideas, concepts or intellectual knowledge. It is called *Prajna Paramita*, Prajna meaning wisdom. Ultimately, the full realization of prajna paramita is that we are not simply a separate self, trying to do good. Rather, we serve the welfare of all beings as a natural expression of the awakened heart."

Over the course of the next year, the Monk would always remind me of the task at hand. "In this year of training you have focused primarily to align your body. I have given you, thus far, simple breath instruction. You must now give your *undivided attention* to your breath to clear your mind."

He encouraged me, "Beginners often experience mental turbulence. In time the mind settles, and we know how to come to stillness. You will surely arrive."

Reiterating his previous instruction, he would remind me, "Count the exhalations and make the out-breath long, continuous and extended or simply follow the breath as it seeps in and out of the nostrils. It is the long, deep extended exhalations that lead to a calm mind."

One afternoon, he said, "One can choose to take this method of harnessing the breath to immortality if one desires it."

I had heard Great-Grandmother talk about immortality but had never considered it for myself. Besides, I was not even really sure what it would entail.

"However," he continued, "the pursuit of immortality involves very complicated instructions." It was as if he knew that I might someday be interested in pursuing such a path. "To prolong life and maintain youth, you must lengthen and slow down the respiration."

I learned to sit with longer exhalations and wondered about the concept of immortality, but the Monk did not bring it up again.

"You must cut away all connections with the outside world as you align first the body and then the breath. Your mind will then naturally come into alignment, and you will know true stillness and true emptiness." With that, he fell into silence.

Just then a huge scuffle from raucous, cackling birds outdoors bombarded the silence and my attention leapt out at the sudden noise. The Monk, however, maintained his unmoved mind. Later, when I heard a dog bark in the distance I realized how difficult it was for my mind not to track sounds in my environment. I worked diligently at keeping my attention with the task of counting the exhalations. I would have to eventually open my eyes while meditating and would have another challenge of not being tossed to and fro with movement around me.

"To remain empty and free, yet to be engaged in the world simultaneously is a wonderful state of mind," said the old Monk.

"Emptiness is not well understood," he continued. "Some people think emptiness means that our head is completely void. It is not. Emptiness is a state of mind beyond words or mental understanding."

After another month of meditation practice the Monk set up a formal interview at the end of each session to check my progress. He sometimes asked me questions, and at other times he simply expounded a teaching. It lasted only a few minutes but I found the short meetings to be powerful. It was a venue for me to demonstrate my awareness and for him to chart my progress.

While the meditation became easier, I should not lead anyone to think that the lessons with the Monk were easy. He was kind but stern. From the very beginning he left out no details. I moved through much difficulty in the arduous three years that I spent with him, but he was patient and exceedingly skillful.

He always spoke to me in Japanese and never in the old tongue. His fluent, proper Japanese piqued my interest. "Who is he?" I wondered one day. "Where does he come from that he speaks in Japanese, yet appears to be a local resident?"

"I know your native language," he said. This did not surprise me, as I had gotten used to his responding to my thoughts. "I speak to you in Japanese because it is the language in your schools, and you must master it to get along in the future." I appreciated that he always looked out for me, not as a surrogate parent, but as my teacher.

"I am from everywhere and nowhere," he stated answering the other part of my query. I constantly wondered about his origin and accepted what he said. The other villagers knew less about him and gossiped amongst themselves. "The ancient one is an Immortal, hundreds of years old," they said.

"Our grandparents and great-grandparents knew of him and swore that he always looked the same no matter how many years passed from one sighting to the next. He is as old as the hills. No one knows where he makes his home. He mysteriously appears and then disappears."

"Yes," I thought to myself, "he is from everywhere and nowhere."

That he could be an Immortal was credible because he demonstrated powers beyond anyone I knew. He revealed very little about his life and only as much as he wanted me to know. He said he had traveled extensively all over Asia and as far west as India. He had collected information directly from healers and wise men from different cultures. The ancient one was versed in many languages and I assumed he was not from these parts. Yet he was so very familiar to me and to Jiraa as well. The Monk had a curious glint in his eye and his voice had such a warm, comforting feel. I searched inside my mind for some hint of who he could be or any memory of him from my past, but to no avail!

CHAPTER 22
THE MYSTICAL ART OF TAI CHI

One May morning after my meditation, I took a leisurely stroll near our home and came upon a wonderful scene. Through the trees and tall grasses I saw the Monk performing a strange exercise. I crept closer and watched for a while. It was some kind of martial art but it did not look familiar.

The men of our village practice a martial art that originated in our islands called *karate* where movements are quite stiff with straight kicks and punches. Karate is an external art, so the attention is naturally directed outward. Here, the Monk appeared to maintain his attention inward. I held my breath and watched in amazement. He moved so slowly that even his kicks were in slow motion. I imagined that the effortlessness of the form he practiced was a direct expression of his mind.

Later that day the Monk came at the usual hour to give me my meditation lesson but I did not mention to him that I had seen him. The very next morning I preceded him to the open field and waited to see if he would show. Sure enough, he came to practice his slow exercise again. I was well hidden and was sure he didn't know I was there. I went to observe him every morning, always preceding him, and eventually I began to learn the movements in my mind.

A few weeks later, the old Monk arrived for our usual meditation lesson and after we had sat for a half hour or so, he said, "I know you have been watching me these last few weeks." I blushed at his knowledge of me and yet he assured me that many students of old began this way. "True students of the art form come to it serendipitously. They do not seek it out. Rather, the art will seek them.

"This martial art is called Tai Chi. All martial arts students come to the *dojo*, place of practice, and must observe for a period of time before beginning training. This is true with karate here on the island. A beginner is required to come to the dojo and sweep the floors and observe for many months before he is allowed to become a student. The school of karate on our island known as *Shuri-te* will be known eventually by another name in the future."

The Monk had precognition and would, from time to time, tell me about future events. "The popular style of Shuri-te on the island will become known as *Shorin-ryu.* Shorin is the pronunciation of *Shaolin,* which refers to Shaolin Kung fu, a martial art in China that will inform the local Shuri-te. There will come to be a form that synthesizes both the Okinawan and Chinese styles.

"You are now ready for meditation in movement," he said returning to our lesson. "It is an excellent thing that you observed for the time that you did. Your mind is well prepared for the task of learning the sequence of movements." I blushed again at his having knowledge of me watching his daily morning practice of Tai Chi even though he wanted me to do so.

"Tai Chi exercise is one of the many methods to quiet the mind and come to awakening, and its most important benefit is spiritual advancement," he taught. "You are ten years old and have been sitting quite well. You are old enough now to advance to this next phase of your training. Plus, we must move your lessons along as quickly as we can."

The urgency of the old Monk to teach me was because we were at a juncture in our history where time was running out. The world was shifting and sacred places on the planet were being spoiled, losing their original pristine environment. With the slow deterioration of these regions, high teachers would no longer be able to assemble in sacred power-places to teach.

I remembered his words on the mountain the day I met him. "No time to waste," he had said a number of times. We needed to ensure the awakening of as many people as possible. We could not work fast enough, and although our people did not have a single clue, a big war was looming.

"Let me demonstrate the Tai Chi exercise for you," the Monk stood slowly and placed himself before me. Although I had seen him from a distance and was familiar with the movements, I was captivated as he began directly in front of me a brief demonstration of the opening posture.

He stood casually his feet approximately shoulder width apart. His eyes gazed into the distance, and his hands dangled alongside the body. He was relaxed and empty. He cupped his hands and slowly moved them out in front of himself tracing a circle, then allowing them to settle back again alongside his body as if he were drawing a ball of energy to himself. He moved fluidly, so slowly and effortlessly, that he looked like a wisp of flowing silk. He then bent his knees, sinking toward the earth, as his right hand drew a circle in front of him. He pivoted steadily on his right heel with his right forearm in a blocking movement. He was demonstrating a defensive posture, protecting his ribcage from an invisible fist punch, which is why his right elbow remained close to his body as he turned to his right. In actual combat the blocking movement would continue to redirect the punch, utilizing the opponent's force against himself. The Monk was a moving source of power.

The following day we walked to the flat meadow on the hill behind our house. The old Monk demonstrated the entire form, all 108 moves, which took almost an hour to complete. It was breathtaking to watch, and I did not yet appreciate the smooth back and forth transitioning from defensive movement to offensive. Truly a martial art, but, for now, I saw the entire form as a beautiful dance.

I wondered why there were so many postures. When he was done, the Monk answered my thought, "The number 108 has a mystical meaning."

"The Heart Chakra has a total of 108 intersecting energy lines that converge toward itself," he expounded. "One of them leads to the Crown Chakra and is involved in the path to Self-realization.

The diameter of the sun is 108 times the diameter of the earth. There are 108 feelings, with 36 related to the past, 36 related to the present, and 36 related to the future."

"And finally," he concluded, "The Buddha's left footprint, when his body was discovered, contained 108 auspicious illustrations." The mystical resonance of the number 108 was alive in the Tai Chi form.

Each day we started first with our sitting meditation practice. We achieved a profound level of Clear Mind, and then walked to the meadow to begin Tai Chi. The small path leading up the hill was quite steep and well worn. The meadow was shaded and had a lush cover of green grass when we started, but, over time, the more we practiced Tai Chi, the more we flattened the grass beneath our feet, establishing and defining a large rectangular area.

This is going to be easy. Just some light stepping, I initially thought. After all, it did look effortless. What challenges could there be? Little did I know how much strength would be required in the legs. Keeping our knees bent quite low throughout the entire exercise was taxing. I was suddenly struck by the memory of when I first saw the Monk sitting cross-legged in our home. Meditation also looked so easy and dreamy. It didn't occur to me at the time that I would have any problem *just sitting*. Tai Chi proved to be the same.

Over time, Tai Chi strengthened my leg muscles and I built power in my arms and hands by using them as if I were moving through water. I was encouraged to feel the heaviness of the air so that I might use the resistance to build inner strength in my arms.

"Where does this exercise come from?" I asked the Monk. I was amazed that one posture moved into the next so smoothly. The transition from defensive to offensive movements was ingeniously seamless.

The old Monk explained, "A hermit of the Henan Province in North China was a strong meditator and learned the entire form in a dream."

With a twinkle in his eye, he continued, "When the hermit awakened from his dream, he simultaneously awakened from the dream of life." Just when the ancient one spoke those words, my consciousness was shifted from ordinary knowing to subtle, sublime awareness. The Monk was a great teacher, and like all great teachers, knew how to select phrases to bring me back to my true, clear state of mind.

The following morning after a brief sit we again made our way up the slope to the flat meadow.

I asked the Monk, "You said the other day that we always begin the exercise by facing north. Why is this necessary?"

"We begin by facing north," the Monk instructed, "because the northerly direction corresponds to the kidneys. Various characteristics such as direction, color, sound, smell, and taste are associated with the internal organs.

"Each of the sense organs relates to an internal organ. The kidneys open to the ears and are related to hearing. They even resemble the ears. Everything is related to everything else in mysterious ways," he shared.

Just as he said that, Great-Grandmother's voice echoed in my inner ear. She had once taught me about the interdependence of all things. "One thing I know for sure," she had said, "is that everything is connected to everything else, like Indra's Net."

Great-Grandmother told me the beautiful Hindu myth of Indra's Net, which speaks to the interdependent organization of the Universe. At each juncture of the Net where threads cross, a perfectly clear gem reflects all the other gems that are infinite in the Net. It is a metaphor used to illustrate how everything is connected to everything else. All our actions no matter how slight, affect everyone else. Everything that exists, or has ever existed, every idea that can be thought about is reflected in each of the gems.

The next day, as he had done before, the Monk began to teach me from the beginning. He extended his cupped hands in front and gently pulled them back toward his body tracing an invisible arc. His wrists remained bent alongside his body. I imitated the movements as best I could.

I was unable to maintain a perfectly clear mind in the beginning stages of learning Tai Chi because I had to *think* to commit the movements to memory. I found too that I held my breath whenever I concentrated with too much effort. I needed to balance concentration with relaxation and my teacher was constantly reminding me to breathe.

Because there were subtleties in just the brief opening, we repeated it again and again. I then took on the gross movements of the subsequent postures and helplessly moved in a disjointed way with my arms moving independently of my legs. I awkwardly shifted from slow to fast stepping, with no particular rhythm, as I tried to mimic the Monk's smooth transitioning from one step to the next.

It was only when I relaxed into Clear Mind that I could follow the Monk's movements with accuracy. It was so much easier for my body to learn without hindrance from my thinking mind.

My teacher explained another benefit of learning Tai Qi after establishing a sitting practice, "It takes great concentration to not lose one's place in the sequence of the 108 postures, but because you first mastered Clear Mind Meditation, you will be able to hold on to the current movement with relative ease, without thinking about the previous or next movement."

In time, with much practice, I refined the movements further and further and integrated what, at first, were independent movements of arms, hands and legs, to a unified movement of the whole body. I pushed off with my right hand as I bent my knees and the turning of my waist actually economized the movement of my right arm as I pivoted on my right heel. There was a relaxed *sinking* of the body and all movements became economical.

Every joint moved in cooperation with the other joints and there was a roundness and wholeness to the movements. I appreciated the almost imperceptible turn of the wrists and hands and the careful stepping of the feet. My body moved as a shadow to the Monk's. The slower he moved, the easier it was to see the nuances, and the subtleties became more and more obvious.

As I transitioned from one movement to the next, the Monk would remind me to maintain a clear mind. "There is nothing clouding your mind as you commit these movements to memory. The mind that is cultivated in meditation openly moves like an easy breeze, not getting stuck on anything."

"In time the body remembers the sequence of the Tai Chi movements and you will enjoy great peace. To hold a soft mind is most important, but you must never become negligent or lackadaisical," he warned. "Only by keeping a serene but alert mind will you know at any given moment where you are in the sequence." I found that I could be relaxed but crisply attentive and vigilant much like I was during my seated meditations.

The Tai Chi exercise was an outer representation of the inner movement of energy through specific pathways known as meridians in the body. During seated meditation, one could move the energy through these meridians with the mind using concentrated inner gazing. In both forms of meditation, it was important to simultaneously maintain sharp attention to detail and utter relaxation.

One afternoon, the old Monk placed his hands over his midback, over the most precious internal organ and explained. "The kidneys are the foundation of Yin and Yang. When we pull our cupped hands toward the body as we face north, we are naturally inhaling the potent kidney energy of the north all the way down into our own kidneys. Both the belly and low back expand naturally during inhalation welcoming the kidney energy of the north into the lower body."

Here was another similarity between Tai Chi and my sitting practice. On the cushion, we breathed all the way down into the lower belly, pulling energy into the region ruled by the kidneys.

Ultimately each of the two disciplines, Clear Mind Meditation and Tai Chi, informed the other. I worked my belly like a pair of bellows in both disciplines. In the Tai Chi exercise I achieved sharp focus while moving, and that training helped me to easily open my eyes during meditation on the cushion. My eyes no longer tracked movement in my environment while I sat, and I was able to sustain a calm still mind despite movement around me. Because of my Tai Chi training, I could more easily carry my Clear Mind off the cushion and into the world, where I was less inclined to be pulled by external events.

I would often hear the Monk's soft instruction, "Keep your eyes gazing ahead of you, at the same time, retain awareness of your surroundings."

As my practice progressed in the meadow behind my house, the borders of our rectangular space extended farther. We were sitting lower and lower in the postures and consequently our steps were longer. It was as if our whole bodies reached and stretched more and more.

Continuing with the critical principles of Tai Chi, the old Monk said, "Maintain a 360 degree awareness. Plant your feet by rooting them on the ground so that you cannot easily be thrown. Step carefully and mindfully. Maintain your equilibrium with economy of motion. Keep your center of gravity low in both your belly and legs. This rooted foundation will give you stability much like that of a tree trunk." These points settled into my mind and into my life. I came to see that the instructions in the world of martial arts could be carried into the world as a way to live.

During inclement weather, we practiced in the small birthing room. The Monk showed me ways to move through the 108 postures by *accommodation* so that I could move smoothly without interruption in a confined space. This involved extra steps forward or backward to complete a simple posture.

"When you step forward or backward, never commit your weight until you know you are on solid ground. Keep your waist supple and free so that you can turn at any given moment.

"We train so that we know when and how to move with force commensurate with what is necessary to effectively turn a situation to our advantage.

"Conserve your energy. Keep your mind clear, breathe fully and naturally and keep your attention in the here and now. Never cloud your mind by anticipating the movement of your opponent," he said introducing the concept of a challenger. After all, this was a martial art even though it felt at times like a slow dance.

The Tai Chi exercise can appear like a soft ballet, but deep inside the practitioner, the art cultivates an iron strength. In many physical disciplines strength is visible on the exterior with no internal power. Here, we learn to develop our internal strength, cloaked in a soft exterior.

After more intense training, I finally relaxed in the performance of the entire sequence. I walked the razor's edge between pristine, spacious emptiness and sharp, focused concentration. One morning, a ghostly figure appeared in front of me as if he were an opponent. I told the Monk what had happened. "A shadowy opponent moved with me during the exercise, and I saw his punch coming while I slid to block it."

"You finally got it," the teacher proudly shouted. "This brings me to the end of the story about the hermit," he laughed. "Months after he had committed the entire form to memory, an invisible opponent appeared."

The old Monk was pleased with my accomplishment. "Your body will begin to understand the actual applications of the movements. You will see why you move as you do to redirect a punch or use an opponent's force to push him off balance and use his strength to your advantage." Sure enough, the sequence made more and more sense as I danced with my invisible opponent.

The next level of training with the Monk involved face-to-face combat where our wrists met. We stood facing one another with a distance of one step between us. Looking into each other's eyes, we simultaneously stepped the right foot forward so that our inner feet were lined up. We bent our knees and brought together the outside of our right wrists, after which we drew circles in a horizontal plane as we shifted back and forth without moving the placement of our feet. This is called push-hands.

"When facing an opponent of equal ability, never be the first to move because you are sure to lose," said the Monk. "We are strongest on the defense."

"In facing a formidable opponent, be cautious, observe and react with swiftness. You can use your opponent's strength against himself. This is the superior quality of all defensive martial arts that cultivate internal power. The cultivation of internal power comes by building true confidence through wisdom and awareness. This power can be used explosively when the moment of need arises not only in physical combat but in mental combat as well.

I learned in the push-hands exercise to *sense* the opponent. The old Monk sat quite low because he was much taller than I. The circling of the hands allowed each of us to apply sudden offensive and defensive moves learned in the long, slow Tai Chi form. I found it fun and exhilarating to try and push him off balance. I began to see that push-hands exercise was a kind of silent interview where my teacher was able to check my progress. He questioned me with an offensive movement, and I answered with a defensive one.

Sometimes I made an offensive move that was not spontaneous, but planned. My teacher could see my mental churning before I executed the movement and easily redirected my push. It is rather a subtle point, but when we *think,* our body tightens and our opponent, if shrewd, can literally feel it.

"Let go of your thinking mind, and trust your body," the old Monk encouraged. He taught me to respond in the best possible way to master any situation.

I had already figured out that the essential Tai Chi instructions are very similar to those in seated meditation and wondered if they shared a similar goal. As if reading my thoughts my teacher smiled and said, "All disciplines that lead to truth have basic similarities. We use both the body and the mind in Tai Chi and in Clear Mind Meditation to achieve our goal of self-mastery. The difference is that in Tai Chi we move with Clear Mind and in meditation we sit with Clear Mind."

That made sense and I could see how inward gazing brought us into our bodies in both instances and how we use the body to remain grounded, whether we are moving or sitting.

Daily meditation had the cumulative effect of shaving away the veils that clouded my vision. More and more the concentrated sitting shed light into the deepest recesses of my consciousness. There were hints that surfaced about many aspects of my life.

On one occasion, the Monk taught, "We practice sitting with a clear mind that has let go of all thought, and gaze at the source point of emptiness with uninterrupted, concentrated effort. Cultivating that empty place illuminates our life.

"By inwardly gazing at the source point of Clear Mind we deepen our practice and cultivate wisdom. Through deeper and deeper insight and understanding, we naturally make corrections of mistaken views and actions. We spontaneously *know* rather than having to be told how to live."

With that instruction, the old Monk and I fell into a deep *samadhi,* an intense state of meditation. Something in his voice when he gave the day's meditation instruction spiraled me back to a time eons upon eons ago.

A dark shadow came over me, and I saw myself as I once lived in a previous life. In a shocking revelation I found myself to be the Emperor of the Sui Dynasty. Tears poured down my face as I wept with utter remorse and sorrow. How could this be? I looked upon my teacher, who in this life was serene and untroubled, and recognized him to be my faithful attendant in the royal court in ancient China. I had ended his life in a moment of petulant anger without any thought for his long, loyal service to me as my Court Magician.

As I cried uncontrollably, the Monk gently opened his eyes and whispered, "We have all run the gamut of roles. You have suffered many lives to reach this spiritual peak. Let me tell you about a famous twelfth century Tibetan master by the name of Milarepa. As a young man, Milarepa committed heinous crimes but he repented and ultimately became a great saint."

I realized then that the old Monk had known all along! I was at one time the cruel Emperor now returned as a High Born One. Even with knowledge of the horrific crime I committed against him in ancient history, the Monk lovingly taught me. He had known that I would come to this realization and offered an explanation of how karma functions even for those who choose dark, narrow paths.

"Milarepa, following the wishes of his mother who was bent on revenge, became a sorcerer who practiced black magic in ancient Tibet. He committed high crimes at the urging of his mother causing the death of many people. But, one day, realizing his grave error he sought the teachings of the highest Buddhist teacher of the time, Marpa, under whom he studied and suffered greatly to repent his misdeeds. Through superhuman perseverance, under the severe teachings of Marpa, Milarepa became a great saint, experiencing enlightenment and bringing the light of wisdom to sentient beings everywhere. The great teacher Marpa taught him principles that had been revealed first by the Buddha.

"So you see, even those who have erred greatly and have committed the most heinous of crimes can choose to come to salvation. Milarepa, attracted by the huge light of Marpa turned away from the dark path to the path of light. It was an arduous journey for him but with a will to change his dark course he was able to return."

I was grateful and in awe of what had transpired. Past lives are a curiosity but what is most important is the here and now. It is this very life, in this very moment that is of the utmost value because it is here that we can take action. The rest is a dream and only this present life is our truth.

CHAPTER 23
THE CONTINUING PATH OF MEDITATION

It was near the end of March 1914, just before our new school year was to begin. I had two more years left of school in our Northern Province. There were only a handful of classmates who were continuing on with En and me. One student who had the intention to join us was forced to return to fieldwork due to his father's illness and many others went off to become fishermen or farmers. I saw less and less of them. I grew closer to En who, like me, had ambitions to venture beyond the simple life in our village. We were fortunate that we could pursue our plans for more academic study.

The old Monk and I met in the late afternoons so I had the days free to join friends during my spring break. On one such morning, I took advantage of my schedule and planned an excursion with En.

We met by the huge gnarled banyan tree at the halfway point between our homes. The spirits that lived in the twisted trunk called us whenever we approached its energy field. We loved to climb it during the day, but on that day the skies grew dark and the tree looked almost like an ogre.

The smell of rain was in the air, and a brisk wind whipped up around us as clouds swelled like thick smoke blowing along the grey sky.

"Oh no, not another typhoon!" moaned the villagers as they scrambled to secure their houses. Jiraa and some field hands ran quickly to place storm shutters on the sides of our house.

Sharp lightning zigzagged above us through the charcoal clouds, and after an interminable time, a thunderous roar followed. A mean storm was brewing.

"We'll lose everything," screeched the farm hands. "All our hard work will be washed away!"

En and I peered into each other's eyes. This unpredictable element threatened the excursion we had planned—a fun trek up the backside of a nearby mountain. We were going to explore a new site.

"Do we go or not?" I asked.

"There's no question," he answered.

"Well, I guess we'll postpone it then," I was disappointed but agreed.

"No. I meant there's no question because why would we let a little storm stop us?" En said.

"That's the spirit!" I shouted above the roar of the rapidly approaching storm. "Why venture out when there's no danger?" Just then, huge, heavy droplets of cool rain came down, refreshing and relieving us from the unusual hot spell we were experiencing.

Feeling adventurous and invincible, we dashed home for head covers. I found a thin, flat piece of wood for protection and waited for En at the allotted place for what seemed an eternity, but he did not show. I suspected his parents probably made him stay home. That was just like them. The exploratory mission we had devised was too enticing to pass up so, after a while, I went on without him.

I wished En could have joined me. Without him, it would be only half as fun. I supposed I could run to his house to get him, but I decided against it. His mother thought of me as an unruly child and disapproved of my friendship with her son. She felt my brother was too lenient and that I lacked a female disciplinarian.

My brother Jiraa might have worried about me, but I had mentioned that I would be studying with a friend. He never argued when it came to schoolwork and he would have assumed I was safe at a friend's house.

Jiraa's life was full. He was busy supervising the farmhands, meeting his own share of fieldwork, living up to the demands of caregiver, playing the role of both father and mother and running the house. How could he possibly know every single thing his younger sister was up to?

The weather now made the journey slippery, but I was determined to forge ahead. What a challenge this was going to be. Without hesitation, I scrambled to the foot of the rain-drenched hill.

As I entered the brush a tiny path appeared. The measly piece of wood that served as a makeshift hat was hardly any protection. So soaked it curled like a banana leaf, so I discarded it. The branches of the tall trees protected me from the heavy rain as I pressed on. I slipped and slid on the mountainside and gripped loose branches that beckoned me. The magnetic tug of these long twigs and branches pulled me forward. The shrubbery reached out to me too, almost like a welcoming. I had a strange sense of elation. This is what I am supposed to be doing, I thought.

As I made my way halfway up the mountain, a grasshopper came out of its shelter to point me in the right direction. "Nature speaks to us if we pay attention," Great-Grandmother's voice echoed in my head.

I followed my little friend to the left, making my way onto a path that became less and less dense until I came upon an area that had been cordoned off by round smooth stones in a semi-circle around an altar. I was reminded of the other sacred grove, overgrown with weeds that I had discovered a couple of years ago. But this place was well-kept and groomed.

"This must be the new location established by the noro and the kaminchu after they abandoned the other one," I surmised. The strange symbols carved upon a slab of stone looked like cryptic designations of past High Priestesses.

Instinctually, with hands in gassho, I ran to what I assumed to be an altar and prayed to pay respects. This had to be the new area where priestesses gathered in secret to perform their rituals and prayers for the clan.

Men were never allowed in their ceremonies and I now understood why En was detained. No men or boys allowed! That was the unbroken rule. I knew I could not tell En about my discovery and felt bad about it since this was to be our expedition.

What these women did was a mystery. I had a hunch that I would be made privy when I met my next teacher, the Noro High Priestess. Why else had I been drawn to this place? Where is she? As I looked around, there was nothing but rain dancing on my head.

I returned home from the mountain and rushed to clean myself up from the mud clinging to my clothes. Jiraa was occupied and didn't notice that I had sneaked in through the entrance at the kitchen. As I was washing up, I thought about the High Priestess. I knew that the time would come soon when I would meet my next teacher. But for now, I was still under the tutelage of the old Monk.

That afternoon, I continued my lessons in the birthing room. "Sit down and let go of all concerns," my teacher said as he often did at the start of meditation. Some days he prompted me with interesting details. Knowing that I had learned to clear my mind sufficiently, I could now absorb elaborate information that would help me strengthen my sitting experience. But on that particular afternoon, my mind kept wandering to the grove I had just found.

"As we sit, the energy from heaven enters the crown of the head, and earth energy flows in through the tailbone. They meet in the body and circulate," the Monk said to bring me back to the moment. For a few minutes, I was able to use this visualization to come back to the breath, but eventually I found myself reliving my morning and thinking about the steps I took up the path and into the sacred clearing.

The Monk always knew when I was elsewhere and was particularly adept at knowing what to say to bring me back to the cushion. "Our posture looks very much like a mountain," he described. "When we sit, the top of our head and tip of the tailbone are magnetic endpoints of our vertical axis. When we stand, earth energy enters through the bottoms of our feet so that we are continually receiving energy from earth whether standing or sitting, and heaven energy enters our crown continuously." There was something about the imagery of the mountain that helped me follow my breath and stay present. It was as if I went from thinking about my journey on the mountain to becoming the mountain.

"So you see," he said joyfully, gesturing with his hand in the air, "Sitting like a mountain while keeping our thoughts at bay brings the mind into alignment. Sitting is the preferred posture but advanced meditators know that a pristine state of meditation can be achieved no matter what position our body is in."

"Although best not to lie down," my teacher chuckled, "or you'll fall straight asleep." His instructions were helpful and always exactly what I needed to hear.

Often he would give me physical cues to work with. "When your mind is restless, elongate the back of the neck so that the chin points slightly downward and raise the sternum a bit allowing the shoulders to fall back naturally. The sternum is the highest point of the breastbone at the center of the chest," he explained, pointing to its location on his chest.

"At the same time release any tension in your body to achieve utter relaxation. Pay no attention to any thoughts or feelings that arise. It does not matter whether your thoughts are good or bad," he insisted. "Do not judge your thoughts. Keep your attention on your breath and do not engage your thoughts."

Just then a ghostly figure intruded upon us. We were dusted by something powdery that soothed me to sleep. My head bobbed back and my eyelids grew heavy. Struggling to stay awake, I asked, "Why am I so sleepy and what can I do about that?" I had dealt with fatigue in the beginning of my sitting practice but I felt like it was something I should have conquered.

"Sleepiness is one of the five major hindrances for all practitioners of meditation," the Monk taught. "There are sleep demons that come to lull you to sleep. Those sleep demons rob you of your wakefulness if you are not vigilant in your practice. You must rally all your determination and perseverance when you come to your cushion. The demons appear only when your mind is full of thoughts that you refuse to let go. You must master your own mind and in time you will be victorious against the sleep demons.

"You might try this technique for sleepiness. Open your eyes wide and concentrate your energy with great effort through those eyes."

Following his instruction, I strengthened my will power to hold my eyes open and issued strong energy out of them. By placing emphasis on my vision, I achieved a state of focused concentration. The sleep demons were so inviting that it was difficult to gain mastery over them, but I used my strong will to hold my ground. The effort of my focused concentration helped me root out my sleepiness and the sleep demons soon took their leave.

Seeing the intense focus that I channeled out of my eyes, the Monk gently guided me furthur, "Now sense the world with your ears."

This simple instruction expanded my narrowly focused visual attention to the huge, round, buoyant world around me. It was a 360-degree awareness.

"Illumination comes of its own when all our senses are open," my teacher continued. Using the perfect analogy, he recounted a passage of an ancient mystical text called *The Secret of the Golden Flower* that describes the sublime example of the acute sensibility of a mother hen as she patiently sits on her eggs.

He enunciated in a whisper, slowly and carefully, "The hen can hatch her eggs because her heart is always *listening.*"

The ancient one's voice grew quieter still and upon hearing his words, which were barely audible, I entered a state of samadhi.

Seeing my pristine state of mind he introduced more passages from the mystical book. "The hen uses heat energy to hatch her eggs, but the heat energy only warms the shells and cannot penetrate deep into the interior, so she conducts the energy inward with her heart."

"The hen does this with her *hearing* in a mystical process. The chick then receives the energy and begins to live," the old Monk murmured.

"Even though the hen leaves her eggs from time to time, she keeps an attitude of *listening* with bent ear so the concentration of the spirit is not interrupted and the energy of the heat is not interrupted, day or night, and the spirit awakens to life."

The cultivation of a mind that is clear and single-pointed in concentration gives us the power to create. When one is able to repeat a singular idea or image, that is to say, when one has clear vision of something with a mind that is devoid of thought, that idea will be manifested.

The path leading to the power to create actually moves us to a state known by the mystics as choiceless awareness, where the desires of the small ego are released and the noble wishes for the welfare of humanity become a priority.

The Monk concluded his teaching by summarizing, "The Buddha said, 'when you fix your heart on one point, then nothing is impossible for you'."

In the state of pristine samadhi, I apprehended the power of creation. For the moment my mind was clear and not dominated by my ego. I was unconcerned with my small self and was grounded in the firm commitment to serve all beings. There were times such as these when I felt advanced in my training. The old Monk's presence coupled with only minor challenges helped me to sustain peace with heightened awareness. But these moments were few and far between.

Wouldn't it be wonderful if I could remain in this state of mind forever? This was the kind of thought that arose after experiencing states of mind infused with such peace. But life has its disturbances. We can count on that and I was sure to slide back again into my unripe self. The elevated notions of myself would quickly vanish and I would feel as if I had made no progress whatsoever. Life is a slippery slope.

In the early stages of my training I found I was able, little by little, to cut away thoughts that arose during meditation. Some thoughts were positive, others negative but all thoughts needed to be thrown away. When my mind was particularly turbulent, I used a special mantra, *gyate gyate, paragyate, parasam gyate, bodhi svaha,* a string of syllables that the old Monk taught me.

"What is the meaning of this mantra?" I asked.

The old Monk answered strongly, "Never mind the meaning of those syllables. You do not need to occupy your mind with definitions and meanings. Those syllables are already imbued with a power to advance you to full awakening."

This was how the training went. One day, I was given key information about the practice and at other times I was admonished for seeking information. Whenever I sought information, I was discouraged to pursue it. On the other hand, when my teacher saw that my mind was clear, he often decided to instruct me.

I later discovered for myself that the string of syllables, which comprised the mantra, came from the Heart Sutra expounded by the Buddha. The Sanskrit name for the Heart Sutra is *Prajnaparamita Hrdaya* which literally translates to the Heart of the Perfection of Transcendent Wisdom.

When I stood up from my cushion to reenter the world from my pristine realm of meditation, I would use the mantra. I made a game of it. What a fantastic tool the Monk had given me! When I walked to school, gyate, gyate, para gyate! I could coordinate the syllables with each step and the mantra echoed in the back of my mind, keeping my mind in check. I employed the mantra continuously under my breath so that my mind was free of chaotic thoughts. I admit there were days when I wearied of keeping my thoughts at bay and I gave in to daydreaming.

"Let go of all thoughts," said the Monk abruptly one day.

He knew I was distracted from the training. "The foundation of this training is letting go of everything. This training is about relinquishing everything until your mind is clear."

I asked him, "Then, why have you given me a mantra? There are times when I work very hard at keeping the mantra going in the back of my head."

"The mantra should not become louder and louder. Rather it becomes softer and softer. The mantra leads you to the stillness of mind that has always been there," he said.

Through repetitive practice of *just sitting,* I grew more resourceful when my mind wanted to run away into fantasy. "We must remain ever vigilant in keeping our mind clear," my teacher warned.

The Monk then gave me a little book on the precepts, the rules and principles of living.

"The ancient masters gave us the precepts out of their kindness and infinite wisdom. When we are young in our practice, we follow precepts in order to still our mind. When we break precepts, our mind is necessarily turbulent. When we are calculating, crafty and sly and we break precepts, we are unable to attain a calm, clear state of mind."

"Worse yet," he said gravely, "when we lie or steal, we set the ground for war. However, when we awaken, the precepts are simply expressed through us so there is no longer a need for these rules. We naturally *become* the precepts."

With this, my formal instruction with the Monk was complete.

"Before I go, I will be giving brief meditation instruction to some villagers and more extensive instruction to your best friend En. After that, I promise to return before your departure to Shuri, when I will bring you the last two important pieces of instruction to complete your training here in the North."

My brother Jiraa could see the changes in me since I had started studying with the Monk and grew more and more curious about the work we were doing.

"Do you suppose the ancient one will teach me too?" he asked earnestly.

"I am happy to give a lesson to your brother," the ancient one beamed with joy. He knew with certainty that my training to cultivate wisdom was seeping into my ordinary life. Why else would Jiraa have such interest?

The truth was, there was more to it. Jiraa still had no idea why he was drawn to the old Monk. He was comfortable around my teacher and felt a warm exchange of loving friendship between them. Jiraa shared vicariously through me a closeness to the Monk, and felt a part of the special world that I shared with my teacher.

"I would like to include some friends and farm hands too if I may," said Jiraa of his instruction. The old Monk was overjoyed. The following day my brother, a few field hands and I assembled before the ancient one. It would prove to be a particularly powerful and revealing meditation.

Please sit in a comfortable position. Although you are welcome to sit on your knees in seiza, the cross-legged posture known as Full Lotus is ultimately the most stable for sitting long hours. The Full Lotus is the end pose of an ancient exercise in India known as yoga.

Many traditions that teach us to clear the mind use a variety of methods. Using the breath is the most direct way to achieving a settled, clear mind.

Bring your attention inside the body now and check your posture. Make sure your spine is straight but not rigid. The posture is taut but not strained. Ensure that the back of the neck is elongated so that the chin lightly points downward. Bending the head keeps us humble. Each of us carries tension in different parts of the body so we bring our awareness inside and breathe life-energy to those areas.

Do not pay any attention to thoughts or emotions that arise. Let all thoughts and feelings sink down into the belly. The thinking brain is heavy with thoughts, but it is only a tiny part of the huge, vast, luminous mind that we actually are, so let go of your thinking and begin to experience more and more your True Mind. The True Mind is clear and empty, a state that is truly indescribable and can only be experienced.

Keep your eyes slightly open and gaze softly a ways in front of you. Be aware of the tip of the nose without staring at it, and that should bring you to 'this place' that is a quiet zone of peaceful awareness.

With that instruction the ancient one slipped into a deep samadhi. He emanated a wonderful energy that strengthened the atmosphere of the house. We sat together for an hour or so in vibrant silence, the group feeling the peace that permeated our surroundings. I sounded a tiny bell that my teacher had instructed me to ring when I sensed the meditation was complete. People wiggled their toes and stretched their arms. We returned to our ordinary consciousness, but sensed a shift. We were more focused and therefore more mindful and aware.

One of the field hands uttered an honest appraisal. "This has been the most difficult thing I have ever done, to sit without a thought in my head. Impossible. And, to sit without moving! Near the end I was in so much pain that I wanted to run away. But I stayed anyway because I have respect for the teacher."

The Monk responded, "With that, you swallowed the bitter medicine. You could have run away and you did not. The best medicine is bitter.

"Our training is neither to grasp nor to reject. With a strong practice we will confront what is in front of us and not run away."

Another field hand who had learned a bit of meditation from his uncle shared next. "That was quite something," he said. "This way of sitting is wonderful, and now I can sit with the kind of single pointed purpose I have learned, not letting one thought arise. I don't even know why I feel compelled to continue. I just feel I should."

The Monk smiled.

When our afternoon session ended, the Monk presented to Jiraa as a kind of 'thank you' for organizing the meditation session a simple cloth pouch tied at the top with string. Jira, surprised at the gesture, bowed and opened his gift. Out of the pouch, he lifted a cricket cage made of the finest bamboo. Inside sat a most unusual looking cricket. Jiraa looked up at the Monk and their eyes locked. There was a powerful glow between them.

Without further comment, the Monk stood and bowed deeply, leaving us to continue holding our attention inside of ourselves. Jiraa sat and eventually entered a state of samadhi, remaining deep in meditation for a long while even as other meditators stood to leave. When Jiraa returned from his spiritual sojourn tears rolled down his cheeks.

We were silent. There was no need to speak. We both under-stood why we had incarnated together. He made no mention of my own role in the story. It was not necessary. The Court Magician-turned-simple-Monk had returned to bless us both.

CHAPTER 24
MEETING THE NORO (HIGH PRIESTESS)

We, in our islands, were somewhat sheltered from the unrest beginning in Europe in the year of the Wood Tiger. The First World War broke out in the summer of 1914, a day after my twelfth birthday in July. The hunger for power in the world to dominate others was great and misplaced.

In August 1914 Britain sent an official request for Japan to become its ally in declaring war on Germany. Japan took this opportunity to begin its expansion in China and throughout the Pacific. The malignant forces for domination and colonization were widespread in Europe and Asia and we, in the small corner of the world, held onto our humanity.

In spring of the year of the First World War, I had entered the seventh grade. I spent the summer practicing meditation with the old Monk and during the month of summer vacation, I explored the island with En.

"Two more years of school and you'll be off to Shuri," my brother said, beaming with pride. After the eighth grade I would enter school in Shuri at the age of fifteen.

I daydreamed about my not-so-distant future when I would sail south to school. I will study to become a teacher and then return to my village to educate the children, I thought to myself. That was my plan for my ordinary life. My other path as a High Born One would become manifest in its own time as it had its own life and timeline. I would know how to proceed when that moment arrived.

I reminisced about Great-Grandmother's tales of fancy goods and exotic animals that could be found in the South, and thought that I, too, would return with sensational stories and goods. I often mused about the high education I would receive in the South. I would be studying the classics along with advanced math and literature. Little did I realize that I was already receiving an incredible education in my village. Nothing could ever compare to the sublime and brilliant nature of my education here, but I did not know that at the time.

When autumn arrived, a dream nudged me to revisit the sacred grove on the mountain. With such intense focus on my studies, I had completely forgotten about my discovery. It had been three years and I smiled when I reflected on my last visit to the area and how the severe rain had not deterred me. I knew that I ought to be dedicating myself to school studies, but I decided to follow my instinct.

The leaves and branches swayed in the light wind as I made my way up the steep incline. The sun was well past the zenith, and I could no longer see the ground I walked on. The vegetation grew thicker and I grasped at the branches around me to hoist me up, carefully wading through the high grasses. Nothing could stop me as I was urged on by a strong compulsion. Using my arms to pull me upward and forward, I continued my climb.

As I got closer, I heard a peculiar sound. It was like a buzzing mixed with an otherworldly languge. It was oddly human yet it reminded me of a particular species of cicada. I listened intently to see if I could decipher what it was.

"Halt!" suddenly the voice changed from the dull drone to a high-pitched explosion. Startled, I lost my bearing and fell backward screaming with fright.

"Waaaaaaaaaaa!" my cry matched the explosive voice in volume and pierced the surroundings.

"You have entered the outer gate of a sacred field," the voice spoke firmly and disapprovingly. "You must not advance any farther." A long silence followed.

A fearlessness came over me as if this very person had transferred her power to me and I quickly got up and dusted myself off.

"Step into the clearing off to your left so I can see you," the voice ordered.

I did and again there fell a long silence. It was as though someone were sizing me up. "Hello, my name is Mahataa," I called, introducing myself, but there was no response.

The silence continued. But since I was quite comfortable in silence I was not in the least bit troubled by any of this. The speaker did not reveal herself to me, but at last the quality of her speech softened.

"I am Noro, High Priestess from Kudaka," she proclaimed in a deep voice.

I remembered one of Great-Grandmother's tales about the Goddess Amamikiyo who descended from Heaven. Kudaka, a tiny island off our southeastern coast, was the first island the Goddess created in our archipelago. Kudaka-jima means island of the gods. According to folklore, the first Noro and kaminchu migrated from Kudaka to our island to bring spiritual knowledge to us.

"I was the first to hold the title of Noro to the King of the Liu Ch'iu Kingdom and was in his employ as mouthpiece for the Original Wise Ones to guide him," she informed.

At one time it was mandatory for the kings of our island to pay pilgrimage to Kudaka because of its legendary significance. After our king was taken prisoner by the Satsuma clan, who invaded in the seventeenth century, pilgrimages to the island came to a halt. Even in recent times, Kudaka Island was rarely visited. There was a belief that people should not venture there unless they had a calling to do so. Some of our islanders were frightened of the inhabitants of Kudaka, or were in so much awe of them that they hesitated to go.

People of Kudaka lived in a culture of silence and rarely spoke. The soft murmuring of natural sounds—wind, waves and birds—was all an ear received. The Original Wise Ones found this geographical location to be most conducive for holding and developing their collective voice and so they used Kudaka Island to bring forth the True Noro to help the inhabitants of the Liu Ch'iu archipelago. Our northern province was another area that was blessed by the Originals because our north was sheltered and could hold the energy of clarity and innocence to welcome and house high teachers.

"It is unnecessary for the people of Kudaka to speak because they communicate through their extra-sensory knowing," Great-Grandmother had explained. "Speech is reserved for uttering sacred tones and not for mundane communication. They say there's no other reason for speaking other than to call the gods."

Because I had no idea the Noro had the power to make herself completely invisible, I assumed she was hiding in the thick brush.

"You will come every morning to this area at the foot of the mountain to learn," she croaked authoritatively, her voice returning to its original hoarseness. "I will teach you True Prayer, a special skill that only select priestesses learn."

It was clear that this next teacher of mine would not reveal herself until she was satisfied that I was worthy of her teachings. She continued, "We will spend every day from the rooster's crow until daylight so that I can teach you important secrets."

My training with the old Monk had prepared me to begin my work with the Noro, High Priestess, but I suffered a moment of uncertainty. Doubt bubbled up.

I blurted, "I was told by the Yuta, the great soothsayer, that I would someday become privy to the secrets of your hidden world, but at the moment I am feeling unworthy. What if you are mistaken about me?"

"The power of your frightful cry confirms for me that you are the one," the Noro exclaimed, emphasizing *frightful* with extra hoarseness. "Although you are the one selected for our teachings, I must be absolutely sure without a shadow of a doubt that you will take the work to completion. Gifted people for one reason or another, after choosing to be groomed in our way of True Prayer, have chosen to turn down another road. Before I reveal myself to you, I must be sure that you will take the teachings and bring life to them."

Fear returned. I had the urge to run away but I collected myself and used my Tai Chi training to hold the energy in my lower belly, that is to say, to ground myself. Seeing that I was holding my ground quite well, knowing that I could handle anything she might say, she explained her curious situation. In effect, she led a double life.

"Let me tell you a little about myself," she said in her deep low-pitched voice. "I am now only a voice. I no longer have my own body." I shuddered but breathed into my lower belly and kept my center of gravity low.

"I will let the owner of the body I occupy speak," she said. There was a rustling in the air and I sensed she allowed the other entity to come through.

A different voice spoke. "I am an ordinary woman who possesses just the right physical vehicle the Wise Ones can use to bring forth the True Noro's teachings. I am not in my current life an actual noro. I serve only as a vessel and am honored to bring you the teachings of the True Noro.

"When I reveal myself to you, I will present myself as the ordinary villager that I am. At the same time you will gaze upon the energetic imprint of the True Noro who once existed in the flesh. I want to prepare you so that you will not be frightened. You will see two persons existing together. I will essentially be asleep when the True Noro comes forward. And when I return to my home, of course, I will revert to my ordinary self.

"I agreed to allow the Wise Ones to use my physical vehicle because the True Noro, elevated to the Realm of the Voices, can no longer descend to our physical plane of existence. In my ordinary life as a commoner, I will not know you and I will forget these lessons which the True Noro is about to give you."

The True Noro then took over again, "You were *saa-daka umari,* born with high spirit rank. I can see the glow around you. And, you have a thread of light from the top of your head that connects to the stars. When you let out your cry today, I could hear the power in your voice. That cry came deep from your *tanden,* the sacred belly. That confirmed for me that you are the chosen one. However, as you move through the beginning lessons, I will know whether or not you actually have the will to bring our great work to its final conclusion. Only then, when I am sure about this, will I reveal myself to you."

I wondered whether I actually had the will to do the work. Again, a bit of doubt remained. There were days when I knew with total confidence about my abilities, and then there were times of uncertainty.

"Having doubt keeps us in check. Over-confidence might make us presumptuous and therefore careless," my mother once told me when I expressed uncertainty about my karma as a High Born One. But then again I remembered the lesson on true confidence as taught to me by the old Monk. He taught me that true self-confidence comes from a quiet, humble place where all is well no matter what the circumstances, whether we are up or down, whether we are winning or losing. "With this kind of self-confidence we can go along with whatever is," he had said.

Then there was the oracle with the Yuta. I am destined to be here, I thought. A moment of nostalgia fell over me and I felt Great-Grandmother's presence. I felt her encouraging hand on my shoulder and knew that all would be well.

"Return here tomorrow morning before school to begin your instruction," the voice said ending our first encounter. I left the strange plot of land and wandered back home.

I returned the next day accepting that I really had no choice in the matter. For the past three years I had received intense instruction from the old Monk. He guided me to develop in profound ways, and I continued to practice the arts of Tai Chi and formal sitting meditation. Because of his teachings, I was ready for this new adventure.

I came upon the Noro High Priestess in the fall of the Year of the Wood Tiger where the association was with new beginnings. I was born in the tiger's mysterious water year when deep potential was laid down, and now the association was with wood and all things new.

The voice of the Noro echoed in my head again and reminded me of an old witch—not at all how I imagined a High Priestess should sound. Craggy and guttural, the voice would surely have frightened anyone else away. The stories about high priestesses told of radiant women who were soft-spoken ethereal beings. Yet this one was a combination of a rather harsh and rough person and a no-nonsense matron, who was both dignified and sober. And the vocal chords certainly belonged to an ordinary villager.

The next morning, even before the rooster craned its neck, before first light, I stirred from sleep and quietly stepped onto the tatami floor that lined the interior of the house. I glided weightlessly so that the wood underneath the tatami did not squeak as I reached the wood panel doors that slid open to the vestibule area. The day before, I had oiled the runners with pine sap to ensure total silence, and I now slid open the wood panel door just enough to let my skinny frame pass.

It was black as a new moon night when I stepped out into the vestibule. I lowered my feet onto the smooth, rectangular cement block, and from memory I slid into my straw slippers that were placed as always in the same spot, in front of the block. I tiptoed to another set of wood panel doors that opened to the outside courtyard, slipped out of the house, crept past the front gate and made my way to the foot of the mountain for my first lesson with the Noro.

My brother knew nothing of my present adventure. He never allowed me to leave the house alone when it was dark. He would never have given me permission to leave the house at such an hour regardless of the reason. Luckily I planned to return before he woke up.

Feeling safe, and encouraged by events falling into place, I made my way. The closer I got to the sacred area, the more I could detect the scent of a subtle delicious resin. The aroma led me to the exact area where I met the voice the previous day. Spread on the ground was a thick animal skin on top of which lay a square cloth. In addition, there was a round, tattered cushion of faded indigo cotton.

"Sit!" the jarring voice commanded from somewhere in the vicinity. She still would not reveal herself. I took my seat in full lotus posture with my back to a small willow tree whose leaves dangled from above. I waited quietly for instruction. For that moment, I was a veritable Buddha underneath that wispy tree.

The Noro kept silent for quite a while. I appreciated that she waited just long enough for the energy to settle. The light wind that stirred during my meditation calmed and the willow branches above hung heavy. It seemed as though all life stood still.

The early morning light would begin its climb, soon to be followed by the sounds of animals, insects and people rousing from deep slumber. But until then, for this moment, even our breath vanished into complete quiet.

The Noro transmitted clairaudiently to me. "No need for words," a lovely voice chimed inside my head. This was exactly how I had envisioned the Noro would sound. My hearing was being stretched in a way that was delightful. A feeling of perfect well-being came over me as I sat motionless, with no hurry, no need for anything. My breath now was breathing me. For a time I was suspended while the Noro transferred teachings directly into my cells through a process that was effortless and joyful. Before I knew it, it was daybreak.

Our first lesson was complete and I knew to return the next day. Although I could not verbalize what I had learned, I was vaguely aware of her teachings, as the transference had seeped into my being. I felt shifted in a positive way. Not only did I experience a renewed sense of well-being but I could feel that the desire and power to help others was strengthened.

The lessons went on like this every day for a while. I sensed my inner light growing stronger with each lesson. I didn't know it then but my body was being calibrated with the proper balance of magnetic and electric qualities. This was something she would explain in a future lesson.

After several sessions of mind-to-mind transmission, the Noro stepped forward, finally revealing herself to me.

There were two persons, indeed, but I didn't find the vision frightening. Instead it was quite magical. The old villager had receded and I could barely distinguish her features while the Noro whose glistening being existed on the surface, caught my eye.

She was as old as the moon, her hair was like pure white billowy clouds, her moon-face reflected the bright sun, and her eyes, black as night, twinkled like stars. She was surrounded by a thin filmy light that shimmered.

I later learned she appeared in the flesh because she needed to look directly into my eyes to transfer the final bits of information necessary for the next portion of study. She did this telepathically. All beings, who have the ability to use telepathic communication, do so when the information is sublime and best expressed this way. Other times, telepathy is used because it is simply an elegant means of communication.

After stepping forward, the Noro receded and the villager took over. It was only right that the villager be given some time to speak.

"I am two persons," the common villager whispered. "In my daily life I am an ordinary woman and work in the rice paddies, but when I am with you I allow the voices of the Wise Ones to direct me," she repeated again her situation.

"The Originals selected the commoner whose body I presently occupy to teach you," the Noro explained, "because she had received some instruction many years ago in the kind of sitting you are doing. Quite unusual that a common person such as herself would have come upon the rare opportunity to learn the high art of Clear Mind. Her body is primed for working with you.

In the next moment, the True Noro retreated again and the common villager came forward to speak. The villager was rightfully given time to explain her situation.

"I was working in the rice fields one afternoon when I felt faint," the villager recollected, "and I made my way to a small clearing. I felt a light hand on my shoulder and when I turned to look, there was no one there. I thought that I should seat myself in meditation under a tree nearby and did so. In a matter of minutes I entered a state of samadhi. During that deep state of meditation I was communicated to in a way with which you are familiar; there are no words, yet you have a deep knowing.

"What I knew was that I was being called to become a noro but not of the usual kind. I would have the powers of the high priestess, but I must keep it well hidden. So I agreed that in my ordinary life, I would have no knowledge of my role."

The villager was given only a glimpse of her karmic contract, and then it was wiped out completely. The Originals had unusual ways of working with people. After she told the story of her calling, all instruction was then turned over to the Noro. It was fascinating to see two persons fading in and out of one being.

The following day, the True Noro began her lessons again. "I will teach you how a very focused thought can result in its manifestation. By holding a continuous thought, the thought will melt into an image. The image then will dissolve into an intention," she continued in a voice that had softened considerably.

"You must first come to Clear Mind and then lean into a thought that you want to manifest. Depending on the power of your ability to hold your mind very clear, the thought will soon become an image or an idea which will then become an intention."

A worry crossed my mind. These manifestation exercises could surely be misused. "Not to fret," the Noro whispered gruffly. "In this exercise, we are protected from all evil because we must have full capability of maintaining an absolutely clear mind. This takes years of focus and concentration. The kind you have practiced with the Monk. In holding and maintaining Clear Mind for long periods, you have accessed a deep place of wisdom. That wisdom is available to everyone if they are able to tap it.

"The overriding prayer put in place by the Original Wise Ones for this kind of *intentioning* is that all things occur for the highest good. You can only help and assist others.

"So, coming back to the lesson, you can begin with an idea or concept and fortify the intention with your will power. Then let go of that thought completely. Banish it. Your mind becomes completely clear of thoughts but your intention remains. You must lean into that intention."

For a first lesson, she suggested I try to manifest something. "Do you see that flat rock over there?" she pointed. "Manifest on top of that rock a leaf from the willow tree behind you."

Developing the skill of moving an object or making an object appear from another location would help me later in locating missing persons or objects. In certain situations I might be able to manifest medicines or tools necessary in dire situations.

There were fallen leaves around me. I could see that the smooth oval stone was quite a distance away. I narrowed my focus on one leaf and made an attempt. But I was trying too hard and nothing happened.

"You must relax completely now that you know what you want to do. Lean on that image of the long, narrow leaf on top of the rock without actually having the thought. Visualize the willow leaf on top of that rock and lean into the image. Do not allow gaps in your attention as you hold fast to the image."

As I put myself to task, I briefly recalled the excursions with En when we had mentally moved small objects on the seashore. We had had so much fun, giggling as we did. But this task before me was not at all relaxing. I was fatigued and told the Noro that I was unable to do it. I felt discouraged.

We met for several consecutive mornings as I attempted the task. It seemed that the goal could not be accomplished. I then remembered what the Monk had taught me and applied *effortlessness* to my sharp, focused attention. Eventually it happened. A willow leaf billowed down, waving through the air until it landed on top of the rock.

I found that the longer I meditated prior to the task of manifestation, the more successful I became. In my deepest concentration I held the image of a leaf without a thought in my head. I relaxed to the ultimate point without falling asleep. There was a midway point where I had the most intense concentration, yet, was able to rest in remarkable relaxation. The Noro had me repeat this exercise again and again until it became easier to perform.

The Noro constantly tested the degree of my powers. She explained that the kaminchu priestesses were born to develop varying levels of skill and degrees of power.

"All kaminchu are born with one of two qualities," explained the Noro one day. "One group of kaminchu have bodies with a special magnetic charge that can reduce the impact of negative events. That magnetic quality has to be carefully harnessed in prayer and then the magnetized prayer is issued with a strong, clear mind. With concentrated prayer, this type of priestess can reduce the negative karma of certain places. These priestesses can go to locations where help is needed and pray on site, or they can travel in their mind's eye to distant places to mitigate the karma before it strikes.

"The powerful electrical charge of the second group brings healing as expeditiously as possible to masses of people after a calamity. These kaminchu render treatment and assistance to people through healing prayer. When you complete your studies with the Yabuu, the medicine woman, you will be able to bring precise healing to large groups of people at once because you will have learned exactly how to treat various cases of illness and injury. With Clear Mind Meditation learned from the Monk and knowledge of healing you will learn from the Yabuu combined with invoking your electrical energy in your work with me, you will be able to overturn adverse situations. You will be able to mitigate calamity and misfortune.

"Noro, who are high priestesses, have more power than the kaminchu and very often the noro have both magnetic and electric powers. Over generations the common priestesses lost the practice of Clear Mind Meditation, an essential tool for gathering and using their energy effectively. Although they worked with the best intentions, they became less powerful without the proper use of Clear Mind. A part of your life's work is to bring back the training of Clear Mind Meditation to the kaminchu."

I was humbled by what the Noro said. That I could take on such a task as to teach the kaminchu was a lofty proposal. But if that were my karma, I accepted it on the spot. I returned the next day for more instruction.

We reviewed the previous lesson about the two types of kaminchu and the Noro said I would learn how to call information to myself about future events–impending disasters, for example. As always, first maintaining a clear mind was essential. Only then would information come. This reminded me of the Monk's teaching on true ideas. The difference with the exercise taught by the Noro was that I would clear the mind and then strongly lean into *receiving news* of any impending events.

One night, after intense training with the method of calling information to myself, I had a dream. Thousands of hens and chicks scurried about in complete mayhem in our courtyard. I heard clucking and screeching, and then the poor creatures burst into flames. I understood it to be a metaphorical vision and an omen for what lay ahead.

For the entire summer I came every morning to the tiny designated area and studied with the Noro to prepare for my karmic work. She explained we were unable to completely nullify disastrous events, but we could mitigate them.

The Noro said, "An example of how a terrible event can be mitigated is in the story of an Indian master who touched the arm of one of his students with a burning twig. The student was horrified but the master explained that he reduced the student's karma by burning him in this way so that he would not die in a terrible fire."

When the weather changed and cooled, the Originals shifted plans. I had not progressed as quickly as they thought I should, so they created a contingency plan. The plan was for me to learn a great deal in an even more compressed period of time.

I had begun my training the moment I was born and was placed by the Originals on an accelerated path. However, even that was not fast enough. The truth was, my progress was affected by my reservations. I was unsure about acquiring the powers of manifestation through concentrated thought. There was a part of me that felt it could be a dangerous enterprise. I was slowed down by my lack of faith that anyone should have such powers, not even I, who held the purest of intentions.

The Originals give full and complete powers to those who were not pushed and pulled by their egos but rather to those who have in their highest interest the welfare of all beings. Even though I had nothing to worry about I was still unsure. I understood my training was safeguarded so that my awakening was a prerequisite to wielding such powers yet I held myself back. I had not yet fully arrived.

So that I would have more frequent lessons, The Wise Ones arranged for the True Noro to continue teaching me in the home of the common villager. They cast a kind of spell over the villager so that the Noro-presence would appear only when I visited for lessons. The rest of the time she was completely and comfortably her common self. The neighboring villagers were also included in this spell so that they would not wonder about my comings and goings.

I visited the villager's home after school and on breaks and sometimes even in the evenings. I asked Jiraa's permission about this new arrangement in my learning and he was quick to approve knowing this was part of the larger karmic plan. My lessons during these last months developed my ability to recognize the subtlest inspirations as they bubbled up.

"You may remember the old Monk's teaching," the Noro said, "by eradicating all ideas, then, and only then can true ideas come."

The Noro was fortifying in my psyche what the old Monk taught me from *The Secret of the Golden Flower.* "You know the meaning of this now," she said, referring to the arising of true ideas.

"As you quiet the mind, allow all thoughts and ideas to fall away, and then out of the blue, a true idea comes. This is how we are inspired by the Original Wise Ones. Do not think. Do not hold even one small thought," the Noro reminded me.

I was fortunate to study with the True Noro, the most powerful and influential noro in our history. From the time she joined the Original Wise Ones in the Realm of the Voices, the role of the noro high priestesses in our islands began to diminish. The leadership of the high noro was almost lost when noro succession began to occur in families. Nepotism was not the true way. It was not the original way. Unless a woman received proper shirashi, divine notification which had nothing to do with common appointments, she was not an authentic noro and could not effectively fulfill the role.

In later years, the kings of Shuri Castle in the South gave the position of noro to their wives without the wives being the least bit gifted. In this way, the kings did as they wished. Here were examples of unawakened humans without any interest in clearing illnesses of the mind engendered by the three poisons of greed, anger and delusion.

Without managing these poisons within his own mind, how could a king rule justly? For a time, the truly gifted women had to become invisible lest they invite harm to themselves. Blending themselves within insulated communities, only local villagers knew about them. Governing bodies could not control the situation by removing the truly gifted noro in order that the appointed ones could rule, because these gifted women were well assimilated. In the beginning the noro were unmarried, but their statuses changed inside their villages so that they became less visible to outsiders.

In addition to the disbanding of the gifted women who had been organized long ago by the Great Kamadaa, the practices of these women came to a halt altogether during the Meiji Era, constraints imposed by Japan from the mid-nineteenth century. It was impossible for an outsider to find the true noro. Apprenticing under these women was a dangerous enterprise.

The noro and kaminchu became householders and their work nearly imperceptible. They met in groups but at odd times and in remote places in the mountains. Many had the gift to make themselves invisible and they moved about without making any sound.

I was grateful to receive the training that had been abolished. The Original Wise Ones brought forth the True Noro to mentor me. I didn't know it but, during my lessons with her, we were both invisible and our voices blended with the natural sounds around us.

I had become privy to secret practices that were forbidden. Yet seeds of truth have a way of surviving. Truth has life, and so these seeds, completely self-sustaining, eventually sprout. They hide in waiting until it is time.

CHAPTER 25
THE SCROLL

The summer of 1915 was unbearably hot but, with the Originals intervening, some of the humidity was lifted and instruction from the True Noro in the home of the common villager progressed comfortably.

As autumn approached, we welcomed the cooler air. Days grew shorter and we enjoyed some respite from the extreme humidity.

Thirteen years had passed since my birth, and I was coming of age. One morning, one of our village kaminchu appeared at our house. "You poor dear," she addressed me, "to have lost your mother at such a young age. I have come to help you with things you need to know in preparation for womanhood." She discussed with me many things that young girls usually receive from their mothers or older women in their families.

"You must not be frightened when you come in to the bleed," the kaminchu said. I had actually already heard the other girls in school speak of it so I was not completely unaware. I would soon be coming to my initiatory passage into womanhood and the kaminchu was kind enough to prepare me in advance.

"There are ancient rituals that accompany the coming of age for young women," said the kaminchu. "Let me know when your moon comes so that a small group of us can gather to say a prayer for you, for you to be fertile, for you to grow strong in your powers."

When my time came, the ceremony was a simple one. Three of the village kaminchu and I gathered together in our house at our altar and lit incense. We knelt together with hands in prayer and the main kaminchu recited a few short verses from an ancient poem to open the gateway to adulthood. The eldest of the three women handed me a gift, wrapped in a simple white linen cloth. The gift was a jifaa, a thin tortoiseshell stick the size of a pencil, to hold my topknot in place. It had been passed from one priestess to another for many generations and held tremendous power. I thanked them and immediately replaced the wooden stick in my topknot with the beautiful tortoiseshell jifaa.

"The jifaa will act as a device to sharpen the incoming messages from the Wise Ones," the kaminchu said. Royalty wore jifaa made of gold. The Samurai wore silver. Commoners wore jifaa made of brass, wood or tortoiseshell.

Although the kaminchu prepared me for womanhood, I still ran about with the boys in the neighborhood. I occasionally wore boys' clothing so that I could blend in with them.

It was the spring of 1916 and a small number of my friends and I entered the eighth grade. We were required under Japanese law to attend school for six years and some of us continued for another two years through the eighth grade if we planned to move on to advanced studies. Academic study beyond the eighth grade was not available in the northern part of the island where we lived. We would have to make our way south by boat because passage by land was difficult.

After the eighth grade I would move to Shuri, the center of education in the southern part of the island in order to receive my teaching certificate. It was rare for women in the poor north to be able to go on to higher learning but I wanted it for myself and not only because my parents had big dreams for me.

All classes in our northern province were taught in Japanese and we were discouraged from speaking in the old tongue. Teachers scolded us whenever we spoke in our native language. This prepared us, I suppose, for our schooling in the South. However, at home and among friends, we freely spoke in our own dialect.

En and I continued to enjoy an adventurous life on our impoverished yet magical island kingdom although we were growing older and began to assume more responsibilities in our respective homes. We were both excellent students. We burned the midnight oil every evening, completely engrossed in our studies.

Our school year proved difficult and the courses more challenging. Somehow I managed my school studies in addition to daily meditation, Tai Chi and occasional adventures with En. Depending on my state of mind, time expanded or contracted to enable me to do it all.

One autumn day as we were returning home from school, En suddenly stopped. "Do you hear the strange rumbling in the mountain? It sounds like a waterfall," he said. We paused to listen.

"It's not the small one near our village," I said. The sound is coming from the top of that mountain." I pointed in the opposite direction.

In a rush of memory, I was transported to an incident years ago when Great-Grandmother showed me a tiny mysterious box a week before her mahasamadhi, the great passing. Great-Grandmother's voice echoed in my ear. "It was passed down to me by my mother Uto who in turn received it from her mother and so on from generation to generation. The Great Kamadaa once opened it ten generations ago but since then it has remained closed." The memory came back to me in a flash.

Great-Grandmother had run a cloth over the tiny box as she whispered, "It contains some kind of message about a mystical waterfall which at the same time exists...but does not exist. The one who finds the falls will be catapulted to magnificent heights of knowledge and power."

Then I remembered her warning, "But the box must not be prematurely opened or something terrible will happen!" Great-Grandmother's voice echoed in my mind. "You must not open this box until you receive shirashi, proper notification."

Great-Grandmother had hoped that she herself might be summoned to open it. However, the gift box handed down by the Wise Ones would not be hers.

"I have not received any sign to open this, but as I approach the brink of my departure to the Land of Spirits, I must turn it over to you for safe-keeping," she sighed before returning the box to its place in the wood beam.

I stared at Great-Grandmother in wonder because she looked so huge as she was confiding in me. It is known among our clan that whenever advanced souls enter a high state of consciousness, they grow very large. In fact my young eyes witnessed Great-Grandmother grow to such a size that she loomed over me like a towering mountain.

Her voice, no longer sad or weak, boomed with strength, "When the old Yuta came to bless you with special herbs at your birth, I knew that the visit of the old woman was a sign. You were going to be the person to open it. I noted to myself then that her special herbs would expedite your development and ready you to open the box."

The images and sounds of Great-Grandmother before her departure came alive in an instant. And suddenly I felt reborn. I knew this was my great shirashi. My karma was unfolding. The first shirashi came to my mother in a dream but now, I had received my own notification.

I ran breathless to the back of the house as En chased after me and watched with stunned curiosity. My fingers flew underneath the wooden border of the house. Frantically searching with both hands, I ran back and forth, but came up with nothing.

"What are you doing?" yelled En. A flood of memories of Great-Grandmother, my parents and Grandmother Machi gushed forth. My tears flowed but not from my inability to find the box. As I wept, I released all the pent up emotions from the loss of my family. I had been kept so busy by my loving teachers that I had not had adequate time to grieve. It was as if I were being released from my old life as a kind of rebirth. I was entering a new world of power and responsibility.

En and I plopped down on a smooth stone bench next to the house. As I began to calm, a green-gold beetle caught my eye as it emerged from the corner of the house. En saw the beetle too and whispered, "My grandfather told me that it is good luck to see a beetle. He said beetles help us in our transformation, metamorphosis and rebirth."

I did not think En fully understood the meaning of those words, but he could have fooled anyone by the tone of confidence in his voice.

My teacher, the Monk, spoke about the beetle, too, and had quoted a passage from his favorite book, *The Secret of the Golden Flower*: "The beetle is associated with spiritual growth. Spiritual immortality is more precious and difficult to reach." His voice always grew mystical whenever he recited esoteric knowledge.

"The scarab rolls its pellet, and life is born in it as an effect of non-dispersed work of spiritual concentration," the old Monk recited. This passage in the book refers to how the sacred scarab rolls a tiny ball out of dung, and because of the scarab's undivided effort of his spiritual concentration as he rolls it, a magic pellet, or embryo, begins to grow inside of it.

"If even in manure an embryo can develop and cast its terrestrial skins, then why shouldn't we, too, through our undivided effort of spiritual concentration, be able to generate a body within the dwelling of our celestial heart?"

Remembering his teachings, I broke into a smile and stood up to catch the beetle. As it flew away, I could see where the green-gold messenger had been pointing. There it was, the wooden box covered now with dirt and cobwebs. Nestled perfectly in the wood beam, it had been camouflaged by moss and lichen with the passage of time. Rain and moisture had caused the wood to swell, sealing the box in place.

En and I scratched around the straight edges of the box with twigs, and finally freed it from its hiding place. I carried it to the stone bench and held it for a while.

"You must not open this box unless you receive proper notification," Great-Grandmother's voice echoed again. But I knew I had received shirashi to open it. My friend En had delivered the notification.

"Take a seat next to me," I invited him as I pried the box open. There was a mysterious glow as I lifted the lid, and the light bounced off of a scroll neatly rolled inside. It was made out of a pale yellowish silk with gold thread. With only minor stains on it, the shimmery silk still retained what must have been its original luminescence.

"Look at how lustrous the silk is. It emanates its own light, doesn't it?" I put the question to my friend.

But there was no response. I quickly looked up from the shimmering contents but En was gone. He was nowhere to be seen. I yelled for him, but again there was no response. A moment ago, I was elated and now I jumped up in fright. I put the box down and ran about yelling for my friend, "En! En! Stop playing games! Come out right now! But I knew in my gut he had not run away and that he had disappeared into thin air.

Was it because of the box? I wondered. I mean, shouldn't En have seen the contents? If it weren't for him, I might never have remembered anything about this treasure. Besides, he did say he heard a strange sound resembling a waterfall. I started to panic. It hadn't occurred to me that he should not see the contents. What was I to do?

I shouted for several minutes and then ran to his house, hoping that on the off chance I was wrong and he had bolted home. No luck. Instead I was left with confronting En's parents, my worst nightmare. After doing my best to tell them what happened without mentioning the waterfall or the box, his parents and siblings dashed out to the back of their house and began yelling En's name. They called his name through the village and all the way to my house, where they searched the backyard. In the end, our search resulted in nothing. I had no explanation to offer and his family was so distressed there was nothing anyone could do to calm them.

En's mother scolded, "How can you say you don't know where he is? You were with him, weren't you?"

I looked down at the ground and En's father took his wife's arm to lead her away. En's siblings just shook their heads. I felt awful. Great-Grandmother was right, "...the box must not be prematurely opened or something terrible will happen! You must not open this box until you receive shirashi, proper notification."

Something terrible had happened indeed. En announced my shirashi but he, himself, did not receive notification. He should never have laid eyes on that scroll. Why did I not know better? Where was my intuition when I needed it?

En's mother returned again yelling, "You're not telling us everything! You were the last to see him. Where is he?"

I could not tell them about the scroll for I was bound by secrecy. What was I to do but to take the blame upon myself. "Yes, I am responsible," I said sadly to En's family. "I do not know where he is but I vow to find him."

En's mother shook her head in anger which masked her true emotion of great fear.

If I were responsible for his disappearance, then surely I would know how to bring him back. Villagers gathered to look for him. They fished in the well, checked the brushes and foliage around the house, and scoured the trees and hiding places.

The next day the elderly village kaminchu was summoned to pray, and the local yuta was brought in to assess the situation with her divination. The famous Yuta in the North Mountains was much too aged to be called upon. The kaminchu gathered other women from our village to perform a ritual. "Quickly! We need to get the boy's *chinuu*," the village kaminchu said. Chinuu was the word in the old tongue for kimono. We used the terms interchangeably but the elders often exclusively used chinuu. En's mother quickly produced a small child's kimono, which was then neatly spread on the bench where En disappeared.

The women clasped hands, and I was asked to join their circle. The innermost circle consisted of En's family who held back tears as they stood around the small piece of clothing. Not one of his family would look at me. Neighbors formed concentric circles around them, while En's older cousin and close friends huddled nearby and prayed. The ritual is known as *mabuyagumi* where we call back one's spirit. This ritual was performed so that his spirit would return to his clothing. We were unsuccessful.

I knew that I must get to my teacher, the True Noro and I rushed to her home only to find the common villager. She looked nothing like the Noro I had spent so much time with. "What do you want, child?" the old woman asked while stirring vegetables in a small iron pot.

"You must help us!" I screeched, hoping my arrival would trigger the appearance of the Noro. "My friend has disappeared!"

"How could I help?" replied the common villager who had no memory of herself as the True Noro. "I don't even know you!"

I was frustrated and annoyed. I turned away briskly and ran back to my house to help with the fruitless search.

Weeks turned into months, and a dreary cold winter approached. The season would be especially unbearable for me. I felt total responsibility for the loss of my confidante, my partner in adventure, my best friend.

Deciding that I was not the chosen one, I returned the scroll to its wooden box and returned the box to its hiding place. I could not decipher it anyway. I was obviously wrong about my notification. I was distraught and mute and refused to go to school.

As I slipped into a deep depression, my dear brother Jiraa tried to console me. "You must eat," he said holding a small bowl of rice and seaweed soup.

But I just turned away, rejecting his offering.

It hurt Jiraa to see me so sad. He asked one of my classmates to bring notes and homework, but I remained disinterested. My teachers even came to the house to help, and because of their efforts, I made feeble attempts to keep up with my studies. In the village, everyone's attention turned to En's family. Neighbors brought them food and kept them company in their darkest hour. I felt so sad that although I wished I could give them comfort, I could not. They didn't know that my pain was as great as theirs.

CHAPTER 26
THE TIGER DREAM

In early December, a ferocious tiger visited me in a dream.

I am seated on the stone bench in back of our house and a striped tiger appears out of the wooded hill. He saunters toward me, and I tremble with fear. My heart pounds as he approaches. Then, he stops in front of the bench and lightly places a kiss on my cheek. My sadness lifts and my fear dissipates.

The tiger speaks, "En will return soon. He is almost ready to come home." In the dream, I protest that En should be returned now and not a moment later. I plead with the tiger to release him immediately.

The tiger replies, "My dear, take a moment in meditation and you will be reunited with him."

When I awoke, I knew that En was safe. I did not know where he was, but, in addition to the tiger's words, the communication I received carried an extrasensory missive that led me to understand what had happened to my friend.

The Immortals call us in our sleep to instruct us. They invite our spirits to be lifted out of our bodies, and we can choose to follow them. However, in En's case, they had no time to waste. He was literally whisked away in an instant, seemingly without his consent. But that can never be. The Immortals are wise and decent and must have obtained his consent another way. Perhaps En had agreed in a dream.

With renewed energy, I ran to the back of the house and pulled the treasure box from its place. I sat on the stone bench and prayed.

En's disappearance was linked to this scroll. Faith enveloped me and I knew that En would return intact. As I unrolled the scroll, I was certain that guidance to decipher the scroll would come. But it was impossible to make any sense of the scroll's supernatural communication. I stared and stared at the strange language of pictographs. I turned the scroll upside down and sideways, but no inspiration came.

My frustration rose and days passed with no insight. En was still missing. As I grew more agitated, my meditation cushion called me. With the box in hand, I made my way to it and sat down, folding my legs into Full Lotus.

"When you are threatened by circumstances or backed into a corner," the old Monk had taught me, "you must sit down and wait. Never waste your energy in fruitless activity. When we spend time scrambling in desperation, our vision becomes narrow and small. We are unable to see from the larger view."

Remembering this teaching, I became calm and alert. I let go of all concerns and replaced them with trust. After an hour of meditation, I stored the wooden box in my small *tansu,* a simple chest of drawers, and retired early. I relaxed with the thought that the glyphs would become decipherable and I would understand their meaning in due time.

My brother was fast asleep when I stirred from my futon mattress the next morning. His deep sonorous breath was a testament to his hard labor in the fields. I gently slid the small scroll out of the chest of drawers and lit the pine candle. I placed loose black and white stones, inherited from my father's Go game board, on the corners so that the scroll lay completely flat.

In an open-eye meditation I gazed effortlessly at the scroll's scribbles and pictographs. This relaxed attitude, together with a mind absent of thought, was essential to access the esoteric knowledge before me. Gazing with a clear mind, I looked at the meaningless glyphs without any pressure to decipher them. And suddenly, there it was.

"It's a map!" I said under my breath. I grew excited but curbed my emotions and leaned back again into relaxed repose. My intuition sharpened, and my vision changed so that I could see another layer that I was not able to see before. Floating inside the map was a mountain trail. When I squinted, the topography came to life. I squinted again and again, and the images of trees and foliage came to life, rustling and breathing with a pulsating vitality. Each time I closed my eyes, my senses sharpened. I discerned the subtle scent of flower essences and heard the faint sound of water. A light wind rising from the map caressed my cheek. In my reverie a vision of En suddenly appeared. He assured me that he was well and that he would return soon but that he needed my help.

"Tomorrow at dawn you must meet me at the stone bench by the house," his voice echoed. "You must sit in meditation on the bench and clear your mind. You must then visualize me sitting next to you," he instructed.

"If you lose your concentration even for a hair's breadth of a moment," En warned, "I will never be able to return." His faint voice now became as clear as if he were already right next to me and he repeated the instruction again.

"You must hold the image of me for an uninterrupted time which could be hours... until I appear. "Bundle up," he warned. "It will be cold. Oh, and please bring a thick blanket and some clothes for me." He sounded embarrassed.

"Of course," I laughed, issuing my answer as a thought. I realized he must have lost his clothes. In the ethereal realm, clothing is of a subtle substance, and En would have had to discard his gross physical garments. Well, there was some humor to be found in this, after all.

Sitting with the kind of focus required to get En back was a momentous challenge. I had sat through difficult trials with my teacher, but never had I been required to sit for this length of time and to concentrate with this kind of pressure. The stakes had never been this high, for a mere moment of inattention could cost the life of my dearest friend.

But I was confident that I would be able to sit with absolute concentration. It is not to say that I had the assurance of a young fool, thank goodness. Being foolhardy only leads to failure. No, I was so determined that I did not allow myself to wonder if I could succeed. I kept my focus on the task and did not let another thought enter. The old Monk had trained me well for the execution of the fifth paramita, the perfection of concentration where the mind does what we want it to.

The instructions I received from the Noro would come to serve me too. I could clear my mind and concentrate with the power of prayer, that is to say, with a strong intention to manifest my friend.

In preparation for the next day, I meditated and took breaks only for small meals and light exercise. Accustomed to my odd ways, Jiraa had no clue about my plan. He went about his usual chores, made food for me and went to work.

At nightfall I positioned myself with my back against my dresser and dozed until the sound of the rooster's crow startled me. I quickly threw on a quilted Chinese jacket left behind by my mother, and wound a thick cotton scarf around my neck. With a bundle of clothes, Jiraa was sure not to miss, tucked under my arm, I shut the wood panel doors behind me, and slipped agilely from the house.

I was nervous as I rushed to the stone bench. But my nerves faded as I sat on my thick cushion to protect me from the cold and brought my legs up into Full Lotus. I checked my posture and placed my undivided attention on my breath to clear my mind. I took a few conscious exhalations as I entered that place of Clear Mind. After a time of holding a mind that was open, bright and clear, the image of En naturally came into focus in my mind's eye. The process required almost no effort. No tension, just intention. The power of prayer took hold. The image of En was strong in my mind, and not another thought or image or emotion crept in. There was no worry, no concern. In fact, I could not be concerned about anything. For to be concerned about anything at all would have manifested as a thought and that thought would have broken my concentration.

So, I just sat and sat and sat. Over time, the image of my friend became stronger and stronger. Sustaining the image of En in my mind caused the image to build and build, growing stronger, having clearer definition, accumulating weight and developing mass until finally he materialized. I could see how single-pointed focus could actually create and manifest. I had even seen this at work with small objects, moving leaves or shells from here to there, but the thought of manifesting something as great as this had never occurred to me. While, on one level, this all made sense, the truth was I was stunned to see En sitting right beside me. I jumped for joy and wept with relief as I told him between sobs how much everyone had missed him and how his disappearance had caused so much alarm and grief.

"Hello," En greeted, grabbing the clothing I had brought. He looked at me with great power in his eyes and I calmed down. He had a certain assuredness that he did not possess before. His youthful sense of unbridled adventure was now gathered into sharp focus and definite purpose. It emanated from his whole being. As we sat together in silence, I received a transference of energy from him, not unlike what I received from Great-Grandmother, just before her mahasamadhi. For a moment, I was frozen under his spell and then the young boy reappeared. He grinned sheepishly.

I had so many questions and wanted to know everything. Where had he been exactly? What was it like? What did he learn? We did not have much time to talk as dawn was turning into day, so En promised to discuss the particulars of his disappearance when we got together again.

At that moment, En was thinking about what to tell his family. He had a lot of explaining to do when he returned home. His face was bright and his voice strong so I knew without a doubt that he was equipped to explain his disappearance to his family without disclosing the truth. Plus, doing so would probably only serve to confuse them.

I accompanied En home and couldn't wait to see the reaction of his family. "I found him," I shouted as his parents and siblings ran to the front of the house, "he was in the hills right behind our home." Everyone screamed with joy and relief. There was clamoring and tears as questions came flooding En from all directions. In the middle of the excitement, I left En's house with peace in my heart. I knew his mother would still never trust me completely but I was satisfied that I had made good on my vow to find him. I was happy to have been able to bring his family a sense of relief and happiness.

I knew that he would convince them of whatever story he told by speaking in a voice that had the power to calm and help them release any suspicions. But that would be just the first step. He would also have to convince them that he would never leave like that again. Otherwise they would never let him out of their sight.

He was successful, and En and I returned to school where teachers and students warmly welcomed us back. En managed to convince everyone that he had simply wandered off into the mountains. Beyond that, the Immortals in the spirit realm did their part to fade the whole incident from the minds of the villagers. Soon, people stopped asking questions, almost as if En had never disappeared. Even my brother who was so ecstatic at En's return seemed to quickly forget the incident.

On our way home from our first day back at school, En told me about his experiences. We took a long path back and I was happy to be spending time with my old friend again. He told me the Original Wise Ones had directed the Immortals to send special guardians to fetch him when the time was ripe to hone his intuitive strengths. Just like I had guessed, he had agreed in a dream to be taken. The day the two of us looked at the scroll, everything came together. He was ready to learn and his momentary glance at the scroll gave him the necessary boost of energy to be whisked away.

"Who did you talk to when you were there?" I asked. "And what were they like?"

"The Immortals," he answered, "are helpful and loving and teach with the greatest patience. They explained many things through mind-to-mind communication. They said, 'Your friend

Mahataa incarnated as the last of the High Born Ones. After her will come great women, but they will not have the abilities she has. Even though your friend is powerful, her task is beyond her capabilities. For that reason we chose you to support her, but your growth needs to be accelerated'."

So the Immortals had whisked En away to bring him to his ultimate psychic capacity in order to assist me. The karmic plan for us was not clear just yet. We had to be patient. But we knew we would be guided and instructed in due time.

"What else did you learn?"

"Well," En said, "the Immortals visit us in our unconscious mind when we can give our undivided attention. Typically those are times when we are fatigued and sleep for long periods. They need lots of time to impart their information, not in words, but with a special kind of communication."

"When we sit in meditation we clear our minds and enjoy deep rest. But in dreams we receive instructions and it is much like being in a classroom where we have so much to learn!"

"It's funny," I said. "We achieve profound rest when we are awake in meditation, but are busy in school when we sleep. That must be why we sometimes wake up so exhausted!" We both had a hearty laugh.

Because the Immortals can move about freely between the physical and spiritual worlds, they are adept at stepping down information to humans. Their information is subtle and must be transformed to a much denser form for most of us to comprehend.

En elaborated further, "But the process of stepping down information is slow and sometimes inefficient. Unfortunately, most people cannot receive the subtle vibrations of the teachings. The physical body is simply too dense so the Immortals find it easier to work with people in their sleep. But the majority of people lose much upon awakening. So, it can take time."

"In my case, they worked quickly," he said.

"What do you mean they worked quickly? You've been gone for months!" I screamed.

"I know. They said in earth-time I have been gone from October through most of December," he said, "but, honestly, I feel like I have been gone for only a day. The Immortals live in another dimension. They must have needed to do a lot of work on me!"

"By the way," he said changing the subject, "I met the Great Kamadaa. She sends you her very best wishes and says that she and Great-Grandmother are watching over you as you progress on your path to complete your mission. She's quite young, you know. I think she must be our age. And she's the most beautiful person I have ever seen, with long hair that is pulled up in a topknot much like we do and she had on a Chinese brocade robe the kind my grandmother wears. There's a depth to her that I cannot explain, almost as if she's a very, very old person at the same time."

"That's all very interesting," I said, jealous and annoyed. I didn't want to hear another word about her beauty so I changed the topic again. "Tell me more about the spirit realm."

"Well let me say that we have all known the spirit realm at one point or another as we have incarnated again and again. It is hard to explain but the atmosphere sparkles, and spirits seem to whoosh about as they are occupied with tasks.

"People who are able to recall their own past lives can also remember bits of this realm. It is a place where the atmosphere is charged so that everyone is in a state of samadhi. Words do not need to be spoken. Rather, communication happens through well organized thoughts. There is no chaos of thoughts, communication is smooth, uninterrupted and succinct. We can receive and issue many thoughts on multiple levels without any thought bumping into another. It is unfortunate that here on the earthly plane our minds can be so chaotic and disorganized."

I wanted to know if there was anything untoward that might have happened to him. "What about any unfortunate events? Everything you've said is so wonderful."

"Well," said En, "as I was whisked away, I did bypass a strange dark tunnel which led to an undisclosed realm. I inquired about it later and was told that one must be careful not to select that tunnel. This is part of why I was taken so quickly. I didn't have time to stop and explore the various realms that I flew past. If we are not properly escorted by light-beings we could get into trouble. They would not discuss with me those strange entrances. So, in answer to your question, nothing unfortunate happened to me but if I had ventured on my own, unescorted, I might have had the urge to follow my curiosity down one of those dark tunnels."

"Why would anyone ever choose a dark tunnel?" I asked.

"Well," said En, "apparently the dark tunnels are enticing to the small ego. And, at the time I was called by the Originals, I had little inkling of my higher self. I was mostly driven by my undeveloped personality."

"Explain further," I demanded, wanting very much to know.

En looked quite serious and said, "Most people who have not managed their own greed, anger and delusion, will certainly find the dark tunnels very, very alluring. They are laced with perfumes and hypnotic music and beguiling visuals that appeal to all the senses. They draw you in and before you know it, you are traveling down the dark road. It is true here on earth as well that we can find and choose dark tunnels to follow.

"That is why it is important to deal with the three poisons so that even the greatest temptation will never cause us to lose our lives, that is to say, our true spiritual lives."

We walked in silence for a while, enjoying each other's presence, until En stopped and took my hand. "You must have regretted allowing me to lay eyes on that scroll," he looked in my eyes, "but if you had not, I never would have had access to the schooling in the spirit realm. I have you to thank. Truly."

En seemed to intuit how deeply I sank into depression after his disappearance. While he received these intense instructions and psychic treatments to step up his powers, I had been inconsolable, feeling completely responsible for his disappearance.

"If you had only relaxed and come back to your training, you would have trusted your dreams and intuition."

He was right but I always had a lingering doubt in me and I told him so. He peered at me with compassion and said, "You haven't stepped into your full powers yet."

"Did you find out how my karma would unfold by any chance?" I asked, hoping he would dispel my doubts and fears.

En responded, "Your time is quite limited to learn all that you must in preparation for your karma. The teachers you have encountered are the last of the great ones. Even the Monk has been given the charge of teaching you for only a period of three years. After that he will have to take his leave. That is his contract. The world is rapidly changing. The three poisons of greed, anger and delusion will foster more wars and misunderstanding. Unless they are reduced inside of man there will always be strife. There are many wars in the offing and it will take greater and greater numbers of people such as ourselves to turn the tide."

Although I was overwhelmed, I asked him to tell me more. "We have a special environment here in the North," said En. "This is one of the few areas of the world where high spirits can easily enter. A handful of High Born Ones like yourself have been placed in other parts of the world in other cultures where the environments are conducive to supporting and nourishing their development. When you and I develop our extrasensory powers to their fullest we should be able to unite forces with those in parallel training to change the destructive course of our planet. That is all I know."

I had been unable to augment the power of my Clear Mind Meditation during En's absence. The cultivation of my power through sustaining Clear Mind needed to grow uninterrupted and the months of my inability to continue the training set me back. This was a drawback for my future karma. But luckily I had a prearranged helper in my friend En.

"Hey, let's take a look at that scroll, again," En said.

We ran the rest of the way back to my house. I took the scroll carefully from my dresser and brought it out to spread the luminescent square of silk on the stone bench. Even though I knew En would not disappear again, I kept my eyes on him as I placed the Go-stones on the outer edges. I let out a sigh of relief when he stayed put.

As we looked at the scroll again, this time with high intuition and great faith, we focused our eyes and began to see through various layers that were there. En was more adept at this method as he was now an advanced wizard of sorts. He guided me in his way of seeing that involved a slightly relaxed squinting. By using the cheeks as a point of focus one could shift perception. This was close to a method I had already learned. The difference was that because there were two of us in intense focus, our collective powers were augmented. We acted like batteries for one another. Between us we generated a level of magnetic and electrical charge that heightened our perception to the point of being able to see and hear things that had not been there before. "There's a small path there, do you see it?" asked En.

I squinted, "Oh yes. And, I can hear the faint echo of chanting. It's increasing in volume."

"I don't hear the chanting," En shrugged, "but the images are getting stronger and stronger." I suspected he could not hear the chanting because they were secret and could be heard only by the High Born One.

The path zigzagged up a kind of slope. "Let's call it our Silk Road!" he laughed, referencing what he had learned in school and appreciating the yellowish-gold scintillating fabric on which the vibrating oracle lay. It glowed faintly while scribbled ancient characters, possibly thousands of years old, floated on top. The characters hovered above rugged terrain on a plane not visible until now. We could finally decipher the writing.

They described specific rock formations near the apex of the mountain. When those sacred stones were reached, certain chants were to be sung. The chants were similar to those I learned from Great-Grandmother, which I could easily adapt by inserting a few unfamiliar utterances. The chanting, if produced by the right voice, would generate a magnificent waterfall. That waterfall would yield magical powers to the one who saw it.

Through my trained inner hearing I recognized waves of droning which turned out to be instructions as to the exact cadence and rhythm for the chant when I reached the rock formations. The scroll also indicated that I should look for a formation that, when seen from a particular angle, would be in the shape of gassho, hands in prayer.

"Do you see the tiny entrance to the Silk Road?" En asked as we both focused our narrow attention on a small section of the luminescent fabric.

"Yes, I see it," I exclaimed with excitement. "It's the path up our own mountain!" we exclaimed in unison.

"But it cannot be," I said. "This map has been passed down from our ancestors who carried it out of Central Asia. They did not know this terrain. It is just not possible."

En and I looked at each other with coincident understanding. The map changes according to the geography in which it finds itself. The waterfall is a mythical place. It takes physical form when our powers of sight and hearing are heightened. This waterfall is discovered by those who can see and hear on a metaphysical plane, where the five senses are developed in their more refined use and can lend themselves to deepen the intuition and heighten the senses.

Soon after En and I deciphered the scroll, I was given instruction in a dream. I was to journey up the mountain path on the winter solstice, the longest night of the year. I would set out at dusk to find the rock formation shown on the silk map. En told me that I might not be able to see the natural sculpture in broad daylight, which is why the Originals had suggested a time when shadows would make certain things clearer.

During our winter two-week break from school in December 1915, I put on my thickest cotton-stuffed kimono jacket and a pair of straw sandals. The well-worn jacket that once belonged to Mother made me think of her and I felt her protection when I put it on.

I announced to Jiraa that I was off to study with a friend and would return by dark. Busy with home projects, he casually nodded an assent.

I carefully rolled up the sacred scroll and with two hands lightly placed it for a second on my forehead. This gesture honored its contents and I bowed to its high source. I had memorized the entire scroll and did not need to refer to it but carried it with me, nonetheless. With the precious relic hidden inside my thick kimono sleeve, I headed into the cold. The sky was already darkening as I left the house.

In the hazy light I made my way up the mountain trail that I knew so well. I could have walked it blindfolded. At the fork in the road where the path to the left led to the sacred grove, I turned right and headed up an overgrown path not traveled by anyone.

The brush was thick and the vegetation so tall that I needed to use the sliver of the moon's glow and the light of Venus to guide me. I made my way along the dark terrain until suddenly I saw a yellowish light that looked like a cluster of fireflies, floating in the air. But I knew that fireflies did not group together like that and wondered what the beacon could be.

As I got closer, I saw it was an oil lantern dangling from a tree branch, rocked by the wind. Someone had undoubtedly left it there for me to light my way back down. Perhaps En had preceded me to light the way, or maybe it was a sign from the Immortals. Whatever the answer, it made me feel less alone.

My gaze sharpened as I looked up the path and I was guided beyond the lantern to the very top. There stood the stony hands in gassho. I imagined it would be ornately carved like a real sculpture, but it was actually quite rough, worn down by rain and weathered by hot sun. Although there was no mistaking the hands carved by nature it could easily have been overlooked, especially in the daylight. Next to the sculpture sat a flat ledge that invited me to climb up onto it. There were no more instructions on the map. I was now on my own.

As I thought to curl up on the flat ledge, I noticed that there was an opening between the two hands. Inquisitive as I was, I peered into the dark space between the hands. Suddenly I was surrounded by the sweetest fragrance and called by faint voices that could have belonged to Mother and Father. I felt a strong tug to enter the space to see for myself if my parents were indeed calling me and then, like a jolt in my head, I heard En's cautioning voice, "Do not venture into the dark tunnels!"

With that warning, I instinctively placed myself in Full Lotus on the flat surface and began to clear my mind. What was revealed to me then was that, when we are closest to the highest truth, temptations come to throw us off our path. We must be wary and alert moment by moment lest we lose our way in a moment of inattention.

In meditation posture I faced the vast nothingness. The edge of the cliff where I sat opened out over an abyss. I closed my eyes for a moment as I checked my posture and aligned my breath. Once my mind had been clear for a short while, I sang the chants that I had memorized from the scroll's instructions and then I sat for a while longer holding very, very still.

Suddenly an image appeared of a young Chinese girl seated in Full Lotus with a flower in one hand and small vial of holy water in the other. She wore ethereal garments that draped over her small frame. She spoke strongly in an ancient voice that did not match her childlike appearance. "The world is moving more and more toward darkness. Nations are conquering nations. An unawakened world has no hope. You have agreed to come now and design a plan to overturn this direction."

She continued, "With the help of your friend you will develop a plan to bring peace to all beings. Your islanders have cultivated the right spirit to effect such change, but it is up to you to harness the energy of the people."

I guessed her to be to the Great Kamadaa because of En's description of her when he met her in the spirit realm. She was indeed beautiful and seemed to possess great wisdom.

I understood that to complete the karmic task that Kamadaa spoke of, I would need the mastery of a few more disciplines. I was both disappointed and relieved that the waterfall did not actualize, and as I walked home, I wondered how long it would be before I would need to return again.

The following day when I saw En, he remarked, "You were given a trial run. You will sit on that precipice one day, and your karmic contract will be crystal clear. The time is close but not now.

CHAPTER 27
THE YUTA (SOOTHSAYER)

Several months had passed since En and I deciphered the scroll. Mastering True Prayer with the guidance of the Noro was time consuming, but I was nearing the end. At first, a large part of the training had been to manifest objects and make them disappear. I went on to undertake more subtle tasks such as suggesting the thought of peace in a person with a hardened heart. Everyone has free choice so we cannot insert changes into people, but we can make suggestions that allow them to change. During this lesson, there was one person that kept coming to mind. Ever since En's disappearance, his mother had become a woman who was contemptuous of others' mistakes and was quick to judge. She had held on to her grudge against me for influencing her son and had been given to gossiping about my brother and me. I thought to see her softened would bring relief to the people around her.

Without having to assume full lotus posture, I took a moment to visualize En's mother as happy, fulfilled and loving everyone around her. I placed her in a light pink bubble in my mind's eye and leaned into the image. At first, it was difficult to send loving thoughts to someone who had been harsh with me but by focusing on softening my own heart and holding compassion I was able to do it. I remembered that we have all run the gamut of personalities, we have been at one time cruel and insensitive as much as we've been kind and loving. When that knowledge surfaced, I realized we can surround not only our friends, but our enemies with loving energy. It is a wonderful tactic to disarm them and at the same time infuses us with the good energy we send.

A few days after my visualization, En seemed much happier and freer than usual. I didn't have to ask and could only imagine that there had been definite changes at home. There is a saying: "When you want to know what is going on inside you, just look around you." This teaches us that our environment is a direct expression of ourselves. By shifting her attitude, En's mother took the responsibility she had to the world around her. Utimately, happiness begets happiness.

True Prayer must come from the purest heart and purest intention. The Originals safeguarded these practices of prayer so that only the highest good should be attained through these methods.

One morning as I was getting ready to go to the common villager's home for my lesson, the Noro arrived on horseback. From a velvet pouch draped across her torso she produced an old tattered book and announced, "You are now spiritually ripened enough to receive instruction on this ancient text. It is time to ask the Yuta in the northern mountains to guide you. This is a book of oracles that will add depth to your clairsentience, your ability to know things.

"Although I am versed in interpreting the contents of the book, it is the Yuta, the soothsayer of the North, who has the highest, most sublime understanding and command of it."

I straddled our mare and followed the Noro through treacherous but familiar terrain. It was the same journey my brother and I had taken a few years ago and I remembered well the road leading to her little hut.

The Yuta was expecting us and, by the time we arrived, she had prepared some hot water to make *mugi-cha,* a roasted barley tea. The Noro and I bowed after a polite exchange and quickly stepped up to her altar, each of us taking three sticks of incense from a tiny box, and lighting the sticks with fire from the hearth. We stuck them in a clay bowl full of ashes and stubs from previously burned incense.

We stood in silence at the altar for a few moments with our hands in gassho and heads bent in prayer to the Yuta's ancestors.

We turned to the Yuta and knelt in seiza. The Noro then offered the Yuta a gift of undagii, my favorite fried doughnuts wrapped in special paper. "Congratulations for your long life!" the Noro said to the Yuta as I echoed the Noro's good wishes. We placed our foreheads to the floor, honoring her longevity.

With a nod, the Yuta thanked us and started to lift herself up from the tatami saying, "Let me get you some tea."

Seeing her struggle, I jumped up and said, "Please let me." The Noro had told me on the ride up that the Yuta was 107 years old and I was amazed that, aside from her difficulty standing, the Yuta was very much unchanged since the last time I saw her. She possessed the same sharp, beady eyes and her hair although slightly thinner now, was just as unkempt as before and was wound in a topknot.

I reached for the hot water kettle and poured the steaming water into the teapot where she had pre-measured some tea. I found three clay teacups and placed them on an old black lacquered tray that had been scratched and was peeling around the rim. It was painted with a faded design of a phoenix.

When I returned with the tray, I caught the tail end of a conversation between the two wise women. "You understand," the Noro said, "Our High Born One has little time to learn all that she must. If I might, please know that it is important to try and condense her lessons. You live far from us and it would be a hardship for her to visit you every day. She could come a few times each week."

The Yuta nodded at the Noro and then, at me, as a sign to set down the tray.

I poured the mugi-cha from the teapot into our teacups and we sat, the three of us appreciating our group karma of being in each others' presence.

"I haven't tasted this in so long," the Yuta laughed as she enjoyed her pastry. We finished our doughnuts and sipped the tea as she told us about her life since she had relocated here. She said the authorities had not come to bother her as she lived far in the mountains. She was free to see clients as she had been doing for the past eighty years or so.

She hoisted herself up and shuffled over to a small bookcase where she retrieved a cloth bag from which she pulled out the *I Ching,* the old book of hexagrams. I remembered the book from my first visit and I could still see that it had the same mysterious energy about it. She held the book reverently and said to me in a gravelly voice, "The *I Ching* must always be stored on a high shelf. Never leave it on the ground. Keep it clean and away from negative influences.

"It is best if the book comes into your hands by way of a gift or by other indirect means. In this way you might infer that you are ready to investigate its contents. What's important is that you are drawn to the book through some uncanny or mysterious means. Perhaps someone mentions it in conversation or you have a sudden feeling about it. In some instances you could purchase it yourself but only because of a genuine need to study its contents."

With that explanation her eyes beamed and she extended the book with a shaky hand. "I bequeath to you this sacred book and someday you, too, will pass it on. It carries the vibrations of all who have touched it and studied its contents, and you will imprint upon it your own personal vibration." I was astonished with her generosity and gasped, "I cannot possibly accept this. It is too precious. Besides, it belongs to you!"

The Yuta insisted, "I heard your cry on the day you were born and I knew my life was complete. You are the right vessel to carry the knowledge I will pass on. I can go peacefully with the assurance that the knowledge I give you will continue uninterrupted. This great book already belongs to you. I consulted it this morning and the book seeks you as its new owner."

I was humbled and I lowered my head to the floor. The Noro nodded and spoke clairaudiently to me, "To receive such a book from someone of her caliber is a sure sign that your karma is ripe for tasting its wisdom."

As soon as I lifted my head the Yuta began my lesson. "The great book of divining is made up of sixty-four hexagrams. Each hexagram contains six lines that render concise answers to questions posed. The book is a sacred oracle that can be consulted by anyone but requires an insightful person to interpret the metaphorical answer.

"The best time to consult the *I Ching* is in the early morning after clearing the mind with meditation. Focus on one question. Better not to have multiple questions. Always be reverent and respectful when handling the book and take care to keep your mind pure and focused on your specific question.

"To begin, throw either yarrow sticks or coins to derive the accurate hexagram. The random pattern of the sticks or the sequence of yin/yang aspects of the coins when thrown builds the hexagram.

"Each of the 64 hexagrams represents a specific image and meaning. The *I Ching* offers explanatory notes attached to each hexagram, notes that are often too vague for the common person to derive meaning from them. The explanations require an ability to think in metaphorical terms. Sometimes the answers are literal, although usually not.

"The book opens to deep knowledge and offers supreme advice. The answers render suggestions for the questioner's highest good, always leaning in the direction of love and harmony for all concerned.

"This book should never be consulted for frivolous reasons," she said. "If your intent is sincere, then you will be given a straightforward answer. If not, you will most likely be given a rebuke of some kind and the *I Ching's* answer to your query may not make sense."

I asked the Yuta if I could ask a question regarding my future, and she nodded and urged me to ask.

"Will I be successful in fulfilling my karma in this lifetime?" I had lingering doubts. The look on the Yuta's face showed concern, and I felt a tingling in my bones.

"You should meditate on that question for two days," advised the Yuta, "and when you return on the third day you will throw the coins, and we will look at the answer."

After clearing my mind each morning I leaned into my question. The Noro had accompanied me on my first visit but I returned alone for the subsequent lessons. I presented the question again and threw three coins a total of six times. The coins have yin and yang sides. The hexagram is built from the bottom up, and each throw of the coins determines whether the lines are solid lines (yang) or broken lines (yin). The hexagram is built from the results of the six throws. The lines yield four possible permutations: two yins and a yang, two yangs and a yin, three yins or three yangs. More often than not, there are two hexagrams that emerge through what are called moving lines.

On the third day we searched the *I Ching* for the hexagrams I had created and looked specifically at the 'moving lines.' I had landed the Hexagram called The Taming Power of the Great that moved into a second Hexagram called The Preponderance of the Great.

TWO HEXAGRAMS
Taming Power of the Great and Preponderance of the Great

"The first hexagram means that you must gather your power. You must cultivate your power without interruption, as it will take a long, long time for you to achieve your goal. To be able to face your karmic task you must remove all of your bad habits which are your doubts and insecurities.

"The second hexagram means that the mission you were born to fulfill in this life may be greater than your ability to realize it."

As the Yuta collected the coins, I thought about her words. She had openly revealed what was in the oracle. However, rather than allow the feeling of defeat to overpower me, I chose to focus on the first hexagram's message that I must do everything to gather my power.

In my next lesson, I was asked to gaze at the 64 hexagrams one after the other so that the wisdom inherent in each would be imprinted in my consciousness. The Yuta and I sat opposite each other with the book on a small table between us. I turned each page and gazed at the hexagram before me with a clear mind. I was not asked to study it. Instead, the wisdom that lived inside of each hexagram and the ability to instinctively know its hidden meanings was transferred to me by the power of the Yuta. This unique way of transferring knowledge was a secret method kept amongst seers and could only be utilized when moving knowledge from the sacred book to the deep consciousness of another.

It took many meetings to imprint the wisdom of the *I Ching* into the deepest reaches of my consciousness. The *I Ching* contained answers to every conceivable question one could possibly ask regarding any aspect of life. The knowledge imprinted in me would help me assess any situation.

One day, after our final transference, the Yuta directed me outdoors. She brought along two blankets and we walked to an area of her garden where the grassy bank was visible and we took our seats. "Focus on any flower or weed. Relax your eyes by nearly closing your eyelids, leaving only a sliver of space to concentrate on the object of your choice.

"All living things, including humans, have a field of energy around them. Lower your eyelids and stare at the object until you see the light that the object radiates. I know you have seen colors around living things your whole life. Now it is time to see more clearly and to interpret colors."

Suddenly I saw something I had never seen before. Perhaps it was the presence of the Yuta that amplified my experience but I had an uncanny feeling that the particular red hibiscus I was focusing on was speaking to me. The color surrounding the flower was shifting back and forth from a light green to a very dark green. The flower was annoyed. I could almost hear it. "Is it possible that the flower is actually communicating with me?" I asked the Yuta in disbelief. I had been seeing light and colors around living things for as long as I could remember but never had I heard plants speak.

The Yuta smiled, "Yes, and we will return to your hibiscus friend in a moment. Looking for color around objects is important but you must also listen for sounds that emanate from things. All things in the phenomenal world can be reduced to vibrations. Colors, even emotions, are vibrations and all vibrations are sounds," she whispered to me.

She said I could *hear* the emotion exuding from living things. "Flowers can laugh or cry. They can impart wisdom or complain to you. You must observe and listen to nature, to insects and trees and plants. In this way your understanding of all living beings will deepen and you will know how to help the world."

I told the Yuta that the colors I see around people are thick and brilliant yet transparent and not of this world. For example, I might see around a person an opaque yellow or a deep purple that is very vivid. The colors are not faint or pastel. They are very strong. I could see such colors, but didn't understand their meanings. "What does each color mean?" I asked.

"The meaning of certain colors will reveal themselves to you. While I could list colors and what they generally symbolize, it is not such a simple thing to say that red always means thus and such and yellow means something else. Interpretation is not so narrow and exact. Most important is the quality of the color and also where the color appears on a person. For example, colors that are vibrant around a person usually indicate a happy and balanced person. Dull colors with a smoky hue might be an indication of illness or imbalance. Blues, greens and violets demonstrate balance and spiritual awareness and are usually seen at the top of the body, around the head. If you see red around the head, this will more than likely indicate anger. But most times you will see a blend of colors and you will have to derive meaning from that.

"It is the job of your instinct and not your thinking to understand the colors which is why it is not possible to simply ascribe exact meaning to each color," she reiterated.

"Colors in the field around the body reflect the person's consciousness. When the color is clear and bright, that usually indicates that the person is more spiritually advanced. This is important for you to recognize. Some people with murky, hazy colors around them will need more spiritual help than others. By meditating on the fields around plants as I have taught you, you will come to understand more and more how to identify just where a particular gradation of color moves from health to illness or imbalance."

"Now back to your hibiscus." The Yuta asked me to look and figure out the meaning of the shifting green color.

"I think green must have to do with jealousy or envy," I said and told her that the color coupled with the sound led me to feel that the weeds around it were taking up too much space. The Yuta nodded her head and directed me to clear the space around the hibiscus. "Be respectful," she called after me.

I was not quite sure what she meant but I carefully pulled out a few weeds that seemed to be hindering the growth of my new friend. When I returned to the Yuta I refocused on the plant. The color had changed to a steady and brilliant clear green. "A very healthy color," the Yuta said.

"Why did I have to be respectful when pulling weeds if they were only making my hibiscus unhappy?" I asked.

The Yuta responded with her philosophy, "When we uproot plants, even weeds, for our own use or when we take the breath from living things in order to place them on our table, we must be reverent. Our wise ancestors had proper rituals and prayers when they hunted, and they never slaughtered more than they needed. When we take food from the earth for our survival, the plants and animals sacrifice themselves willingly and lovingly. Man should not kill for sport. What comes from the earth belongs to the earth. It is a gift to us and should be treated as such."

Moving along, she said, "So you understand sight and sound. There is also touch. When we touch things, we know temperature or texture. But we can also simply hold our hands over things and sense heat or cold and allow the objects to speak to us. All of nature speaks and, if we train ourselves to listen, we can hear. Because you already have an innate gift, your meditation skills will open you to nature's teachings."

We sat in silence for a while and I could feel my lessons with the Yuta were coming to an end. Sure enough, the next day, the Noro accompanied me to the Yuta's home. She said, "I must send Mahataa now to study with the Yabuu, our medicine woman. Bowing deeply the Noro placed her forehead to the floor and said, "Thank you so very much for your great effort at transferring your knowledge and wisdom to our High Born One."

"It has been my pleasure," said the Yuta who invited me to sit for one last counsel. The Yuta had worked quickly and I was sorry to part so soon, but happy to have my lessons extended even if for a few more minutes. I took my seat opposite the Yuta and she said, "After you are finished with your schooling here in the North and after completing your training with your mentors, you must quickly depart for the South. There, you must establish yourself not only on behalf of your parents to begin advanced academic study, but you must find a temple near Shuri and bring with you the teachings that the Monk has given you.

"The True Noro has given you the gift of mitigating calamity. You can begin that work in the South, where you will gather a group of persons strong enough to initiate such a project. Many things you must set in motion for the future! When your work with the Yabuu, medicine woman, is finished you will be able to call specific healing procedures and methods from the high healers on the inner plane to come to the rescue of our people when it becomes necessary.

"The Yabuu will also teach you how to treat vast conditions of inflammation, stagnation, poisoning, pain and trauma. That, together with the work you have done with Great-Grandmother, the Monk and the Noro you are able to heal not only on the level of the physical body but the emotional, mental and spiritual as well."

I thanked her and bowed deeply, placing my hands in gassho. "You and I are one," I said to the Yuta. "All that you have taught is alive in me. I have no words to adequately express my gratitude to you. I have taken to heart your request and will leave as soon as my schooling is finished here in the North. What you have given me is great and precious." The Yuta smiled and we ended our exchange bowing without another word.

CHAPTER 28
THE YABUU (MEDICINE WOMAN)

I went to see the Yabuu the very next day with a note from the Noro requesting that she accept me as an apprentice. The Yabuu was the last of the three powerful women of my culture with whom I would be studying. Each gifted woman brought to me an enhancement of my senses, which strengthened my clairsentience, my sixth sense of inner knowing.

The Noro had helped me use my mind like a muscle. I was now able to lean into my intentions and with the training I received in Clear Mind Meditation I could sustain that leaning, giving me the ability to manifest.

The Yuta, soothsayer, had helped me sharpen my sight and my ability to comprehend situations. I could now discern hidden meaning in events and could help others through difficult life passages. She helped me hear in a different way, introducing a method of communicating with all living beings from plants and insects to higher animals.

I was now approaching the last of the matriarchs, our Medicine Woman Yabuu of the North. Carrying my letter of introduction, I arrived at the Yabuu's small thatched dwelling.

"Hello!" I called out as I got closer. Already I could smell the powerful brewing of herbs. I caught sight of the Yabuu helping someone hobble out of the hut. Her long hair that had once reminded me of an even mix of black and white sesame seeds was decidedly much whiter now. Her hair was still tied in a ponytail that fell below her waist. She appeared to be in her seventies but the

Noro said she was well into her nineties. Perhaps it was her special medicines that kept her looking more youthful than her years.

She moved about swiftly and I could see her small bicycle stored on the side of her house, an indication that she was still quite active. Probably another reason she maintained her youth.

I remembered the first time I met her during my visit with Great-Grandmother. She had told us about her aunt, a well-known yabuu, who had raised and mentored her, and left everything to her.

Great-Grandmother later told me that the Yabuu's parents had been herbalists also and had moved their practice to a smaller island in the archipelago. They moved away with their five children leaving behind the Yabuu, their sixth child, with the aunt, the mother's sister, who was barren. The Yabuu grew up as an only child with her aunt who became a surrogate mother. It may seem strange but this kind of practice was common in our culture. When women were barren, siblings would offer one of their own to them. It was not uncommon for those children to feel discarded by their families despite the love they received.

As I approached the Yabuu, I could see her jaw was square and tight from clenching her teeth. I wondered if it was a habit that came from extreme focus or if there were feelings of abandonment that she locked away and refused to talk about. "Follow me." My thoughts were immediately interrupted by the Yabuu's gruff voice.

She led me into her hut where the strange smells of oils, vinegar and incense together with dried herbs assaulted the senses. Without a word, the Yabuu walked off to prepare a cup of tea leaving me to browse the small area. I found the smells were coming from a cabinet filled with crude clay pots housing dried herbs. I wandered outside and peeked at a bench just beside the entrance where jars of herbs were suspended in various solutions. I could see some of the lids were not tightened properly letting the smells of those decoctions waft through the air to mix with the other odors.

The Yabuu came holding a tray of tea. She said nothing but stared at me with penetrating eyes which I took to be an invitation back inside where she served the loquat tea she had brewed. I held the cup to my nose as the tea's fragrance was strong enough to help override some of the heavy smells in the air.

"Please accept this letter of introduction from the Noro," I finally said handing her the carefully written note as I sipped the herbal tea. The Yabuu glanced at the paper and threw it aside.

"So you are the High Born One," she said. I noted her curt manners but decided that she, too, must have felt the urgency to teach me, because she began to do so without any form of introduction.

"Most important for you is to see each patient clearly. After you complete your studies here, you will be able to read a patient's emotional predispositions. Each of our emotions is associated with an internal organ. When a patient displays anger or fear, there are possible imbalances in the liver or kidneys respectively. You must be careful to look for other signs and symptoms so that you will know how to render appropriate treatment. You had better stay alert. I will only say things once. I am not going to repeat myself."

She brusquely turned away. I was unhappy that she was not going to be my friend. I preferred to be taught by an amicable teacher, but I had to bear in mind that I was here to learn everything the Yabuu knew and was not here for the sake of friendship.

The Yabuu had never married. Her work kept her completely occupied. When she was not seeing patients, she refined yoga postures that she taught to alleviate pain and readied various herbal decoctions in the event she would need to prescribe them.

Although shiny from the daily application of sesame oil, the tanned skin on her slight frame was a bit wrinkled. Her deep-set eyes were trained to penetrate the most difficult conditions. They had a shrewdness with which to dissect things. With that ability she could see the beginning of disease before its physical manifestation. Years and years of practice developed her intuitive skills. She used all of her senses to diagnose. She felt the pulses of her patients and, when appropriate, asked for urine samples to confirm her suspicions. Color, smell and clarity of urine were diagnostically relevant. Even though we were not becoming friends, I was able to learn about the intricacies of the medicine she practiced by watching her work.

What do you think about the elderly man who walked in a moment ago," asked the Yabuu while we were in the back preparing an herbal decoction. "What colors were on his face? What was your sense about him?"

I thought for a moment and had noticed a subtle greenish hue on his temples. His skin was very dry. His voice was weak and he was hard of hearing. I relayed this to the Yabuu who then said, "That is a fine observation."

The Yabuu continued, "The greenish cast on the patient's temples is a sign of liver imbalances and the dryness of the skin, a possible blood deficiency. His hearing problem relates to weak kidneys." She told me to help the old man lie down in a small space on the tatami floor of her clinic and searched her medicine counter to pull together some herbs to strengthen his liver, spleen and kidneys.

She cut thin round pieces of ginger root and placed them on the patient's back. Then, she put small cones she formed with her fingertips of processed mugwort on top of the ginger slices and lit them. The burning mugwort had a familiar scent since the curing method had been used in my own home.

"Another way to determine his condition is to feel his pulses on both wrists," said the Yabuu. She demonstrated pulse-taking on the patient and said, "Feel his pulses while I gather his medicine." I did as I was told and then stepped aside once the Yabuu was ready to give the patient his medicine. She was kind with him and explained what he would be receiving. With a half smile, she sent him on his way. Once he left, the Yabuu simply stopped talking to me. That is how our lessons ended every day. She would just stop teaching which I came to understand meant our day was complete. I would then leave only to return the next day.

The Yabuu's home was dedicated to healing. Reference books neatly lined one wall, and jars of dried, pulverized and fresh herbs soaking in various solutions lined another on several shelves. No other yabuu in our northern province owned books. They all learned through apprenticeship. I was indeed fortunate to learn from her, however difficult a personality she presented.

She grew medicinal plants in the gardens that surrounded her home and she produced a variety of herbal oils. "Oh, yech!" the Yabuu let out a screech one afternoon. One of her herbal oils had gone rancid. When she removed the top of the bottle where the herbs were soaking, the room instantly took on a noxious odor of mold, vinegar and rotting leaves.

She quickly dashed to the back of the house to bury the mal-odorous medicine.

"You must never use fresh herbs in oil unless you are planning to use them soon!" she admonished me as if I were responsible for the foul concoction, even though I had yet to learn about prepar-ing oils. I just nodded in understanding as I could not protest. She was my teacher, after all, and I had to be obedient. But I must say it grew increasingly difficult to see her being friendly to everyone else but short with me.

One of her favorite patients arrived just in the midst of the Yabuu's disgruntled stance. The woman carried a small basket of fresh seaweed and tofu in exchange for a treatment. This made the Yabuu happy and her irritation dissipated as she invited the woman in. The Yabuu casually turned to me to finish her lesson about the herbal preparation in a pleasing tone. "It's actually better to use dried herbs when we make these oils if we're going to keep them for a while."

As soon as she led the woman to the treatment area I had a vision of the Yabuu as a very little girl playing with one of her sisters. The sister shared an energetic similarity with the woman who had just arrived. When they faced each other and spoke there was an arc of white energy connecting their crowns and emanating from one heart to the other a beautiful emerald green light. On top of that, the joy on the Yabuu's face when she greeted the woman was the same as the joy on her face as a young child in my vision.

After the patient's departure, I asked the Yabuu if they were related even though I knew they were not. My hope was to draw the Yabuu out and perhaps get her to talk a little about herself. The Yabuu smiled and shook her head, "Seems like it, doesn't it?" she said.

"Almost like you were sisters," I said.

"Funny you should say that," the Yabuu said as she crushed some dried leaves, "she does remind me so much of my older sister." She looked off in thought.

"That must have been difficult," I sensed the mix of joy and sorrow emanating from the Yabuu's chest. "Being separated from your family at such a young age."

The Yabuu looked down at the leaves she was crushing. "Oh, I was very sad and unhappy for a long time and nothing would bring me out of my grief. I was given away when I was five and couldn't understand why, even though they tried to explain it to me. My older sister cried and cried and so did I. It wasn't until years later that I saw her again. But she remains my most favorite sibling."

"You are fortunate that your parents and siblings are alive," I responded. "And, you know where they are. You can visit them. My parents were lost at sea and no matter what, I will never see them in this life." The Yabuu turned to me with a look on her face that had softened considerably. "Life is about loss," I said. "We lose each other at some point or another."

"Yes, it's true," said the Yabuu. "Sometimes we grieve our entire life and that is not a good thing."

"Unless," I offered, "we transform the energy of grief to bring good to the world around us. Great-Grandmother told me that the women warriors knew how to transform the energy of their emotions." The Yabuu nodded and patted me on the shoulder, "That is the end of our lesson for today."

The next day, I was instructed to collect fresh mugwort leaves in the hills near the Yabuu's home. I was going to learn to process them by tying bundles and hanging them up to dry. On the west side of her house the Yabuu had strung nets to hold the drying bundles. Mugwort, known as *huchiba* in the old tongue, had multiple uses. Huchiba could could be freshly diced and mixed into rice when making rice gruel. It was used also to make medicinal herbal teas for many purposes such as building blood. The noro and kaminchu priestesses drank huchiba tea to sharpen their premonition through dreams.

My brother prepared lots of huchiba dishes for me because he knew that they would help me learn through dreams and aid in my spiritual development.

The Yabuu mostly used huchiba for use in a burning technique, called yaachu, to treat patients. "These crushed, pulverized leaves are fashioned into small cones and burned sometimes on coin sized ginger or garlic slices or sometimes directly on the skin at specific points," the Yabuu said. "Burning the mugwort not only heats the points upon which the herb is burned but the smoke from the burning mugwort can ward off evil spirits."

As we wrapped the leaves in thin gauze, the Yabuu explained that during rainy season the bundles would be dried indoors from the heat of the wood-burning stove. I learned that it took two to three years to properly dry mugwort. "After that," the Yabuu said, "the leaves are crushed by hand in a huge bamboo sieve." The Yabuu then took down a few dried bundles and showed me how to crush and separate the leaves from the twigs and branches. We were then left with a small amount of a refined, cotton-like substance perfect for burning which the Yabuu stored in a large clay jar.

"I heard stories from my aunt about your great-great-grand-mother Uto," the Yabuu commented one afternoon as she prepared a decoction. I realized this was the first time the Yabuu had spoken about my family or me. "Uto brought much knowledge of heal-ing to our island, teaching herbal medicine and various methods of hands-on techniques. My aunt apprenticed with one of the healers taught by your great-great-grandmother, who in turn, transmitted the knowledge to me. I am grateful to your ancestor and I am happy to return the gift to you."

I was surprised by the Yabuu's compliment and sensed the energy between us had shifted profoundly. The next day as I walked up to the hut, the Yabuu greeted me cheerfully. She looked lighter and happier.

"Today, you will learn how to prepare and prescribe herbal medicines. Many of the powders, twigs and dried leaves come from other shores, but some of them are grown right here in my garden. Eventually you will be able to identify them, which is not an easy task. Your senses must be crisp."

I hoped she meant that I would be spending some time herb gathering and learning to identify outdoor species, but my heart sank when she said, "But first things first. You will clean the cabinet over there with the rows of clay pots of dried leaves and roots." She pointed to a dark area of the house. She saw the disappointment on my face and barked a laugh, "We'll spend some time outdoors soon but, for now, you must wipe the outside of the pots and retrace the names of the herbs that have faded on the exterior of the pots. The ink and brush are on the side of the cabinet. Be sure to look carefully at the names. As for the herbs, be sure to taste them and smell them. Let them speak to you, and you will learn that each has its own personality."

I wasn't keen about this project at first, but in a short time it became interesting and fun. The personality of each herb transferred its unique characteristic to me as I handled them. I found myself amongst friends. Ginger, for example, is gregarious and highly sociable. And indeed it is an herb that is used in most herbal formulas because it moves the other herbs along. Picking up another herb, I felt spreading in my hands a regal energy and a sense of reverence wafted over me. There were only a few pieces of the herb inside the jar and on the outside were faintly drawn characters. It was Ginseng, a wise old sage that, when prepared into a tea and ingested, gives energy and long life. As I touched the jar I could feel the herb communicate its wisdom to me.

Then I came across a jar of fresh squid ink. The Yabuu had just acquired it from a neighbor who brought over a fresh squid. The ink sac had to be gently removed and transferred to the tiny jar.

"We will make a black ink soup for a patient who is weak from blood loss." There was a woman in our village who had tremendous fatigue after childbirth. The Yabuu showed me how to prepare the soup and at the end of the day I accompanied her to the woman's home. There, the Yabuu applied sustained pressure on a point on the woman's leg. This particular point known for curing diseases was usually burned with the yaachu method but the patient was too weak, and so the Yabuu chose to use pressure instead. The woman also drank the ink soup made with two herbal blood builders together with fish shavings and small slivers of cooked pork that the Yabuu had prepared.

Once I was done cleaning out the cabinet and was getting a sense of all the herbs, the Yabuu cautioned, "More important than learning the use of the herbs is learning when *not* to use them. An herbal medicine that is excellent in the treatment of one condition could harm the patient in another."

The Yabuu owned a small weights-and-measures instrument so that she could replicate the exact prescription of the ancient healers. Each herb in a formula had to be carefully measured. There was a certain beauty to the herbal formulas devised by the old masters. Each herb ingested singularly might be mildly powerful but when brought together in a specifically measured formula, the combination provided a remarkable synergy that could cure a condition that the individual herbs taken singularly could not.

After a few more weeks of training, the Yabuu brought out an ancient book of charts showing all the points on model bodies that I needed to memorize. These original charts were small in size and were organized into a loose compendium. Because the charts had been painted onto a sturdy cloth, they were in good shape with only a few tattered edges. These original drawings came from the old Tibetan healers, and the Yabuu took great care in handling the relic.

"It is possible that the Tibetans had mapped the energy flows long before the Chinese," said the Yabuu. For comparison the Yabuu brought out more recent charts of Chinese origin. The Chinese charts were more understandable because the pathways of energy on model bodies were clearer and more systematized. However, the Chinese charts she had in her possession were more fragile because they were produced from paper made of fibers from pressed wood and grasses.

As I held the charts, I was suddenly visited by a vision of Mongols of the Steppes of Central Asia using the burning method to cure disease. I concluded from the vision that the method of curing had been transferred from the Mongols to the Tibetans as well as to the Chinese.

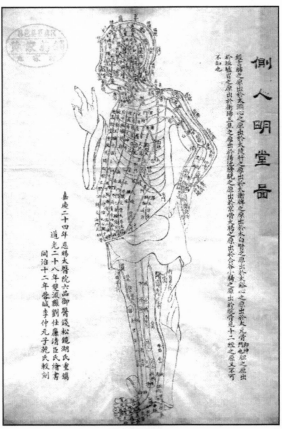

ANCIENT ACUPUNCTURE CHART

"You can see the points along these pathways that we apply the burning method to," the Yabuu said as she traced the energy pathways. "And, these points can also be punctured. The ancient healers of Tibet and India knew about these openings in the body and it is likely that they used a form of acupuncture at one time," said the Yabuu.

"These openings known as acupuncture points are different from regular pores on the skin, and energy from the atmosphere can be interchanged with the gases emitted from these points."

It seemed as if the knowledge the Yabuu possessed was infinite. One thing she could not give me was her long experience. Nothing can replace experience.

"The ancients taught that nature reflects us," she said. "By observing nature the ancients could see that what happens in the outer environment happens also in our inner environment.

"Look how a tree grows up from the ground and spreads its leaves outward. We have energy in our body that moves and spreads its energy like the tree does." The Yabuu was referring to the liver organ. The ancients taught that liver energy moves upward and outward in the body spreading out like the branches of a tree. When the liver functions well, the overall energy of the body is smooth and free flowing. When the liver is disturbed, anger, depression or stagnation results.

I thought momentarily about En's mother and how she effected positive change in the people around her by making changes inside herself. I shared this with the Yabuu and asked a related question, "If we take care of trees around us, can that heal our livers?" I was thinking that if by changing ourselves inwardly, we can directly affect others, then, perhaps by caring for the environment around us we could directly affect the inner environment.

The Yabuu was quiet and thoughtful for a moment before speaking. "Just like when a tree is given the right amount of sunshine and water and minerals in the earth, it thrives, so do we when we develop and nurture all areas of ourselves. If we observe the natural world around us we can see the nourishing cycle that supports life. Every aspect of the tree, the branches, the leaves, the roots, is nourished by the elements. In this way, we give life to all parts of our self. Nature is our teacher."

I thought about what the Yabuu said and reflected on all of my different teachers and how they had each helped me nurture the various parts of myself. Like the nourished tree, I too was giving life to all the parts of myself.

Although my first impressions of the Yabuu were not so positive, I eventually came to appreciate her not just as a teacher with information, expertise and experience but also a teacher with depth and wisdom.

"Come taste this decoction," said the Yabuu one afternoon.

"Ugh! This is awful!" I yelled. The Yabuu laughed. She had become something of a prankster. "That is the reason we make compresses. When herbs are too strong and bitter to be taken internally, we use the decoction for compresses that are very effective when applied to the body." She then showed me how to make ginger compresses that were applied hot to the body to relieve colic, which is an obstruction in the abdomen, and to restore warmth to cold joints or invigorate circulation in stiff, cramped muscles.

I found myself saying to the Yabuu, "When my full powers are in place, I will be able to merely visualize these healing methods for patients and be effective. The methods you teach me can be used in long distance healing and I need to learn the actual process so that I will be able to visualize it exactly."

The Yabuu grinned and I blushed. The words had just come out of me as if someone had spoken through me on my behalf. Perhaps it was so that I would know this truth but also so that the Yabuu would know our lessons were coming to an end.

She turned to me with penetrating eyes, that now looked at me with a warmth and compassion they did not seem to have when I first walked into her hut. "We have almost completed our time together, but before we do, I have a favor to ask of you."

I nodded. The Yabuu had gone from being reserved and hard with me to being open and someone who could ask for my help. I was only too happy to do whatever she asked.

"When you arrived here, you told me that you learned the workings of the *I Ching* from the Yuta. Perhaps you could throw the coins to see if you can find the exact location of some special roots."

Our island produced over 400 varieties of herbs and the Yabuu tended almost 100 of those, some on her property and some outside in the woods near her home. "I would like your help in finding the rare ginseng root. Your great-great-grandmother Uto is rumored to have planted the ginseng somewhere in this vicinity but I have never seen it.

"I can help you," I answered, "but it will not be through the *I Ching* that I will find the root. Great-grandmother took me to the bamboo forest to look for bamboo shoots when I was little and we accidentally stumbled upon a strange looking root that Great-Grandmother thought to be ginseng. I am guessing that is where Uto planted it. But the bamboo forest is thick and one can easily get lost in it. With the blessings of the Yuta I will gather my power to call the ginseng as she taught me. I will see if the ginseng root can speak to me and call me to it."

The next day I meditated and cleared my mind. I then used my sixth sense to receive an answer to questions I had put into motion the previous day regarding the location of the root. I knew that as soon as I received an answer, it would be time to search the forest.

It was not until the day after my request when I awoke from a dream that I knew the ginseng's exact location. In my dream Great-Grandmother came to me holding a conch shell to her ear. We were deep in the bamboo forest. She spoke to me, "My mother Uto planted ginseng in a patch of ground mysteriously primed to nourish its growth. Can you hear it?" Then I began to hear in my inner ear the sound of a root growing underground from an area near the edge of the forest. Slowly the sound barely audible at first began to build and very soon I could hear the snapping of hundreds of roots growing. I awoke from the loud mixture of sounds of branches breaking as hundreds of roots snipped and popped through the earth creating an incredible cacophony.

Jumping out of bed, I grabbed a burlap sack and shovel in search of the location. As I took a short hike into the bamboo forest I began to feel plants communicating with me. Near the edge of the forest, just as my dream indicated, I came upon a very large patch of ginseng root. It was more than I imagined. "The Yabuu will be thrilled when I return with a sack full!" I thought to myself.

When I rushed back to the Yabuu's house, I eagerly opened the sack to show her my findings. Kneeling in seiza, she picked up the burlap sack and looked at me with tender eyes. "Thank you for these roots. I will gladly receive a small portion of these but the rest are for you to dry and sell to our neighboring yabuu in the outlying villages. The money you make from the sales can be used to pay for your schooling in Shuri. I know your brother has been saving a bit of money for you but now you will have what you need to make your start in the South."

I was astonished and perplexed at the same time. "But I have found these roots for you to use in the clinic because you need them," I protested.

She answered, "And I am able to use a few of these, thank you kindly, but the rest belong to you. You found them," she smiled and shrugged almost playfully. "Besides, I will be able to dig for more roots when you show me where the patch is." We both laughed and I agreed to leave her the location of the roots before I left.

Our last few lessons were dedicated to yoga postures and nutrition. "Our patients need more than our medicines and treatments," said the Yabuu, "especially those with joint pain.

"We spend our whole lives bending forward. In order to counterbalance the forward bending we must bend backward. Field hands who carry heavy bundles of grasses and branches on their backs and farmers who bend all day long to tend their rice paddies are helped immensely by yoga postures."

"Yoga along with healthful habits such as adequate hydration, nutritious foods and appropriate rest prepare the physical body for spiritual unfolding.

"Our diet consists in very little meat, as you know, and we consume mostly wild plants, purple potato and vegetables with occasional fish, rice and millet. More important than anything is our motto to fill the belly only eighty percent. Everything we do to cleanse, purify and strengthen the body moves us toward spiritual advancement.

"Drinking sufficient amounts of water rids the body of poisons, but hydration also plays a role in spiritual development. You will soon learn about water's connection to spiritual advancement. We drink tea but often neglect the drinking of simple pure water. We must make an effort to do so."

The Yabuu saved the information on the Triple Burner organ as her final lesson because she wanted the knowledge to be fresh in my mind. She knew I would be learning details about this special organ when the Monk returned to give me his last lessons.

"The Triple Burner refers to the three burning spaces inside the body. The first space is the Lower Burner that includes the organs of elimination. The second is the Middle Burner that encompasses the organs of digestion. The third space or Upper Burner refers to the organs of respiration and circulation."

The Yabuu knew that the points along the Triple Burner meridian could be stimulated for treating physical symptoms such as lung conditions or digestive problems but this unusual organ housed hidden secrets—deeper, spiritual uses—that would be revealed to me later by the old Monk.

During my study with the Yabuu, I did not see the Monk at all. He had been mentoring En who had learned very quickly. Perhaps the speed with which En moved through his meditation lessons could be attributed to the instruction he received to develop himself in the spirit realm when he was whisked away. However, because En did not possess certain karmic elements required to complete the entire curriculum of Taoist Alchemy, the old Monk took him only through the basic instructions of Clear Mind Meditation. Without instruction in Taoist Alchemy, En would not have the possibility for immortality.

Feelings were already stirring in me about what I might choose. Would I choose immortality when the time came? What if I felt destined to choose the life of the Bodhisattva, the one who would incarnate again and again to ensure that all beings were assisted on the path to awakening?

When it was time to depart, I put my hands in gassho and bowed deeply to the Yabuu, my dear friend. "Take good care of your health," I said to her.

"Of course! And, you too. Write me when you have a little time and let me know how you are doing," she said affectionately. I waved goodbye and as I headed down the path, her hut got smaller and smaller until it was no longer visible. She stood outside her doorway waving until I disappeared. My heart was glad to have known her, to have learned from her. My connection with her was strong and I knew she would remain in my heart and mind for my whole life.

CHAPTER 29
TAOIST ALCHEMY

I spent the next weeks traveling from village to village on our old mare selling the ginseng roots to farmers and healers. I put almost all of my earnings away for my future trip to Shuri and still managed to purchase the most exquisite green tea powder from a merchant visiting from the South. I even purchased the accoutrements of a tiny bamboo whisk and small measuring ladle. I bought the tea with the old Monk in mind. I knew I would be spending another short period with him and thought to offer him a delicious bowl of tea to show my gratitude at our very last meeting.

It was March 1917 and I was preparing to graduate soon from the eighth grade. My brother Jiraa was beaming and he called our neighbors for a small meal to celebrate. They arrived with small coins of hard-earned money in humble handmade envelopes to send me off.

"You will come back, won't you, to teach us?" they asked. They were proud that I would be the first girl of our village to set sail for school in the South.

I told them it would be an honor for me to return as I hoped to come back and offer more interesting courses in our school of the northern province. I imagined that like Great-Grandmother who had described fascinating objects traded in the South, I, too, would return with items to show them, items they had never seen before.

In the chill of the early March air the Monk returned to give me lessons on Taoist Alchemy, the first of two final pieces of knowledge I would acquire before my departure. I was to learn how Alchemy related to a special internal organ in Chinese Medicine, and how the use of its energetic correlate could lead to immortality. As we had done so many times before, we settled into the birthing room together in Clear Mind Meditation before he started his first lesson.

"In ancient history," the Monk began, "Taoist priests in China, who were very interested in immortality and longevity, experimented with developing a potion, an actual physical drink, made of metals. These alchemists thought the potions would lead to immortality but these potions failed. Instead of gaining immortality, people died after ingesting decoctions made from cinnabar, a red mercury ore and various other elements.

"Taoist priests and court magicians of the ancient world then convinced the Emperor that the Elixir of Immortality could be found in the eastern mists. For that reason, the Emperor sent out expeditions into the Pacific waters in search of the Elixir and the Land of the Immortals. Those expeditions landed here in this archipelago."

"Yes. I remember I was the Emperor!" I said excitedly.

The monk paused and said, "There is only one life and that life is what you are living now." This was his way of bringing my attention back to the present moment. His message was that we ought not be distracted by anything!

He explained that there's no point in putting emphasis on a life that is no longer relevant. Perhaps we might still carry imprints of those past personalities but best not to identify with someone we no longer are. So with an attitude of non-identification with the past personality, he continued.

As he spoke I felt a twinge in my heart and I told him that I had heard such stories from Great-Grandmother. She had said, in fact, that our islands did indeed house the Elixir somewhere, hidden.

The old Monk nodded, "Yes, and I have arrived to give you that Elixir." He said this the same way he introduced most critical information with a casual calmness.

In jest I replied, "I hope whatever you've brought is not as awful tasting as some of the decoctions brewed by the Yabuu. She mixed some vile medicines!"

He chuckled and said, "Immortality is a state of mind that is achieved not by medicines. Immortality is a mind that has transcended duality." I had no idea what he meant but trusted that I would come to understand.

He continued, "Although the high physicians in Chinese Medicine were most interested in the cultivation of spirit and less concerned with the physical body, the physical body is of primary concern. Without the body we could not birth the spiritual True Self."

As he mentioned the True Self, the birthing room suddenly transformed itself into a kind of golden palace. The Monk who sat in Full Lotus posture seemed to be hovering slightly above the tatami mat and I, too, felt as though I were going to lift off. It was a most unusual feeling. I gently closed my eyes to fully experience the sensation of levitating, allowing the joy and peace to waft over me, and when I opened my eyes he was gone. Our first lesson was over. The Monk had slipped away.

The next day, my teacher introduced an organ in Chinese Medicine called the Triple Burner and compared it to the Three Cauldrons in Taoist Alchemy. "We have in Chinese Medicine an organ that is not truly an organ. It is called the Triple Burner and refers to three areas of the body: the lower abdominal area, the middle of the torso and the upper chest region."

During this lesson, I had another curious experience. As the Monk described those areas, I could feel a tingling sensation in those three areas in my own body and, in fact, those areas glowed on the monk's body. It was as if our physical bodies were mysteriously in accord with the information being taught.

"Yes," I said emphatically. "The Yabuu instructed me on the Triple Burner organ during one of our last lessons." The old Monk nodded knowingly and continued, "The ancient Chinese physicians refer to these spaces as *burning* because these areas of the body have to do with the chemical transformation, or burning up, of food and drink combined with vital life force where the coming together of these elements causes combustion. This process generates heat.

It keeps our body at a specific temperature and provides the energy to live."

"In Taoist Alchemy the three burning spaces are referred to as the *Three Cauldrons* which have similar but not exactly the same locations. The burning spaces in Taoist Alchemy refer to the lower abdominal area, the upper chest region and the brain. The middle torso is not included in Taoist Alchemy because that area has to do with digestion of food and drink and has less to do with metaphysical function."

As the Monk described the functions of both systems of the Cauldrons and the Burners, I said, "I understand that when you mention the *Burners,* you are referencing Chinese Medicine and when you talk about the *Cauldrons,* you are referring to Taoist Alchemy. I see, too, that both the Burners and Cauldrons deal with the changing of substances from one form to another."

"Quite right," said the old Monk. "In fact, in Chinese Medicine the Burners extract the essences from food and drink that we consume and release the unusable downward through the bowels. The essential substances are then distributed throughout the body.

"In Taoist Alchemy the esoteric fire and esoteric water percolate the seed in the lower belly and the refined form of the seed mists upward. The differences between the two, the Burners and the Cauldrons, are of dispersion and ascension respectively of energetic substance." He would explain this process in more detail later.

Between the lessons, we would have intervals of meditation so that the information he gave could settle into my cells. We can understand a concept intellectually but it takes time to bring it into a *place of knowing* inside ourselves. For that reason, the monk's lessons were carefully planned so that I was given ample time inside of an entire day to process what he taught through hours of meditation.

Over the course of his teachings, visitations in my dreams by spiritual beings increased at night. There were ancient Taoist sages and ancestral matriarchs who came to me, each presenting tiny pieces of the splendid panoply that I must come to embody. The huge collection was beyond the reach of words or explanations.

Dreams can be like that. The experience is like having a word on the tip of your tongue, where you *know* what something is, but it escapes you. You *almost* have it, yet, it remains elusive.

In one of my lucid dreams I was training again with the Yabuu. In the dream, she placed cones of processed mugwort on the low back of a patient, and the heat and smoke of the burning mugwort magically opened the patient's back. Suddenly the body was transparent and I was able to see clearly the energetic structures. I saw the Cauldrons and the Burners just as the Monk described and the pathways of energy we call meridians. The meridians existed as part of the energy body that was juxtaposed on the physical body. I saw refined mist rising through the Cauldrons and the essences from food and drink being distributed from the Burners.

The following day, as I received further instruction about the sacred seed, I began to experience the stirring of the seed in my own body. The herbal powders that Mother had mixed into a paste and smeared on my Third Eye soon after my birth had opened the seed in my belly and it lay in wait for fifteen years. The seed had been brought to life long ago and the monk explained that it was now time to develop and refine it.

The monk continued, "There is an interface between the physical body and the energetic body so that the seed in the Lower Cauldron actually exists in that interface. The seed is a partially physical and partially spiritual substance.

"I got it!" I cried out. "The seed is in the world of the *in between.*"

The old Monk nodded and continued, "The Upper Cauldron in Alchemy refers to the area of the head and opens to the Third Eye. In fact, the Alchemists call the Upper Cauldron The Chamber Behind the Mid-Point of the Eyebrows. Another name of this sacred area is the Chamber of the House of the Spirit."

My attention went to my Third Eye. With eyes closed I recalled the protection ceremony conducted for me by my family where the indigo stain on the midpoint of the eyebrows stayed on my forehead for many months. It was the first time the Monk spoke about the idea of a chamber behind the Third Eye. My consciousness was subtly shifted by the idea and by turning my gaze inward I experienced the vastness of my inner world through the portal of the Third Eye. It was the feeling of infinity where outer space is experienced as inner space.

When I opened my eyes, the Monk had a slightly different appearance. He seemed to embody an actual Taoist Sage and his robes had taken on an ethereal glow. He whispered, "The ancient magicians and wizards used the information of the Cauldrons to claim immortality. The physical body does not live on. Rather, our spirit, after a process of refining, emerges from the top of the head. At that moment the physical body can be abandoned and its energetic structures left intact. One could then use the spiritual body that remained when needed. Some move to the Realm of the Voices and others continue to dwell in the ethereal plane."

The ancient one slipped into silence again, and we sat for a long period of time. He must have felt that this was enough information and took his leave. That night, in a beautiful dream, I sat under a tree where monks began to gather. There was a bearded Sage dressed in a flowing robe who did not speak but whose presence commanded the atmosphere. A peculiar fragrance emanated from the tree and as we sat in meditation we breathed in the subtle scent and were transformed. Spiritual knowledge entered us through our sense of smell and the more relaxed we became, the more easily we were able to absorb information difficult to comprehend. Suddenly leaves began to fall from the branches of the tree. Each leaf was carried effortlessly as if on a pillow of air until it rested on the grass around us. Before long we were surrounded by leaves and eventually those leaves blossomed into flowers. The Sage nodded at me and suddenly I knew that it is through utter relaxation that knowledge is taken directly into the cells, bypassing the thinking brain. That knowledge will then settle easily inside the consciousness and become knowable and usable.

In the morning, the old Monk, completely refreshed, swooped in to begin his lesson. "I spoke to you about the Triple Burner in Chinese Medicine and the Three Cauldrons in Alchemy, and you learned their shared locations. My lesson today is about the two most important elements in Alchemy, water and fire.

He materialized water in a tiny glass vial and created a burst of fire in another. The trick was brilliantly executed and I had no idea how he managed it. Although I did not wonder for too long because as soon as he spoke, my attention was once again gathered in sharp focus.

"The elements of water and fire are the foundations of life. These are physical substances, and at the same time they exist as esoteric substances. Just like the seed, the esoteric expressions of water and fire exist in the *in between*." He borrowed my phrase 'in between' and I was happy that he found the phrase useful and accurate.

"In the Lower Cauldron a special extra kidney exists in the space between the ordinary kidneys. It is a third metaphysical kidney called *Mingmen* that is suspended between the two physical kidneys. Mingmen has a psychic location rather than a purely physical one. That is to say, it too exists in the 'in between' along with the esoteric manifestations of fire and water and the sacred seed. The Mingmen is a mystical gate that opens and closes or more accurately put, inhales and exhales, simultaneously with our breathing. So, you see, this is what I have already taught you very early on in your studies about the kidneys. Our bodies breathe not only with our lungs."

I remembered his earlier instruction. It occurred to me that we breathe through our pores too. My mind drifted to a vision of my life in the womb like a sea anemone with water inside and outside and then when I was born onto dry land I had air inside and outside. I floated with these imaginings when the Monk's voice pierced my daydream.

"As for breathing down into the lower belly in your Clear Mind Meditation practice, have I not said to you that you must work your abdomen like a pair of bellows?" I suddenly understood that the pumping action of the lower belly as we breathed had a magical influence on the seed.

The seed, which holds potential of the highest Self, continues to mature in the Lower Cauldron. There, the fire and water of the Mingmen act on the seed, percolating and producing steam, causing the more refined seed substance to rise like mist. The seed transforms from a more physical state to a more spiritual state, misting upward.

"The Taoist sages of the ancient world referred to the seed that matured, as an embryo, and in later stages of development they called it a fetus," taught the Monk.

"In Clear Mind Meditation, we breathe down, sinking our thoughts with the breath into the Lower Cauldron. There in the belly, the thoughts function like wood and are burned up as fuel by the esoteric fire of the Mingmen."

I remembered my dream the night before and relaxed completely, allowing the Monk's information to be drawn into all my cells. I listened with an open heart as he continued.

"The fire and water of the Mingmen refer to esoteric fire that generates esoteric water. At the same time the esoteric fire resides in esoteric water and is also fueled by esoteric water. These mystical truths are the basis of transforming the spiritual seed into the True Self." His words floated into my psyche while the part of the brain that analyzes and tries to comprehend lay dormant.

My teacher was perfectly happy with the way in which I was receiving the information and said, "No need to completely understand this at the moment. You will experience these metaphysical truths in the alchemical process of birthing your True Self. We will move through that process together."

The ancient one had a serene look on his face as we sank together into deeper states of meditation. We spent the rest of the afternoon in Clear Mind as I allowed the knowledge to penetrate the marrow. The Monk stood to leave as I continued a bit longer in a state of samadhi.

In our next lesson, the old Monk continued instructing on the Lower Cauldron. "The Lower Cauldron is like a combustion engine that must keep the heat and steam going from the combination of fire and water to nurture the seed's fragile beginnings.

"It is a critical time as one can easily lose the seed through carelessness in one's approach to spiritual development. The Lower Cauldron is the densest area and from this murky bottom rises the lotus."

"I like the analogy of the lotus," I said to the old Monk, "but what comes to mind is the story you told me long ago about the scarab."

The ancient one had taught that the scarab rolls a tiny ball out of dung and because of the scarab's undivided effort of spiritual concentration as he rolls it, a magic pellet, or embryo, begins to grow inside of it. The Monk had quoted from a mystical book, "If even in manure an embryo can develop and cast its terrestrial skins, then why shouldn't we, too, through our undivided effort of spiritual concentration, be able to generate a body within the dwelling of our celestial heart?"

My teacher was happy that I remembered word for word what he had taught me. The lower belly was indeed a remarkable area. The spiritual seed ripens there, becomes an embryo, develops into a fetus as it mists upward through the Middle and Upper Cauldrons and then pops out of the head as the True Self. My understanding was merely intellectual at that moment and not the real thing. We sat in silence, both of us moving into Clear Mind Meditation, grounding the energy in our Lower Cauldron and nourishing our body and mind.

"There is a reason why the Alchemists refer to the maturing seed in the belly as a fetus," he said the following day. "Each of the Three Cauldrons is a womb where the seed is cultivated and refined."

"For a number of years you have been sending the breath down into the belly through Clear Mind Meditation and through the Tai Chi exercise. The seed has been quickening for this length of time, and you can begin now to send the breath through the two major pathways, the Du Mai and the Ren Mai. Those are the spinal and midline meridians." I recalled these two major pathways from the dream I had when the Yabuu and I peered into the back of the patient. I remained relaxed throughout the Monk's instruction as I closed my eyes and visualized the movement of the energy through those meridians in my own body.

"Breathe up the spine and down the front mid-line. With subtle awareness we are able to circulate the energy in both directions. We can breathe up the mid-line and down the spine as well. The energy alternates by mysterious magnetic forces with the application of our will."

The Monk suggested that I pull the breath from the tailbone up the spine to the midpoint of the eyebrows and then move the breath down the front midline. I worked consciously sending the breath as he instructed. It was more than a mere visualization. The power of the will was necessary in this endeavor to quicken the cultivation of the spiritual embryo.

"When a woman gives birth, the infant moves downward from heaven to earth. In birthing her True Self the spiritual fetus moves upward from earth to heaven." My teacher then smiled as if revealing a deep secret.

"Because you have incarnated in a female body, it will be much easier for you than for those born in the male body. Women's bodies are better equipped to carry the seed to fruition because they have a space to actually hold the seed in their belly, which is designed to give life. Women's bodies are designed to house the seed.

"Men have a greater challenge because the design of the male body is less conducive for this work. They could easily lose the seed altogether because their anatomy has no real home for it. Because men have no physical womb to nurture these fragile beginnings, they must work much harder to circulate the breath through the central and spinal meridians. However, because of this great effort, they are apt to be catapulted to an extremely high level.

"Since women generally choose to bring forth children, it is more difficult for women to actualize the True Self because parenting comes with its challenges of constant distractions. Yet, many brave women after procreation have come to this path and followed it to completion."

I shared with the old Monk what Great-Grandmother had taught me on the subject. She said, "We women are very lucky. We have the choice to give birth to children or to give birth to our True Self right out the tops of our heads."

The old Monk smiled upon hearing this and said, "Immortality is granted to those who can birth their True Self out of the tops of their heads. I will give you a demonstration when we next sit together." I was amazed that he had not only birthed his True Self but could give a demonstration whenever he wished.

"When I return I will also give you the highest Visualization Meditation that has been kept secret among the Taoists through the ages." The old Monk took his leave and I did not hear from him for several months. Some villagers whispered that he had left to be with the Immortals. Others thought he might have died. I didn't think about where he had gone and instead remained in the present, continuing my Tai Chi and Clear Mind Meditation. When the Monk finally returned, I had been so absorbed by my practices that I would have believed he had been gone for only a day.

CHAPTER 30
THE MONK RETURNS

"Konnichiwa!" A voice called out a joyous greeting and echoed as if spoken from the top of a high mountain. I recognized the caller and immediately ran to the entrance to greet my old teacher. So it came to pass that the old Monk appeared in my life once again. There he was in our vestibule one afternoon while I was washing sweet potatoes for the evening meal, a few hours before my hungry brother would be home from the fields.

The Monk looked different. He was more radiant and a light emanated from his whole body. He was almost ghostly and less sub-stantial. He seemed to glide around and because his robe touched the ground, I could not see his feet. His eyebrows were as white as snow as they had always been but were longer now and swept the sides of his cheeks. His beard, too, had grown and wisped halfway down his chest.

I placed my hands in gassho and bowed deeply.

"You have developed quite well without any further instruc-tion," the old Monk beamed. While some things had shifted with his appearance, he still had those sparkly eyes.

"As promised, I have returned to give you the last secret method of Taoist meditation. It is a series of visualizations that will allow you to birth the True Self."

I knew he had chosen not to give me these visualizations pre-viously because if I had gotten them too early I would not have reaped their full benefit. In fact, without preparation of strong focus in Clear Mind Meditation most people are not able to hold the images strongly enough to profit from them.

As we sat on the birthing room floor together, I had no memory of putting down the potato I was washing or of drying my hands. I had no recollection of making my way into the birthing room, but here I was. I was able to push those thoughts from my mind and assume the posture of Full Lotus. I then aligned my breath to sink the energy so that all heaviness of the body settled in my legs while the upper body remained light and agile. Then, the visualization meditation began.

The Monk instructed me to let go of one section of the body at a time. He mentioned that in Clear Mind Meditation the eyes are slightly open so that one remains connected to the world, but here in this visualization, the eyes are lightly closed with hands gently relaxed on the lap. We both entered a state of samadhi. Without such a sublime state of mind, it would be impossible to move through the stages that the Monk was now leading me.

"Allow your whole body to relax and sink," he whispered. In samadhi I was able to receive the barest of instructions as I intuited them before he spoke.

"All structures and all internal organs sink downward." I felt all tension leave me from head to toe. At the same time a subtle energetic thread from the crown of the head held my spine erect, preventing complete collapse. My vertebrae seemed to naturally stack one on top of the other and there was no effort to hold my physical frame. My mind was clear and I sharpened my focus as I settled body and mind. I felt him communicate, "Fall completely into a relaxed state."

"The fetus is beginning to rise. Can you feel it?" The Monk's voice was barely audible. "This image is pre-installed in your psyche so now just allow it to slowly come alive.

"We will now refer to the Lower Cauldron as *the Lower Elixir Field* where the first stage of distillation of fire and water occurs. Your low back and abdomen open with the inhalation and close with the exhalation.

"Observe your breath and use effort to open and close the Lower Elixir Field. On the in-breath the low back expands out as does both sides and front of the belly."

"Put just a little more effort on the out-breath, bringing the belly to the spine and lightly squeeze those areas. You are working your sacral pump.

"Squeeze very gently a few more times, and then return to the observation of the breath in the Lower Field."

I knew from our lessons that this method of opening and closing the Lower Field is called fanning the fire. The reason for the conscious effort of expanding and contracting the lower area is to bring stimulation and focus to it. The Lower Elixir Field is the main reservoir of the vital life force. Consciously breathing into it strengthens its foundation.

I also knew that people mistakenly try to build the Upper Elixir Field, the Third Eye area, without preparation. If the foundation of the Lower Elixir Field is weak, not sturdy or not powerful enough, the energetic structure, much like a building, will fall.

Because I was grounded in my meditation practice, there was an ease to what we were doing. The old Monk and I advanced toward the unknown but I had no fear, only joy. I could sense a combined radiance that filled the room around us and as we breathed, the Monk brought our attention to the Middle Elixir Field, the chest.

"Focus on your lungs in the center of your chest. As you inhale, expand the chest equally in all directions without force. The exhalation is natural and slow and long. The lungs become little wings, fanning the fire in the Middle Elixir Field. Here in this Middle Elixir Field the heart also resides. The lungs support and fan the heart to always express its truth and in so doing, the esoteric aspects of the lungs and heart are cleared of any emotional debris of sadness and grief. The heart and lungs can now only reside in love and this newfound lightness allows the energy to keep rising.

"Stay with your relaxed breathing, your mind still clear, and as you fan the fire in the chest, listen for the intelligence of your body that will tell you when it is time to move the breath to the

Upper Elixir Field, the Third Eye. Do not rush as you should not move your attention there until the distillation is complete in the Middle."

I could feel all sadness and unresolved grief drain from the Middle Elixir Field of the chest and at the moment when the last morsel of emotional imbalance had gone I was ready to move upward.

Together we moved to the Third Eye. And as we did, I sensed our energetic influence radiated all around and knew that we could alter the course of our planet. Everything I had worked on had led up to this point and I could feel my task beginning to emerge.

But I could also feel that I was at a crossroads. I realized I could take this visualization to the next step where my True Self would appear, or I could wait and utilize the huge energy required for such a feat in a future life to bring others along to influence our planet. To claim Immortality now would mean that I would join the Immortals without reincarnating again in human form. I could certainly help humanity from the spiritual spheres but what about En and our joint purpose? My choice was clear. I would incarnate again in human form and continue my work as a Bodhisattva alongside En and others who had made the same decision.

I sat with the Monk as we enjoyed the perception of endless time in the birthing room as we appreciated things being *just so*. We *became* the intermittent chirping of birds, the smell of wet earth and the tiny lavender and yellow flowers that showed themselves among the grasses. We sat together for quite a while and then I began to feel a tingling at the crown of my head.

I opened my eyes to see the old Monk, whose True Self had popped out of the top of his head. Rays of light streamed from his crown, and the Realized One, his True Self, sat on the top of his head like a shimmering Buddha. He had kept his promise and demonstrated for me exactly how this was done. The old Monk was completely still, silent and luminescent.

"Sprouting our True Self and achieving immortality are one," he whispered.

THE MONK RETURNS 257

I nodded. I experienced the grandeur of knowing the True Self yet I would not birth it as the old Monk had demonstrated. I would take the wisdom from this experience into my next life. I am a Bodhisattva. Of this, I am certain.

In that suspended moment of sublime awareness I rose to make my way to the kitchen, gliding with economy of movement to gather the offering I had put together. I wished to present to my beloved teacher a parting tea and sweet.

I brought out on a lacquered tray my mother's beautiful porcelain tea bowl together with green tea powder in a small wood container, a small wooden ladle and a bamboo whisk. I placed in front of the monk a square of rice paper upon which I previously had placed two small pieces of dried persimmon to be taken before his tea. I effortlessly measured the green tea powder by scooping two tiny ladles into the tea bowl and reached without any self-consciousness for the hot water pot and poured just enough hot water into the bowl. I then briskly whisked the slightly bitter tea for him and presented the bowl from the tray.

The Monk placed his hands in gassho as he enjoyed the dried persimmon I had prepared and took the bowl of steaming tea in his cupped hands savoring the supreme flavor of the green tea. After he sipped the last remaining drop of tea he said:

Every day is a good day for drinking this clear and bright tea
There is no place it cannot be drunk
Even though it is bitter one moment and sweet the next
It is always freshly brewed.

I bowed deeply to him, bringing my forehead to the floor. He smiled as he stood, placing his hands together in gassho, and bowed. He then turned to take his leave.

I stood up only to find myself standing in the kitchen holding a damp potato. No time had passed and there was no trace of my old teacher. What a daydream, I thought to myself but when I walked past the birthing room, there was my mother's lacquered tray and two bowls of finished tea.

As I cleared the tray, I remembered Great-Grandmother's explaining that the Elixir sought by the Chinese expedition in 608 AD was actually here in our islands. I understood why the expedition came up empty. The Elixir was not in the form of a potion, but rather, in the form of sacred information.

CHAPTER 31
LAST TRIP ON THE SILK ROAD

The day after my final lesson with the Monk, I went to tell En all about it. As I approached his house, I saw his older cousin planting seeds in the garden. I ran up to him to ask if En was home. "Who's asking?" he said without stopping his task or turning around. "It's Mahataa," I said, "his oldest and best friend." The cousin kept digging the soil and I could see that he was laughing. Just as he turned around I realized that the boy I was talking to was not En's older cousin but it was En. I had forgotten how much he had grown. It had been years since we had spent consistent time together. We had met on occasion at school and run down to our favorite beach on some afternoons but because of my busy schedule with my mentors it was not at all like it used to be a few years earlier.

En and I met when we were seven and now we were turning fifteen. In my mind En was still that seven year old boy but he had grown as tall as Jiraa and his voice was deeper. My voice had also changed but in an entirely different way. I would guess that, like Great-Grandmother told me, my voice was growing more and more powerful.

"You didn't recognize me," En smiled. I shook my head and admitted he was right. "It's all right. You look different too." I guess I did. I was taller than when I had last seen him and my hair had grown quite a bit. Instead of keeping it tied in a ponytail, I had started pulling it up in a thick topknot with my favorite tortoise shell jifaa. My dress had also changed as I could now fit into some of my mother's kimono. On that day I was wearing one of her favorites.

It was the kimono she had worn during our last New Year's celebration together. I had also thrown on Great-Grandmother's obi belt to accent the kimono and felt as though I were wearing blessings from both Mother and Great-Grandmother.

I would be leaving this kimono behind rather than packing it for my trip south because I would be dressed almost exclusively in the school uniform while I was in Shuri. I wanted to wear it today because today was special. Today would be one of the last times I would see En. "I remember that kimono. Your mother wore it during a party at your house years ago. It was stunning then as it is now. You wear it well," En said.

"I can't believe you remember!" I said as I thanked him for his compliment. He seemed to blush a little and for a moment neither of us knew exactly what to say. I then remembered why I had come and began telling him about the monk's last visit. As we talked, any awkwardness from not having seen each other for a while disappeared and it felt like old times. "Why don't you come and sit in the birthing room with me," I suggested.

"Yes!" said En, "I'll wash up and let my mother know." I told him I would precede him to my house and throw on some casual clothes so we could sit together. It would be our first opportunity in so long to relax and enjoy each other's company.

As childhood friends, En and I had explored the mountains and sea and now we were reconnecting as maturing friends. We met in this life due to strong karmic ties. Our mission on this planet coincided but we didn't yet have details.

Our precious teacher, the Monk, had disappeared without any huge farewell. He left like a butterfly that had alighted upon us for a short while and then took its leave. We were rich in our experience because of him.

"Hello, I'm here!" called En as he made his way to the birthing room. We both settled on our cushions facing each other and began our meditation practice. We lost track of time as our attention sharpened with the breath work, and our awareness grew so huge we sensed the entire world around us.

It felt wonderful to sit together and after a time, when it felt right, I lifted the tiny bell and rang it to end the sit. In the fading overtones of the bell's reverberations we both knew there was one last task to be finished. En whispered, "You must make the journey again up the mountain. The summer solstice is upon us. You should consider making your vision quest."

I felt ready and slowly stood, placing the meditation cushion under my arm. I gathered the sacred scroll from the chest of drawers and En stood to accompany me to the foot of the mountain. When we got to the entrance of our Silk Road he turned to me and raised his hand to my forehead, lightly placing a finger on my Third Eye.

"You are protected as you take this journey," he said as if he were speaking on behalf of the Originals. He silently turned away, holding a strong meditative image of me in his mind's eye.

I reviewed the contents of the silk scroll and made my way through the tall grasses. As I hiked up the familiar trail, out of nowhere, a mysterious, cloaked figure appeared at the side of the narrow pathway. The image was ghostly and as I approached, I saw that the cloak was made of an otherworldly fabric and hid the face of an old woman. I knew who she was the moment I saw the shadow of a Chinese phoenix perched above her on a branch. The cloak shaded her face and our eyes did not meet but she gestured with her hands, encouraging me on, throwing fragrant dust of crushed herbs over me as I passed. Farther along the path the voice of the True Noro resounded in my head, "Lovely to see you advancing to your high karma." Then she spoke faint congratulations as I silently conveyed gratitude to her. I felt the strong presence of my family too as they surrounded me with love and protection.

I came to the juncture in the trail and turned right, making my way to the top. The stone gassho sculpture was bathed in sunlight and I rushed to climb onto the flat ledge in Full Lotus. In moments my mind was clear. Meanwhile, in the village, on the stone bench behind our house, my best friend just sat and sat, bringing clarity to his mind. He took and held the image of me in his mind's eye. His *holding the space for me* in his mind's eye assisted in grounding me and I continued to sit in perfect clarity.

I recalled the instructions on the scroll and chanted the sacred tones once again. I moved through the various phases of samadhi, entering deeper and deeper levels of concentration. There was no sense of time, no vision, no sound, no thought. Everything in the external and internal world dropped away.

Suddenly, out of the complete quiet and stillness, came an image of Great-Grandmother in the sky. She was seated in seiza telling my birth story when a gush of water came spewing out the top of her head with tremendous force. Ghostly figures were seated around her, and one by one these figures emanated rays of light from their heads. The collection of figures multiplied until there were hundreds, and these hundreds sat in concentric circles around Great-Grandmother. The image was vast and luminous and just as quickly as it filled the entire silent world, it faded away. Then, without warning it happened.

The thunderous roar of a magnificent waterfall filled my ears and, as I looked down from the stony ledge, a cascade of white water gushed from beneath me and foamed upward in thick mist. The waterfall was deafening and intense. The reflection of the bright sun created three brilliant rainbows in its spray and I understood the combined power of water and fire.

I recalled in Great-Grandmother's tale about the great High Born Matriarch Sandaa who had told the clan that the one to discover the sacred waterfall would be instantly catapulted to a place of profound wisdom and would have a mission that the Original Wise Ones would disclose. Sandaa had also said the one who finds the waterfall would hold a state of mind as clear and powerful as water.

Then another vision came. A group of 108 persons clustered together in Clear Mind Meditation with each person holding the intention for world peace. As they settled into Clear Mind, another group appeared and then another until the groups extended beyond our archipelago. The groups of 108 people, each displayed unique geometric patterns as the waterfall continued crashing and cascading. The roar of the waterfall ceased and there was silence. I was left with only the sound of the sea in my ear.

During my time on the mountain, my friend En remained on the stone bench maintaining an uninterrupted image of me in meditation. I had done this once for him and now he was providing it for me. When I heard the roar of the waterfall he, too, experienced its power. At that moment, I saw En in my mind's eye being lifted off the ground. His eyelids flickered and he generated a great light that merged with mine on the mountain.

Our mission had become clear. We were to organize groups of 108 persons ripe for sustaining Clear Mind. The groups would hold one intention for world peace and would come together in several select places on our planet to penetrate the world's collective mind. War begins in the minds of men, why not peace? Here was the mythical net, Indra's Net, promising that our every action, every thought affects everyone else.

I had been given the final piece of the matrix to complete my mission. I knew intuitively the training of people had already begun in different places on our planet. We needed only join forces at a designated time that would reveal itself. Teachers would work in this way grooming and cultivating students in meditation with meticulous attention. And this process could take decades, perhaps a century, certainly beyond my own lifetime.

I was exalted for the time that I experienced the vision, but on my way down from the mountain I began to feel sadness that our mission could not possibly be realized at this time. It was extraordinary and, more than ever, the world needed it now, but we had to prepare the ground for it and that would take significant time. There was a big war looming. The seeds of destruction had already been sown and while we had the necessary skill to avert it, we did not have the time to ready enough people in Clear Mind Meditation. En and I would have to complete our karmic mission in another incarnation.

One thing is certain. We take all our wisdom acquired in one life into the next. Great-Grandmother had told me, "When we leave this life we cannot take any of our material possessions, but we take our wisdom and knowledge."

She had encouraged me by saying, "For this reason we need to advance as much as possible in our present life so we can use our high mind in a subsequent one." She had left me with the courage to persevere. We need to hold the thousand-year view which means we work diligently, never losing sight of our goal even though it is beyond the reach of one lifetime. I would go soon to Shuri and train others in this task of peace.

The night after my vision quest, I had the nightmare I had had a few years earlier. Thousands of hens and chicks ran helter skelter in our courtyard. They spontaneously burst into flames and thousands of innocents lost their lives. This dream reconfirmed for me impending doom.

I knew none of our poor villagers were aware of the stirrings for such a war that would bring great calamity and misfortune to our islands. The Originals did their best to insulate this ground of the north where the high teachers had incarnated. No bombs would fall in our northern province and our lives here would be spared but our houses would be burned down and our people would be greatly affected.

It was 1917 when I readied myself for my departure south and the karma for war was churning with no way to prevent it. The seed for World War II had already been planted in World War I, which began in the summer of 1914 and ended in 1918. Germany would be defeated and forced to pay repatriation by the Allied Forces which would bankrupt the country causing her to suffer great humiliation. Those conditions would sow the seed for the rise of the Nazi regime. There would be aggression worldwide with Japanese imperialism in China and other parts of Asia, with Mussolini in Italy and Franco in Spain.

Even with such destructive events in the world, we were still living our lives as normally as we could. Having knowledge of tumult and unrest in the world kept us sober and mindful.

I planned to return to the North after the completion of my studies in Shuri, to sit in purposeful meditation. I wanted to offer my clear mind as an expression of peace.

En and I would part ways soon. I had already packed for Shuri what little clothing and books I owned. En, too, would leave after me to make his way to China, his true homeland that he had yet to discover. Before saying our farewells, we agreed to meet for one last walk to our favorite spot by the ocean.

On the way, we spoke about our immediate plans for school. I told him I was looking forward to my new adventure in learning and he confessed he was nervous about heading to China. He had learned a bit of the Chinese language from his grandparents and he was hopeful that it would be enough to get by.

We eventually arrived among the cicadas and tall grasses, and we cut away from the larger path through the brush to find ourselves on the pristine shoreline.

"So we're supposed to meet in another life but how will we recognize each other?" asked En. That was an excellent question. First of all, we weren't even told which country we would be born in. Thinking it over, I said, "We should invent some kind of secret sign so that we will recognize each other."

En agreed, "How about a hand signal when we think we've found each other?"

"Maybe a word in the old tongue that we can utter," I offered. We went back and forth with ideas.

As we strolled along the shoreline wriggling our toes on the edge of the sea, we recalled all the fun we had shared. We spotted some ahsa, green moss, on the craggy rocks to bring home. Just as I bent to gather it, I saw an oyster in the shallow water. "What good fortune!" I shouted. "Let's share it right now." I pried it open with a sharp bamboo stick I happened to have in my pocket.

"Oh my gosh!" gasped En as it broke apart. Inside was the most exquisite, lustrous pearl. We each took a bite of the oyster and I rinsed the pearl in a pool of seawater. I held it up for both of us to admire.

"This is my gift to you," I said giving the pearl to En. "It will always remind you of our island and of me and of the task we have yet to complete." The pearl glistened as I held it in the sunlight. It was like a metaphor for the illuminating wisdom we had both attained in these early years. En smiled as he took it from my fingers and promised to treasure it always.

"I have something for you too," he said. From his shirt pocket, he pulled a pressed dried flower. "A few nights ago, the Immortal who taught me in the spirit realm returned this flower to me. I had acquired it while I was there but I left it because I didn't think I was allowed to carry it back. I had never seen flowers like this before and thought they were the most exquisite I had ever seen. The Immortal explained during one of my lessons with him that these flowers were abundant in the country of the 'West of the West.' He said I was welcome to pluck one so I did. I then pressed it in one of my books."

En continued, "Know that this flower is dried but not dead. It is imbued with the energy of the realm from where it came. You have been my best friend and my guide and to show how much our friendship has meant to me I would like to offer this to you," he said extending the flower.

"Oh, it is beautiful," I said as I accepted his gift, which had both a physical and ethereal presence. It was a brilliant red and I had never seen such a shape before. The green of the stem and leaves were clear, reminding me of the vibrant colors I saw around living things. As I looked at the flower my heart opened and I knew what our plan should be.

"You'll show me a pearl and I will lift up a flower," I said. "That is how we will recognize each other." And there, it was decided. We knew we could not carry material objects into the next life and that we would have to be resourceful.

En nodded, "You are my western flower." "And, you, my eastern pearl," I replied. With that, we ran on the smooth sand looking for interesting seashells to admire. It was the last of our typical afternoons at the beach where we were enveloped by joy and peace for a moment in time that would remain preserved in our deep unconscious until our next life.

When I returned home, I rushed to press En's flower in one of my books. Naturally I selected the *I Ching* and decided to throw the coins for the exact hexagram's page where I should press the flower. I turned to The Cauldron that moved into a second, Coming To Meet.

The interpretation of the first hexagram's moving line states: You will succeed in finding strong and able helpers who complement and aid you in your work. It is important to hold to self-abnegation and not be led astray.

This meant that En and I would be supported to succeed. To clearly know our mission in our next life was a gift bestowed upon us by the Wise Ones. We were Bodhisattvas, servants to humanity, and would return at the allotted time to continue our collective journey.

CHAPTER 32
JOURNEY BY SEA TO SHURI

"It's time to change your name," Jiraa said to me while discussing my imminent departure to Shuri. To enter school in the south I was required to have a Japanese name. I also needed to dress in the Japanese school uniform and could no longer wear my villager's kimono.

"You can select a name that you like or take a name I have found for you," Jiraa said. I liked the idea of having Jiraa choose. After all, he had acted as a surrogate parent for all of those years so it seemed fitting that he would name me. So from that moment, I became Sumi. My new name meant settled and clear in the Japanese language. Its meaning reminded me of my teacher, the precious old Monk, and I thanked Jiraa for his superb selection.

After the eighth grade at the age of fifteen, having come through my studies not only at the local school in the village of Gushiken but finishing also under the tutelage of the old Monk, the Noro, the Yuta and the Yabuu, I sailed away on the *pon-pon-sen,* a small putt-putt boat with a tiny engine. It was a day's travel from the northern end of the island to Tomari Port in the south. The teachings I had received as a young girl would be synthesized and distilled in me so that, at another time, I would be able to transmit those teachings to others.

The evening before my departure, Jiraa fixed my favorite meal. "I'll make some special soup for you tonight," he had said. Just the other day a neighbor had come with some *chinkwan,* a small pumpkin, and a large *shibui,* a kind of squash. Jiraa knew it was my favorite soup. He also prepared some stir-fried *gunbo,* burdock root, he found in the mountains.

After our meal, he handed me a small woven purse with some folded money for my schoolbooks and travel costs. I would ride a *jinrikisha,* a cart pulled by a runner, when I arrived in Shuri to get to the School for Young Women. And, I needed money to pay for that among other things.

I bowed to my brother with tears in my eyes. No one could have asked for a better older brother. I was sad to be leaving him. "Wait here," I shouted as I ran to my room to get the gift I had gotten for him. With some of the money I had earned from my sales of the ginseng roots, I had purchased a handsome shirt and a pair of trousers. I thought Jiraa would marry soon and start a family of his own. I wanted him to have a good, clean outfit to court the woman who would stand by him. How fortunate she would be to have him as her husband. Jiraa blushed at the explanation of my gift but I knew he was grateful.

The next morning, I tearfully waved goodbye to my brother. Also to see me off were the Noro, the Yabuu and my best friend En. The Yuta had already made her transition but she was there in spirit along with the old Monk. I waved to them all as they stood on the shore flying handkerchiefs in the air. I could see what looked like white flags for a long while as my boat putted away. The Noro would soon be leaving the village to resume her dwelling in the spirit realm and the Yabuu would pass on in the coming year. My friend, En, whom I would never see again after we said our goodbyes at the seaport committed in his heart to meet me in another life.

"What adventures we shared," I sighed to myself. It was painful to turn south to a new life that no longer included the people who came closest to the center of my heart. I ached with memories and dreams.

Although I loved my new name, my first and truest name, Mahataa, given to me by my father, would remain in my heart, holding with it the memories of my family and my early years in my small village. Holding my true name close I was able to pay tribute to the Originals, to my high teachers and to my ancestors.

My karma decrees that I must embark on an ordinary life as we enter a time of relative darkness. The northern province will begin to slowly lose its magical atmosphere as modernization creeps in. People will begin to desire more and more the material things that the South offers. The South is our island's door to the world where its port receives foreigners and goods that will dilute the spiritual power of our islands. The northern villagers' attention to their inner world will begin to wane and their fascination with the external world will become more and more enticing until finally, the inner world will become a strange land.

I see our peninsula of the North becoming less and less inviting to high spirits. In fact, I was the last to receive direct teachings from them. I was the last to actually contact and witness these high ones who appeared in the flesh to impart their knowledge and offer assistance in heightening the power of the senses to see, hear, taste, smell and know in ways beyond the mundane. These teachings to which only a few were privy were considered secret only because dull minds could not be taught to use the senses in these elevated ways.

There are temples and monasteries on our island and in neighboring countries where the tiny flame of Clear Mind Meditation is being kept alive. The teachers within those places are meticulous in training their students in the way the old Monk taught me. I am not alone in keeping this fragile flame alive. Others in remote places through good karma have received the teachings. The temples and monasteries, like the mysterious ambiance of our Northern Province, have the right atmosphere to invite and hold the teachings.

Outside of temples and monasteries, small groups of persons coming together for the sole purpose of clearing the mind is the first step in moving toward the goal of peace. Each person has the responsibility to clear the self of greed, anger and delusion. Without great effort in clearing oneself of these three poisons, peace cannot be achieved, neither for the individual, nor for the world. Accessing our Clear Mind, cultivating and deepening it, is our work and once that is securely in place we can lean into the prayer for world peace.

I see through my inner eye a small temple in Shuri where monks are practicing similarly to the way I was taught by the old Monk. That temple was built sometime in the early fifteenth century and still functions as a meditation center. I will be able to sit with other meditators with whom I can continue my training during my sojourn in the South.

We light-bearers in temples and monasteries need to exercise extreme caution in times ahead to hide our light until we intuitively know when to stand up and shine brightly. Hiding our spiritual light allows for its growth without hindrance so that we might use it most effectively when the time is ripe. Like a seed in gestation, all things in life have periods of rest and uninterrupted growth before emerging.

We must be strong in continuing to fan our own inner fire just as the ancient noro of every village tended the fire in the hearth for her people. Common people around us will be oblivious, will wage war and will fall into pettiness. We must keep our wits about us, be silent and observe.

A collage of memories pours over me as I sit back on my tiny putt-putt boat on my way south, of Mother and Father waving goodbye to me as they boarded their Chinese junk, of the time my best friend En and I moved seashells with our mind, of the old Monk who showed me how to sew, of all the experiences that brought so much to my path of light. But I must withdraw inward soon, dimming my light, knowing that I will need to suspend my knowledge for the time being.

As I recall details of my birth from the deepest places inside of me, I am transported to a time long ago. As I drift into sleep, I recede back into time, and it is the summer of 1902 again.

The old tiger, in one great roar, shakes the ancient wind on
    Gokoku mountain.
The new spring morning's light illuminates the sky.
From the beginning of the year many people gathering, for
    what do they pray?
For the four seas knowing true peace, giving life to the
    Patriarch's Zen.

Shodo Harada Roshi
Zen Master and Abbot of Sogenji Monastery
Okayama, Japan
January 1, 2010
In the Year of the Tiger
http:www.onedropzendo.org

ACKNOWLEDGEMENTS

I would like to give special thanks to creative editor, Molly Kochan Ouanes and creative consultant, Paul Sugiono, Ph.D. for their keen sensibility and exceptional contributions. I want to also thank Christine Imori for her long hours of preliminary editorial help that laid the foundation for the book and Julia Stein for the organization of the chapters; to Illustrator, Shuho Kiki Giet for her drawings in the book, her long hours of researching images and important suggestions to help complete the book. Many thanks to Sachi Kaneshiro for her kindness in proofreading the manuscript a number of times with editorial corrections and many wonderful suggestions, to Miyara Seiko for her countless hours in researching historical facts and gathering useful data regarding Okinawa of the early 1900's, to Maeda Nao, a Noro High Priestess of Kudaka Island who granted me a lengthy interview in April 2008 and provided me with valuable information about the priestesses of the Ryukyu Islands, to Ken Cohen for instructions in Taoist Visualization techniques, to Shodo Harada Roshi, my spiritual teacher, without whose teachings on meditation and whose profound wisdom, this book could not have been written, to close friends too numerous to name who lent inspiration and love, to each member of the One Drop Zendo of Los Angeles for supporting me on and off the cushion, and to Edwing and Dr. Mikio Sankey for their encouragement.

ABOUT THE AUTHOR

Jikun Kathy Sankey, aka, Kathleen A. Sankey, OMD, LAc, is a Doctor of Oriental Medicine and Licensed Acupuncturist in the State of California. She was licensed in 1985 and received her doctorate in 1986. She served as an Examiner for the Acupuncture Examining Committee under the California State Board of Medical Quality Assurance from 1985 to 1990.

Dr. Sankey has been in private practice since 1988 treating patients with acupuncture, nutrition, Chinese and Western herbs, and Jin Shin Jitsu.

She began Vipassana Meditation at the California Vipassana Center in Northfork, California in 1992 and participated in retreats for three years. In 1995 she began training in a Rinzai Zen Monastery known as Sogen-ji in Okayama, Japan, with Zen Master Shodo Harada Roshi where she continues to train in Japan and on Whidbey Island, Washington. She is currently involved in the Rinzai Zen Koan Curriculum under Shodo Harada Roshi. She received her dharma name, Jikun, from Harada Roshi at Sogenji in April 2000.

She heads the One Drop Zendo of Los Angeles which is a zen group affiliated with Sogen-ji Monastery in Okayama. She has also opened her zendo for weekday sitting.

In addition to her acupuncture license, she holds a B.A. in French language from the University of Hawaii, and two certificates from the University of Paris at Sorbonne where she spent one year of study.

GLOSSARY

acupuncture: Traditional Chinese medical treatment involving the insertion of needles into specific points on the surface of the body to stimulate the flow of energy (chi).

ahsa: Okn. Green moss (or algae) growing in holes of jagged rocks covered during high tide and exposed during low tide.

Alchemy: (sources: Elizabeth Reninger; Wikipedia) In Taoist practice, a set of procedures and principles meant to prolong human life. In Taoism, there are two types of alchemy:

Outer Alchemy is the branch of alchemy that used elixirs, which would produce immortality when swallowed. The most important ingredients were cinnabar (red mercury ore) and gold. As Taoism developed, the belief that immortality must be achieved by ingesting an elixir was supplanted by the doctrine of Inner Alchemy.

Inner Alchemy relied on symbolic meditation to achieve immortality.

Amamikiyo: Okn. In folklore, the Goddess who descended from Heaven. Kudaka, a tiny island off the southeastern coast of Okinawa, was the first island the Goddess created in the Liu Ch'iu archipelago.

ascetic: Characterized by the practice of severe self-discipline and abstention from all forms of indulgence, typically for religious reasons.

basa: Okn. Extremely fine textile like Chinese gauze.

basho-fu: Okn. (sources: Bashofu Hall; Kenny Ehman) The art thought to have been brought to the L'iu Chiu archipelago during the 13th century from South East Asia, where similar types of weaving have been discovered. The lightweight fabric is produced from special banana leaves of plantain trees. This technique provided the perfect type of clothing for the warm and humid climate of Okinawa.

bingata: Okn. (source: Wikipedia) Literally, "red style." Okinawan traditional dyed cloth, made with stencils and other methods. It is generally bright-colored and features various patterns, usually natural subjects such as fish, water, and flowers. Bingata dates from the Ryukyu Kingdom period (c. 14th century). It is believed to have developed as a synthesis of Indian, Chinese and Javanese dying processes.

blood deficiency: Chinese medical diagnosis: an insufficiency of blood with signs of anemia, dizziness, dry skin or hair, scant or absent menstruation, fatigue, pale skin and poor memory.

buchidan: Okn. A small altar area housing a memorial plaque with inscriptions of ancestors. The altar area also has an incense bowl, incense sticks and small dish to place food offerings. (Jpn.: Butsudan)

cauldron: Energetic space located in three parts of the body: the lower abdomen with the navel in front and the point for the gate of life in the back; the chest area; the head/brain area.

cha gan ju: Okn. Greeting: hello.

champuru: Okn. Stir fried dish of vegetables, sometimes with the addition of small strips of pork or chicken.

chinkwan: Okn. Small pumpkin.

chinuu: Okn. Traditional Japanese garment worn by women, men and children. (Jpn. Kimono)

Confucius: (source: Stanford Encyclopedia of Philosophy) 551 BC – 479 BC. Chinese thinker, social philosopher who had a simple moral and political teaching: to love others, to honor one's parents; to do what is right instead of what is of advantage. He thought that a ruler who had to resort to force had already failed as a ruler. "Your job is to govern, not to kill." He taught reciprocity: to do unto others, as you would have them do unto you.

dojo: Jpn. Place of practice for martial arts. Literally means "place of the way."

elixir: In Outer Alchemy, a magical potion that bestows immortality when swallowed. In Inner Alchemy, the life-prolonging energy attained through spiritual purification.

Engawa: Jpn. Long plank approximately 80 cm that lines the entrance to a house.

Formosa: Former name for Taiwan, an island in the South China Sea. Named Formosa, meaning "beautiful isle," by the Portuguese.

funshii: Okn. Wind and water philosophy for construction of houses and buildings. (Jpn.: Fusui)

gassho: Jpn. Hands in prayer. (Okn. Utoto)

genmai-cha: Jpn. Brown rice tea.

Go: Jpn. Board game of strategy for two players using round black and white stones. The object is to gain territory on the board by controlling (surrounding) a larger portion of the board than the opponent. Originated in China.

gunbo: Okn. Burdock root. (Jpn. Gobo)

gyate, gyate, paragyate, parasam gyate, Bodhisvaha: Skrt. (source: Sogenji chant book) "The Prajna Paramita is the great transcendent mantra, is the great bright mantra, is the utmost mantra, is the supreme mantra, which is able to relieve all suffering and is true, not false. So proclaim the Prajna Paramita mantra, proclaim the mantra that says: gyate, gyate, paragyate, parasam gyate, bodhi svha!" Literal translation by Edward Conze: "Gone, gone, gone over, gone altogether beyond. O what an awakening, all hail!" Refers to "going across to the other shore from ignorance to enlightenment."

guru: Skt. Spiritual teacher.

habu: Jpn. Venomous snake found throughout Southeast Asia, Japan, Philippines, Taiwan.

hai sai: Okn. Greeting: Hello.

hara hachibu: Jpn. Motto to fill the belly only eighty percent.

Heart Sutra: (sources: Wikipedia, Sogenji Monastery chant book) Well known Mahayana Buddhist sutra for its brevity and depth of meaning. (Skt.: *Prajnaparamita Hrdaya* which literally translates to the Heart of the Perfection of Transcendent Wisdom.)

hexagram: (source: Sacred Books of the East, translated by James Legge) A figure composed of six stacked horizontal lines where each line is either Yang (unbroken, or solid line), or a Yin (broken, an open line with a gap in the center). The hexagram lines are traditionally counted from the bottom up, so the lowest line is considered line 1 while the top line is line 6. Used in the *I Ching*, which contains 64 hexagrams. Hexagrams are formed by combining the original eight trigrams in different combinations. Each hexagram is accompanied with a description, often cryptic, akin to parables. Each line in every hexagram is also given a similar description.

Hinukan: Okn: Goddess of the Fire of the Hearth.

Huchiba: Okn. Mugwort. Known in Japanese as Yomogi.

I Ching: Chn. (Sources: Sacred Books of the East, translated by James Legge) Known as The Book of Changes. Philosophical and divination book dated from the period when Chou Dynasty replaced Yin Dynasty. Although the *I Ching* has its origin in Chinese culture, the underlying truth inherent in all 64 hexagrams is the same the world over, and is found at the heart of all spiritual and wisdom teachings.

jifaa: Okn: (Source: research by Seiko Miyara) A thin stick to hold in place the topknot on the head. Royalty wore jifaa made of gold. The Samurai wore silver. Commoners wore jifaa made of brass, wood or tortoiseshell.

jinrikisha: Jpn. Mode of transport where a runner draws a two-wheeled cart which seats one or two persons. Known also as rickshaws and were commonly made of bamboo.

kachashi: Okn. Lively, free and spirited dance at parties.

kaminchu: Common Priestess(s).

kampu: Okn. Topknot.

karate: Jpn. (source: Wikipedia) External martial art developed in the Liu Ch'iu Kingdom prior to its 19th century annexation by Japan. It was brought to the Japanese mainland in the early 20th century during a time of cultural exchanges between Japan and Okinawa. SEE: Shorin-ryu

katii: Okn. Midwife. (There are a number of terms for midwife in the various Okinawan dialects.)

konnichiwa: Jpn. Greeting: Hello, good day.

koto: Jpn. (source: Wikipedia) Traditional Japanese stringed musical instrument. Approximately 180cm in width. Thirteen strings are strung over 13 movable bridges along the width of the instrument. Players can adjust the string pitches by moving these bridges before playing, and use three finger picks (on thumb, index finger, and middle finger) to pluck the strings.

kshatriya: Skt: (Wikipedia) The warrior caste, a member of the second of the four Hindu castes. The traditional function of the Kshatriyas is to protect society by fighting in wartime and governing in peacetime.

Kudaka Island: Okn. Located in the east cape of Chinen off the southern coast of Okinawa, 5.3km away. The island is 7.8 km in circumference. Small island thought to be the place that Amamikiyo, the creator of the Liu Ch'iu Islands, descended from the sky.

Lao Tzu: (source: Wikipedia) Literally, "old master." Traditionally assumed to have been born in the sixth century BC. He is considered the author of the earliest Taoist philosophical text, the *Tao Te Ching*, the Classic of the Way and Its Power.
There is a close association between Lao Tzu and the legendary Yellow Emperor, Huang-Ti.

Lemuria: (source: James Churchward, author of The Children of Mu) The name of a lost continent that existed in ancient times and sank beneath the ocean as a result of geological, cataclysmic change. The continent was thought to be located in the Indian and Pacific Oceans. An ancient civilization which existed prior to and during the time of Atlantis. Lemuria is sometimes referred to as Mu, or the Motherland of Mu. At its peak of civilization, the Lemurian people were both highly evolved and very spiritual.

Liu Ch'iu Kingdom: Name in ancient history of the Ryukyu archipelago which includes the string of islands from the south of Kyushu to the north of Taiwan.

mabuyagumi: Okn. Ritual to call someone's spirit back. "Mabuya" means soul or life force. There is also a Native American ritual to "call back someone's spirit" which demonstrates the connection between Okinawan and Native American cultures.

mahasamadhi: Skt. Where a spiritual adept consciously and intentionally leaves one's body at the time of death. This is not the same as the physical death that occurs for ordinary persons.

mantra: Skt. A sound, syllable, or group of words that, when repeated continuously, are considered capable of creating spiritual transformation.

meridians: The twelve major pathways through which energy (chi) flows, supplying nourishment to the body. Acupuncture needles are placed in points along these lines of energy.

mingmen: Chn. Metaphysical "third" kidney suspended between the two physical kidneys. Referred to as the Gate of Life, a mystical gate that opens and closes simultaneously with respiration and is relevant to the workings of esoteric water and fire in the body; also informs Taoist Inner Alchemy.

miso: Jpn. Fermented soybeans made into a paste to make miso soup, a traditional Japanese soup.

mugi-cha: Jpn. Barley tea.

mugwort: Common name for artemesia vulgaris. Used in herbal medicine and also dried to obtain a cottony substance to burn on acupuncture points.

Nakijin Gusuku: Okn. (source: Okinawa G8 Summit Host Preparation Council 2000) Nakijin Castle. Located in the outer reaches of Motobu Peninsula. Symbol of Okinawa's ancient past, Archeologist estimate that construction began at end of 13th century. The castle's interior once supported several buildings used to house the King, his family, vassals, a small army, and supplies. Many horse bones were unearthed indicating that stables existed. One of Nakijin Gusuku's most striking features was its enormous size. The castle's total land area covered approximately 14 acres, making it the largest gusuku (castle) to have existed during its time.

noro: Okn. High Priestess.

padmasana: Skt. Full Lotus Posture in Yoga. The end posture, the King's posture in Yoga and is also the pose ideally assumed in zazen meditation.

paramitas: Skt. (sources: Pema Chodron) Means to cross over to the other shore. May be translated as perfection, perfect realization, or reaching beyond limitation. Through the practice of the six paramitas (Perfection of Generosity, Self-Discipline, Patience, Joyous Effort, Concentration, Wisdom), we cross over the sea of suffering (samsara) to the shore of happiness and awakening (Nirvana). Each of the six paramitas is an enlightened quality of the heart, a glorious virtue or attribute—the innate seed of perfect realization within us. The paramitas are the very essence of our true nature.

phoenix: (source: Mark Schumacher) According to Chinese tradition, a mythical bird not related to the phoenix of Western mythology, which arises from ashes. The Chinese phoenix is often paired with the dragon. During the Ming and Ching dynasties, the phoenix symbolized the empress and the dragon symbolized the emperor. According to ancient Chinese lore, the appearance of the phoenix on the wutong tree was a testament to the peaceful rule of a virtuous emperor.

po-po: Okn. A crepe-like pancake, likely introduced to the L'iu Chiu archipelago from European mariners trading in the Pacific in the 18th and 19th centuries.

Prajna paramita Hrdaya: Skt. Literal translation: the Heart of the Perfection of Transcendent Wisdom. (See: Heart Sutra)

saadaka umari: Okn. Born with high spirit rank. Curiously, the term sadhaka is a Sanskrit term meaning seeker or spiritual practitioner. (source: H. H. Avatar Swami Baba Sri Nataraj)

sadhana: Skt. Spiritual practice or discipline.

samadhi: Skt. (source: Wikipedia) A state of intense concentration achieved by meditation. A non-dualistic state of consciousness in which the consciousness of the experiencing subject becomes one with the experienced object, and in which the mind becomes still, one-pointed though the person remains conscious. In Buddhism, it can also refer to an abiding in which the mind becomes very still but does not merge with the object of attention, and is thus able to observe and gain insight into the changing flow of experience.

sanpinja: Okn. Jasmine tea.

sanshin: Okn. (source: Wikipedia) Musical instrument and precursor to the Japanese shamisen. Often likened to a banjo, it consists of a python skin-covered body, neck and three strings. Its close resemblance in both appearance and name to the Chinese sanxian suggests its Chinese origins.

Secret of the Golden Flower: (source: Wikipedia) Ancient esoteric treatise transmitted orally for centuries before being recorded on a series of wooden tablets in the eighth century. It was recorded by a member of the Religion of Light, whose leader was the Taoist adept Lu Yen.

seiza: Jpn. (source: Wikipedia) To sit in seiza-style, one first kneels on the floor, folding one's legs underneath one's thighs, while resting the buttocks on the heels. The ankles are turned outward as the tops of the feet are lowered so that, in a slight "V" shape, the tops of the feet are flat on the floor and the big toes are overlapped, and the buttocks are finally lowered all the way down.

shibui: Okn. Winter melon. (Jpn: Togan)

shirashi: Okn. Divine notification.

Shorin-ryu: Okn. (source: Wikipedia) School of karate. Chosin Chibana was the top student of the great master of Shuri-te (original fighting style), Anko Itosu, who was the top student of Matsumura Sokon, a renowned warrior of his time, bodyguard to three kings of Okinawa, he has been called the Miyamoto Musashi of Okinawa and was dubbed bushi (warrior) by his king. He synthesized the knowledge of Okinawan arts with Chinese martial arts that he learned on his travels and taught it as a coherent system. In 1933 Chosin Chibana chose to call his style Shorin-ryu in honor of the Chinese Shaolin roots.

Shuri-te: Okn. Martial Art that preceded Shorin-ryu.

Silk Road: (source: Wikipedia) The long and arduous routes by which traders, missionaries and others traveled between China and the ancient Middle East, so named because silk traveled to the Mediterranean along these routes. The Roads stretched across northwest China into central Asia and then southward to what is now Afghanistan, Pakistan, and India, and finally westward toward the Middle East and the Mediterranean.

solstice: Either of the two times of year when the sun reaches its highest or lowest point in the sky at noon, marking the longest and shortest days of the year and the change of seasons.

Tai Chi: Chn. (Literally, "Great Polarity") Martial art exercise, executed slowly and with precision. Meditation in movement used for strengthening the body and mind.

taiko: Jpn. Barrel shaped drum struck with wooden sticks.

tanden: Jpn. The lower abdominal area and one of the three locations in the body used in the practice of Inner Alchemy. Also important: location of primal chi that martial artists tap for self-development and call upon for combat.

tansu: Jpn. Chest of drawers.

tatami: Jpn. Traditional type of Japanese flooring made of rice straw to form the core with a covering of woven soft rush straw. Tatami are made in uniform sizes. Usually, on the long sides, they have edging of brocade or plain cloth although some tatami have no edging.

Triple Burner: In Chinese Medicine an organ that refers to three areas of the body. It has no equivalent in Western conventional medicine. Also known as the Triple Warmer or San Jiao in Chinese. The Triple Burner has three parts: the Lower Burner (organs of elimination), Middle Burner (organs of digestion) and Upper Burner (organs of respiration and circulation).

tumai kuru: Okn. Purple sweet potato.

Uchinanchu: Okn. Native of Okinawa.

undagii: Okn. Deep-fried doughnut.

Upanishads: Skt. (source: Wikipedia) Literally means, "sitting down near," and implies listening closely to the mystic doctrines of a guru or a spiritual teacher, who has cognized the fundamental truths of the universe. It points to a period in time when groups of pupils sat near the teacher and learned from him the secret teachings in the quietude of forest hermitages. Upanishad means brahma-knowledge by which ignorance is annihilated. Thought to have been written around 800 – 400 BC. Forms the core of Indian philosophy. An amazing collection of writings from original oral transmissions where we find all the fundamental teachings central to Hinduism.

utoto: Okn. To pray; prayer.

Vedas: Skt. (source: Wikipedia) (means "knowledge") A large body of text originating in ancient India. The texts constitute the oldest layer of Sanskrit literature and the oldest scriptures of Hinduism. Comprises the Upanishads, a sacred text of a mystical nature.

yaachu: Okn. Method of burning dried mugwort on acupuncture points to stimulate the points which have specific actions on the body.

yabuu: Okn. Healer(s) who can be male as well as female, although male healers were extremely effeminate. Medicine woman.

Yoga: Skt. (source: Wikipedia) A system of exercises practiced as part of the Hindu discipline to promote control of body and mind. Hindu discipline aimed at training the consciousness for a state of perfect spiritual insight and tranquility that is achieved through the three paths of actions, knowledge and devotion.

yuta: diviner(s), soothsayer(s)

(Author's note: Regarding Chinese terms, I opted for the Wade-Giles version versus Pinyin because Wade-Giles spelling is most easily recognized, eg., Tai Chi versus Taiji or Chi versus Qi.)

Made in the USA
Charleston, SC
18 January 2012